GRAVE-
YARD
PLOTS

Books by Bill Pronzini

"Nameless Detective" novels:

Bones
Double (with Marcia Muller)
Nightshades
Quicksilver
Bindlestiff
Casefile (collection)
Dragonfire
Scattershot
Hoodwink
Labyrinth
Twospot (with Collin Wilcox)
Blowback
Undercurrent
The Vanished
The Snatch

GRAVE-YARD PLOTS

The Best Short Stories of
BILL PRONZINI

St. Martin's Press
New York

TWO WEEKS EVERY SUMMER. Copyright © 1980 by Bill Pronzini. First published in *Ellery Queen's Mystery Magazine*.

THE HANGING MAN. Copyright © 1981 by Bill Pronzini. First published in *Ellery Queen's Mystery Magazine*.

CHANGES. Copyright © 1980 by Bill Pronzini. First published in *Ellery Queen's Mystery Magazine* as TIMES CHANGE.

CAT'S-PAW. Copyright © 1983 by Bill Pronzini. First published as a limited edition by Waves Press, Richmond, VA.

SKELETON RATTLE YOUR MOULDY LEG. Copyright © 1984 by Bill Pronzini. First published in *The Eyes Have It*.

SANCTUARY. Copyright © 1985 by Bill Pronzini.

Designed by Doris Borowsky

Library of Congress Cataloging in Publication Data

Pronzini, Bill.
  Graveyard plots.

  I. Title.
PS3566.R67A6   1985   813'.54   85–11730
ISBN 0-312-34457-0

First Edition

10 9 8 7 6 5 4 3 2 1

CONTENTS

Preface   ix

Cain's Mark   1

A Lot on His Mind   24

The Pattern   32

I Don't Understand It   42

Proof of Guilt   51

Multiples (with Barry N. Malzberg)   63

Sweet Fever   69

Putting the Pieces Back   75

Smuggler's Island   81

Under the Skin   99

Caught in the Act   105

Strangers in the Fog   113

His Name Was Legion   123

Rebound (with Barry N. Malzberg)   129

Black Wind   140

A Craving for Originality   146

Peekaboo   157

Two Weeks Every Summer   163

The Hanging Man   171

Changes   186

Cat's-Paw (A "Nameless Detective" Story)   191

Skeleton Rattle Your Mouldy Leg (A "Nameless Detective" Story)   216

Sanctuary (A "Nameless Detective" Story)   245

PREFACE

It is common knowledge that no one reads prefaces to short story collections.

That being the case, I'm writing this one to please myself. Which is as it should be, because that's why the stories in this book were written in the first place.

Oh, the money factor entered into it, of course; I'm a professional writer and I make my living mostly from fiction, so every dollar helps. But it is also common knowledge that no writer ever gets rich writing short stories (and that only one author in the mystery and detective field, Edward D. Hoch, can make a satisfactory living doing them exclusively). In the main these stories were exercises in "self-expression"—a euphemism meaning some pretty good ideas occurred to me and I wanted to see if I could turn them into worthy pieces of short fiction.

And I had a devil of a time selling some of them, too. What I consider a good idea all too often fails to coincide with the opinions of magazine editors. Take "His Name Was Legion," for instance. One editor I sent it to said that the biblical references were "too mystical" for the readers of her publication, whatever that means. Another editor said there was too much sex "for a family mystery magazine." (There's more sex in your morning newspaper than there is in "His Name Was Legion." And it has always struck me as a tad hypocritical for a "family magazine" to piously reject stories on the grounds of sexual content, mild or overt, while specializing in all sorts of fictional murder, mayhem, and felonious behavior.) I finally sold the story to *Mike Shayne Mystery Magazine* for 1½ cents per word—the munificent sum of $35.00. Writers definitely do not get rich writing short stories.

On the other hand, some stories that I figured would be a difficult sell found acceptance on their first submission. "A Craving for Originality" is one. It is a writer's story, pure and simple—a satire on hack writers and hack writing—and fits into no particular category or market. I sent it to the late Frederic Dannay at *Ellery Queen's Mystery Magazine,* without much hope because it isn't really a crime story, and he amazed me by buying it almost by return mail. (Fred continually amazed me. He would buy stories I thought had little or no chance and reject those I was certain he would like. It got to be a kind of game, after a while—too often a frustrating one for me. All in all I managed to sell him 25 stories, of which maybe 10 I felt were "sure sales" on submission.)

Anyhow, the 23 stories in these pages are my favorites among the more than 150 pieces of short crime fiction I've published. (A few other favorites appear in the 1983 "Nameless Detective" collection, *Casefile.*) They span seventeen years of my writing life, from 1968 to the present; and they run the gamut of criminous story types: straight suspense, psychological suspense, "impossible crime," detection, fantasy, horror, satire, even what might be termed a Western. One—"Strangers in the Fog"—was nominated for a Best Short Story Edgar by the Mystery Writers of America. Seven—"Cain's Mark," "Sweet Fever," "Smuggler's Island," "Strangers in the Fog," "Rebound," "Cat's-Paw," and "Skeleton Rattle Your Mouldy Leg"—were selected for inclusion in the annual anthologies, *Best Detective Stories of the Year* and *Year's Best Mystery & Suspense Stories.* "Proof of Guilt" was adapted for a segment of Roald Dahl's *Tales of the Unexpected* TV series. And "Cat's-Paw," one of the three stories here that feature "Nameless" (the other two are "Skeleton Rattle Your Mouldy Leg" and an original, "Sanctuary") received a Private Eye Writers of America Shamus for Best Short Story of 1983.

Obviously I'm proud of all these stories, or they wouldn't be here. I wish I could say that I hope you like them as much or almost as much as I do, and that they give you a couple of hours of pleasurable diversion. But I can't say that. No one reads prefaces to short story collections, so there's no point in it.

Is there?

—Bill Pronzini
San Francisco, California
January 1985

GRAVE-
YARD
PLOTS

CAIN'S MARK

The first thing Cain did when he arrived in San Francisco was to steal a car.

He stepped off the through-Portland bus at the Seventh Street Terminal, carrying a blue airline overnight bag; it was a few minutes after midnight. He walked through the terminal, without haste, turning south to Mission Street and then east along there to a shadowed, unattended parking lot between Sixth and Seventh. He prowled among the scattered few cars still parked there until he found a dark blue, late-model sedan that satisfied him. From the pocket of his tan overcoat he took a thin piece of stiff, oddly shaped wire and bent to the door lock. Moments later, he slipped in beneath the wheel, placing the overnight bag on the seat beside him. He probed the ignition slot with the wire, and after a few moments more the sedan's engine began rumbling softly. The entire operation had taken perhaps two minutes; if anyone had been watching, it would have looked like he was entering his own car with his own set of keys.

Cain put the sedan in gear, switched on the headlights, and drove out of the lot, crossing the double yellow lines illegally to turn west on Mission. He picked up Bayshore Freeway South at Tenth and Bryant, eight blocks away. Traffic was light at this hour, but Cain remained in the center of the three lanes, maintaining a moderate speed.

Some twenty minutes later, he left the freeway at the Poplar

Street exit in San Mateo. He drove through the dark, quiet, deserted streets, crossed El Camino Real, and entered the prosperous, well-landscaped community of Hillsborough. On Devaney Way, Cain made a left turn and went three blocks. In the middle of the fourth, he eased the sedan to the curb in front of a sprawling, two-story red-brick home with ornate grillwork balconies. On the left side of the house, just ahead of where Cain had parked, was a crushed, white-gravel drive, bordered on both sides by a six-foot hedge. He could not see the front door of the home because the hedge extended down to parallel the street in front, broken only by a grillwork gate to the rear of where he was parked. But he could see the open, empty garage clearly; a pale, hooded light burned over the door.

Cain shut off the headlights, but left the engine running. It was an extremely quiet engine, and he had to strain to hear it himself; he was sure no one in the red-brick house—or in any of the adjacent or facing houses—could hear it. He set the parking brake, and then slid across the seat to the passenger side. He wound down the window there, then lifted the blue overnight bag onto his lap and zippered it open and took the .45-caliber automatic from inside.

He held the automatic on his right thigh and looked at the luminescent dial of his wristwatch. One-ten. Cain slid down in the seat until his eyes were on a level with the sill of the open window.

At twenty-seven minutes past one, headlights appeared on Devaney Way, coming toward him. Cain drifted lower on the seat. A red directional signal, indicating a left turn, came on below the headlights as the car—a cream-colored Cadillac—approached. Cain nodded once in the darkness, his fingers tightening around the butt of the automatic on his thigh.

The Cadillac turned smoothly onto the white-gravel drive, red stop lights winking. Cain watched as the driver—the lone occupant—maneuvered the car into the open garage. Cain, ears straining, heard the faint slam of a car door moments later.

He raised up on the seat, placing his arm on the window sill, the automatic extended toward the garage. A shadowed figure emerged from inside, stopped, and there was a faint whirring sound as the automatic garage door began to slide down. Then the man turned and Cain could see him clearly in the pale light from above the door.

He squeezed the trigger on the automatic three times, sighting along the barrel. Each of the three shots went exactly where Cain had intended them to go: into the garage wall above and slightly to the left of the man there.

The man threw himself to the white-gravel drive, rolling swiftly toward the green hedge on his right. Cain dropped the automatic into the overnight bag, slid over under the wheel; with his left hand he released the parking brake, with his right he dropped the automatic transmission into Drive. The rear tires on the sedan screamed against the pavement, as Cain's foot bore down on the accelerator. He had time for one quick glance in the direction of the garage; the man lay partially hidden in the shadow of the hedge, head raised slightly, looking toward him. And then the sedan was moving away, gathering speed. In his rearview mirror, Cain could see lights being flicked on in neighboring houses. He took the first corner, left, and when he had cleared the intersection he switched on his headlights. Two more blocks and a right turn, and Cain reduced his speed to the legal limit of twenty-five.

Just short of half an hour later, he reentered the San Francisco city and county limits. He exited the Bayshore Freeway at Army Street, turning right off there on Harrison, and parked the sedan in front of a warehouse driveway. He got out then, taking the overnight bag, and walked quickly up three blocks to Mission Street; he caught, almost immediately, a Municipal Railway Bus downtown.

He left the Muni at Sixth and walked up to cross Market. On the corner of Taylor and Geary, he entered the Graceling Hotel, registered under the name of Philip Storm, and was given a room on the third floor. Inside the room, he removed the gun from the bag, oiled and cleaned it, and reloaded the clip from a box of shells. When he finished, he replaced the automatic in the bag, put it under the bed, and lay down on top of the sheets.

It was almost dawn before he finally slept.

The man who had been shot at in Hillsborough was named James Agenrood.

Following the shooting, he sat in his mahogany-paneled, book-lined study. He was alone; his wife, who had been badly frightened, had taken several sleeping pills and gone to bed.

Agenrood poured brandy from a crystal decanter into an expensive snifter and tasted it without his usual enjoyment of the imported liquor. He had regained his composure, but his nerves were still agitated.

He tasted the brandy again, and then slid the telephone toward him across the desk, dialed a number. It rang several times; finally, a sleepy voice said, "Hello?"

"Len?"

"Yes?"

"Jim."

"This is a hell of a time of night to be calling anybody, Jim," the sleepy voice said irritably.

Agenrood took a measured breath. "Somebody tried to kill me tonight," he said.

"*What!*"

"Yes. About an hour ago."

There was silence for a moment, and then the voice, which was no longer sleepy, said, "Do you have any idea who it was?"

"No."

"Professional?"

"I'd say so. He seemed to know my habits, that I always go to the Club on Wednesday nights, and that I usually get home around one-thirty. He was waiting out on the street."

"Just one man?"

"I think so."

"Did you get a look at him?"

"It was too dark."

"How about the car?"

"Dark sedan, maybe last year's," Agenrood said. "I saw part of the license plate. DRD."

"Did you call the police?"

"No. I made sure the neighbors didn't either."

"I'll get somebody on it right away."

"I'd appreciate it, Len."

"Listen, Jim, whoever it was isn't affiliated with us. You know your standing with the National Office."

"I didn't think he was."

"Just so you know."

"Thanks, Len."

"I'll drop by your office tomorrow."

"All right."

"And Jim . . . be careful, will you?"

Agenrood laughed, but there was no trace of humor in his gray eyes. "I'll do that, don't worry."

He cradled the receiver, lifted the decanter of brandy again; he poured another drink—his fifth since the shooting. He sat staring into the snifter. His face, in the pale light from his desk lamp, was an inscrutable mask etched of solid stone.

Cain awoke at eleven the next morning, dressed leisurely, and then called room service and ordered a pot of coffee and some buttered toast. When it arrived, he carried it to the small writing desk. In one of its drawers he found notepaper and plain white envelopes and several soft-lead pencils.

He printed a short, two-paragraph note on one of the pieces of paper, folded it, and slipped it into an envelope. He addressed the envelope, sealed it, finished his breakfast, put on his overcoat, and went out to the elevator.

In a drugstore two blocks from the Graceling Hotel, Cain bought a twenty-two-cent stamp. There was a mailbox on the opposite corner, and he dropped the envelope inside after noting on the front the times that mail was picked up there.

Before returning to the Graceling, Cain bought a newspaper from one of the sidewalk vendors. In his room, he read it carefully. There was no mention of the episode in Hillsborough. Cain had not expected that there would be; for one thing it had happened well past midnight, too late for the morning editions; for another, and more importantly, he knew that Agenrood would not have called in the police. But he read the paper thoroughly just the same.

He lay on his bed, thinking, for the remainder of the afternoon. At five o'clock, he went out to a nearby restaurant and ate a light supper. On the way back from there, he stopped at a parking garage that had a telephone booth. He inserted a dime and dialed a number from memory. A man's voice answered.

"Hello?"

Cain did not say anything.

"Hello?" the voice repeated.

Cain held the receiver away from his ear.

"Hello? Hello? Who is this?"

Cain hung up and left the garage.

The distinguished-looking man who sat in James Agenrood's private office at Consolidated Trades, Incorporated, tamped the dottle from his briar pipe and said, "Let's have a look at this note, Jim."

Wordlessly, Agenrood passed a folded sheet of paper across his marble-topped desk. The distinguished man picked it up, unfolded it, and read:

Agenrood:

What happened Wednesday night can happen again, if there is a need for it. And if there is, you can be sure a garage wall will not be my primary target.

Stay by your phone this weekend.

The distinguished man folded the paper again and laid it carefully on Agenrood's desk. "No signature," he said.

"Did you expect there to be one?"

"Easy, Jim."

"I'm all right."

The distinguished man refilled his pipe. "What do you think he means?"

"It's obvious, isn't it?"

"Maybe."

"He wasn't trying to kill me the other night at all. He's not a professional assassin."

"Unless he's freelancing."

"That's possible, I suppose," Agenrood said. "In any case, he knows a lot about me. I don't know how, but he's got my private telephone number at home."

"He called you?"

"Yes."

"When?"

"Last night."

"What did he say?"

"Nothing. Nothing at all. I could hear him breathing on the other end of the line, and then he hung up."

"How do you know it was him?"

"It was him," Agenrood said.

"You haven't talked to the police, have you?"

"I'm not a fool, Len."

"I didn't mean to imply that," the distinguished man, Len, said. "I've put Reilly and Pordenza on it. They're good men."

"Sure."

"They learned that a dark blue sedan was abandoned in the Mission District some time Wednesday night. It had been stolen earlier in the evening from a downtown parking lot. First three letters on the plate were DRD. It looks like that was the one he used."

"That bases him in San Francisco," Agenrood said. "The envelope this note came in was postmarked there."

Len nodded.

Agenrood said, "Did Reilly and Pordenza learn anything else?"

"No."

"Well, whoever he is, he's got to be known to the National Office," Agenrood said. "Only somebody within the Circle could find out as much about me as he seems to know."

Len rubbed his nose with an index finger. "Can you think of anybody who has a grudge against you? Anybody you pushed, no matter how lightly, at one time or another?"

"None that would try anything like this."

"Give me their names anyway."

Agenrood wrote several names on a sheet of paper from his desk and gave the list to Len. He glanced at it briefly and tucked it into the pocket of his olive silk suit. "Are you staying home this weekend?"

"What else can I do?"

"I can put a couple of men on your house in case he tries something."

"No, Len," Agenrood said. "How would that look?"

Len nodded slowly. "Yes, I see what you mean."

"I don't think he'll do anything until after he talks to me," Agenrood said. "I'll be all right."

"If he calls, you let me know right away."

"I will."

Len stood. "Try not to worry, will you? We'll find him before long."

Agenrood did not speak. The two men went to the door. When Len had gone, Agenrood closed the door and stood looking at it for a long moment.

"I hope so," he said finally, in a whispering voice. "I sincerely hope so."

*   *   *

On Saturday night, shortly past eight, Cain left the Graceling Hotel for the first time since Thursday evening. There was an icy wind off the bay, blowing ethereal wisps of fog overhead; he walked quickly. On Pine Street, near Powell, he entered a quiet, dark cocktail lounge. He ordered a draft beer from the red-vested barman, and then carried it with him into the rear of the lounge to where a public telephone booth stood between the rest room doors.

Inside the booth, Cain set the glass on the little shelf beneath the phone and dialed the same number that he had on Thursday night.

Presently, there was a soft click and a man's voice said guardedly, "Yes?"

"Agenrood?"

A brief pause. "Yes?"

"Did you get my note?"

Another pause, longer this time. Then, "I received it."

"Did you understand it?"

"I think I did."

"Good," Cain said. "I thought you would."

"Just who are you?"

"You don't really expect me to tell you that, do you?"

"All right, then. How much do you want?"

"Two hundred thousand dollars."

Cain heard Agenrood suck in his breath.

"Did you hear me, Agenrood?"

"I heard you."

"Well?"

"I don't keep that kind of money."

"But you can get it readily enough."

"Suppose I don't agree?"

"What do *you* think?"

"You're making a large mistake," Agenrood said. "I represent——"

"I know who you represent."

"Then you're a fool."

"Two hundred thousand dollars," Cain said.

"If I pay it, you won't live to spend it."

"If you don't," Cain said, "you won't *live*. Period."

There was a long silence.

"Well, Agenrood?"

"I'll have to think it over."

Cain smiled. "You do that."

"How can I get in touch with you?"

Cain continued to smile. "Stay by your phone, Agenrood," he said, and replaced the receiver.

James Agenrood paced the wine-colored carpet in his study nervously. He said, "He called about eight tonight, Len."

The distinguished man stood holding a snifter of brandy by Agenrood's desk. His features were grim. "And?"

"He wants two hundred thousand dollars."

Len said, "My God!"

"He's deadly serious. It was plain in his voice."

"What are you going to do?"

"I don't know," Agenrood said. "That's why I asked you to come by."

Len rolled the brandy snifter between his hands. "If you pay him," he said slowly, "it won't be the last time. If he knows you're worried, worried enough to come up with the money once, he'll be back. Again and again."

"Yes. I was thinking the same thing."

"I'd like to say Reilly and Pordenza have something further," Len said. "Or that somebody on that list you gave me checks out as possible."

"But there's nothing, is there?"

"Nothing at all."

"Then I've got to pay him," Agenrood said. "Either that, or—" He left it there, moistening his lips.

Len walked across to the wine-colored drapes covering a large picture window. He stood with his back to Agenrood. After a time he said, "That would be very dangerous, Jim."

"I know."

"You're established now, both here and with the National Office. And you're important to us, Jim. Very important. I think you realize what I mean. If something went wrong . . ."

"I know that, too," Agenrood said.

Len turned and met Agenrood's eyes. "I don't advise that alternative," he said.

"Do you think I like the idea of it any better? But it doesn't look like I have much choice, does it?"

Len did not say anything.

"Will you help me, Len?" Agenrood asked.

"I don't know."

"I've never asked you for a favor before."

"No, you haven't."

"I want two men, that's all."

The distinguished man worried his lower lip. "How do you know he'll leave himself open? He's done the rest of it very shrewdly."

"If he doesn't, I can arrange it."

"Are you sure?"

"No," Agenrood said. "I'm not sure."

"When is he supposed to contact you again?"

"He didn't say. I don't think it will be too long, though."

"I see."

The two men stood quietly for several minutes. Agenrood said then, "More brandy, Len?"

"Yes."

Agenrood poured more brandy for each of them. They stood drinking in silence. Finally, Len said, "All right, Jim. *If* you can arrange a quiet place, out of the way. *If* you can do that."

Agenrood inclined his head and, wordlessly, they continued to stand drinking their brandy in the dark study.

*   *   *

The telephone booth in the lobby of the San Francisco Hilton Hotel smelled of lime-scented after-shave lotion. Cain did not like the smell, but he kept the door shut nonetheless. He said into the receiver, "What's your decision, Agenrood?"

"All right," Agenrood said. "I don't have any other alternative, do I?"

"You're a wise man," Cain told him. "When can you have the money?"

"By Tuesday."

"Fine."

"How do you want to pick it up?"

"You bring it to me. Personally."

"There's no need for that."

"There's a need for it," Cain said.

There was a long silence, and then Agenrood said, "Whatever you say."

"If you don't come yourself, I'll know it."

"I'll come myself."

Cain nodded in the booth.

Agenrood said, "Where do I go?"

"Are you familiar with the Coast Highway, just south of Rockaway Beach?"

"Yes."

"There's a Standard station on the highway there that has gone out of business," Cain said. "Loy Brophy's is the name of it. Park in there, by the pumps, at midnight Tuesday. When you see headlights swing in off the highway, and they blink off and then back on again, follow the car. Have you got all that, Agenrood?"

"Yes. Is that all?"

"Just one more thing."

"Yes?"

"Make sure you're alone."

Cain left the Hilton Hotel. A block away, he hailed a taxicab and told the driver where he wanted to go. The driver looked at him curiously for a moment, and then shrugged and edged out into the light Sunday afternoon traffic. Cain settled back against the rear seat, lit a cigarette, and thought out carefully what he was going to say when he arrived at his destination.

James Agenrood said, "That's all of it, Len. Just as he told it to me on the telephone."

The distinguished man shifted in his chair. He took the briar pipe from his suit pocket and looked at it for a moment. "It sounds like he's covering himself from all angles."

"Not quite."

"No," Len agreed. "Not quite."

"He won't be able to see inside my car unless he pulls right up next to me at the pumps. And even if he does that, it will be dark enough in the back seat to hide anybody down on the floorboards. He'd have to get out and walk right up to the car, and he's not going to do that, not there on the highway. He's got some other place in mind."

"Suppose that other place is one that's well-lighted, with a lot of people around?"

"I don't think so, Len," Agenrood said. "If that was his idea, he wouldn't have set it up for Rockaway Beach; that's a pretty dark and sparsely populated area. And he wouldn't go through all that business about blinking his headlights off an on, and then leaving with me following him."

Len nodded thoughtfully. "Maybe you're right."

"I think I am."

"Why do you suppose he wants you to bring the money personally? You'll see his face that way."

"I don't know," Agenrood admitted. "He has to be a little crazy to try something like this in the first place, and there's no way of telling what could be going through his mind. Maybe it's just a precaution against a trap and he's covering himself the way you said."

"Maybe," Len said. "And maybe he intends, once he has the money, to finish what he started Wednesday night."

"Yes," Agenrood said, taking a breath. "But it doesn't really matter, does it? If that's what he plans to do, he won't have the chance."

"I don't like it. It's damned risky."

"No riskier than turning him down, and then having to look over my shoulder every time I go out for a package of cigarettes until you locate him. *If* you locate him."

Len filled his pipe. When he had gotten it lighted, he said, "Reilly and Pordenza?"

"I know Pordenza. He's very capable."

"So is Reilly."

"All right, then."

"He told you he'd know if you didn't come yourself?"

"That's what he said."

"He might plan on watching your house, then."

"I thought of that."

"But we can't do anything there."

"No."

"How do we get Reilly and Pordenza into your car?"

"They can come across the rear of my property and slip in through the back entrance to the garage. I'll have the garage door closed, and if he's out on the street somewhere he won't be able to see inside. They can get in and out of sight before I come out."

"That sounds okay."

"I guess that's it, then."

"Yes, that's it. But listen, Jim, I don't want to lose you, and neither does the National Office. Go easy Tuesday night."

"I plan on doing just that," Agenrood said. "Everything is going to turn out just fine."

"I hope so. Because if there's any trouble, I can't help you, Jim.

As much as the National Office likes you, they won't go to bat for you if there's a foul-up."

"I'm aware of that."

"Good luck, then."

Agenrood smiled faintly. "And good hunting?"

"Yes," Len said. "And good hunting."

At twenty minutes past nine on Tuesday night, Cain left the Graceling Hotel and walked to the corner of Taylor and Eddy streets. There, he entered a gray stone building; over the building's entrance was a yellow-and-black sign that read: RIGHT-WAY RENT-A-CAR—$25 PER DAY, 5¢ PER MILE.

It was five minutes till ten when he emerged from an adjacent parking facility, driving a new, light brown, two-door hardtop. He had had no difficulties.

The luminescent dial of Cain's wristwatch read ten-forty when he parked the hardtop less than half a block beyond James Agenrood's red brick home on Devaney Way in Hillsborough. He eased his body down on the seat, remaining beneath the wheel; he adjusted the rearview mirror until he could see clearly Agenrood's garage, and the pale light that burned above its electronic door. He was not worried about being seen there, or of anything happening to him so near Agenrood's home; but he kept his right hand on the automatic in the pocket of his overcoat just the same.

Agenrood came out at eleven-thirteen; Cain saw his face clearly in the garage light. He was alone. He disappeared into the garage, and moments later the cream-colored Cadillac began to glide backward to the street. Headlights washed over the hardtop, but Cain was low enough on the seat so that he was sure Agenrood could not see him. The Cadillac swept past, and through the windshield now he watched it turn the corner at the first intersection and then vanish from sight.

Cain remained where he was for five minutes, timing it by his watch. Then he straightened on the seat, started the hardtop, and drove off in the direction Agenrood had taken.

Cain turned off Sharp Park Road, south onto the Coast Highway, at twenty minutes before twelve. He drove through Pacifica and Rockaway Beach; the Pacific Ocean lay smooth and hushed and cold on his right, like a great limitless pool of quicksilver in the shine from the three-quarter moon overhead.

He began to slow down when he saw the black-shadowed shape of the closed Standard station ahead of him. He came parallel to it and then made a left-hand turn across the highway and swung up onto the square of asphalt in front of the station. The cream-colored Cadillac sat dark and silent by the forward pumps. Cain touched the headlight switch, shutting the beams off; immediately, he flicked them back on again. He drove across to the opposite side of the asphalt square, waited there to allow a large truck to pass, and then swung out onto the Coast Highway again, resuming a southerly direction.

He looked up into his rearview mirror and saw Agenrood come out of the Standard station and fall in behind him.

Inside the cream-colored Cadillac, one of the two men hunched down on the floor of the back seat—Pordenza—said, "Where do you think he's heading?"

James Agenrood's hands were slick on the steering wheel. "I don't know," he answered.

"Well, I hope he gets there damned quick," Pordenza said. "I've got a charley horse in my leg."

"Just stay out of sight."

"Don't worry, Mr. Agenrood."

"We know what we're doing," Reilly put in quietly.

Agenrood watched the crimson lights two hundred yards ahead of him. A fine sheen of perspiration beaded his wide forehead. They continued for another mile, and then the left directional signal on the hardtop winked on; the car began to reduce its speed.

Agenrood said, "He's going to turn."

"Where?" Pordenza asked.

"There's a narrow dirt road up ahead. It winds up into the hills, to some private homes scattered across the tops."

"Anything between the highway and those homes?"

"No."

"That's it," Reilly said.

The hardtop turned onto the dirt road. Agenrood followed. They began to climb steadily; the road twisted an irregular path, with several doglegs and a sharp curve now and then. High wisps of fog began to shred in Agenrood's headlights, and he could see that at the crests of the hills, where the private homes were, it was thick and blanketing.

The hardtop came around one of the doglegs and its stop lights went on, flashing blood-red in the gray-black night. Agenrood said, "There's a turnout up ahead. I think he's going in there."

The hardtop edged into the turnout, parallel to the upper end, where a slope was grown thickly with bushes and scrub cypress. "He's stopping," Agenrood said.

"Pull up behind him," Pordenza directed from the floor of the back seat. "Leave a car's length between you."

Agenrood complied. When he saw the headlights on the hardtop go out, he shut his own off. It was dark then, but the moonlight— though dimmed now and then by the tendrils of fog—bathed the turnout with sufficient light to see by.

"What's he doing?" Pordenza asked.

"Just sitting there."

"When he gets out of the car, let him get clear of it by a few steps. Not too many. Then let us know."

Agenrood could hear faint stirrings in the back seat. He knew Reilly and Pordenza had moved one to each of the rear doors. They were waiting there now, with one hand on the door handles and the other wrapped around their guns.

"When we go," Reilly breathed from the back seat, "you get down on the front seat. Just in case."

"All right," Agenrood said, and the sweat on him was oily and cold now, flowing wetly along his body.

Cain sat very still beneath the wheel of the hardtop, his eyes lifted to the rearview mirror. There was no movement from inside the Cadillac; at least, none that he could see.

With his right hand, he took the automatic from the pocket of his overcoat and held it tightly in his fingers. He put his left hand on the door latch, and then took a long, deep breath, released it, and opened the door and stepped out onto the dusty surface of the turnout. He held the automatic low and slightly behind him, so that it was hidden from Agenrood's view by his leg.

Cain's muscles tensed, grew rigid. His eyes, unblinking, never left the Cadillac. He took one step away from the car, another, a third step toward the Cadillac.

Three things happened simultaneously.

There was a hoarse, muffled cry from inside the Cadillac; Agenrood's body disappeared, falling sideways; the rear doors of the Cadillac flew open and two men came out, very fast, guns extended in their hands.

Cain threw himself to the ground, rolled once, twice, came up on his knees, bracing himself. Twin flashes came from either side of the Cadillac; the two explosions were so close together the sound of them became one. Dust splashed up to one side of Cain; at the same instant, he felt a jarring impact high on the left side of his chest, a quick cut of pain, then the area went numb. But he did not lose his balance, and his eyes were clear. The automatic bucked twice, loudly, in his hand. He saw the man on the driver's side of the Cadillac whirl and fall, crying out.

The second man ducked behind the fender on the passenger side. Cain tried to turn his body there and couldn't; his entire left side was without feeling now. The man on the passenger side rose up cautiously, extending his gun, aiming, and then three rapid shots sounded from the scrub cypress on the slope. The second man stood up briefly, pirouetted, and vanished from sight.

The automatic dropped from Cain's fingers and he let his body sag forward until he lay huddled in the cold dust. He heard the whirring whine of the Cadillac's starter; then there were several shouts and the sound of running feet. A door was wrenched open. The Cadillac became silent again.

Cain tried to smile, but he was unable to move his facial muscles. He closed his eyes. A single pair of running feet approached him, and he felt a hand on his shoulder and heard somebody speaking to him. He could not understand the words.

Blackness began to unfold behind his eyes, and then there were no more sounds at all.

The private hospital room in Pacifica had greenish walls and smelled of ether and antiseptic and, faintly, of the day nurse's rose-water perfume. Cain sat propped up by several pillows on the single bed; his chest was bare, and the upper half of it was swathed in bandages.

There were two other men in the room. One was tall and had a long, thin neck; the other was short and studious-appearing, and wore a large pair of horn-rimmed glasses. They sat on two white metal chairs at the foot of the bed.

The studious-appearing man said, "You're a damned fool, Cain. You know that, don't you?"

"Am I?" Cain said briefly. He was looking out of the window; it was a warm, clear day and he could see the Pacific Ocean, glass-smooth in the distance.

The studious man opened a leather briefcase on his lap and removed several sheets of paper filled with neat lines of typing, single-spaced. The man looked at Cain, then looked back at the papers. "Do you know what this is?"

"No," Cain said.

"It's a report on one Steven Cain," the studious man told him. "A very comprehensive report we had compiled."

Cain continued to look out of the window.

"It says you were a colonel in the Marines during the Second World War, twice decorated for valor on Leyte and Okinawa. It says that you graduated at the top of your class at the University of California, where you majored in law enforcement following the war. It says that you joined the San Francisco Police Force in 1949 and while you were a patrolman in the Mission District you once captured four men in the act of robbing a factory payroll. It says that you were the youngest man in San Francisco police history to be promoted to the Detective Squad, and the second youngest to make division lieutenant." The studious man paused, looking up at Cain again. "There's more, a lot more. It's a very impressive record you've got, Cain."

Cain did not answer.

"Impressive enough to indicate an acute intelligence," the studious man said. "But I don't see any sign of intelligence in this crazy stunt you pulled off here. I don't see anything at all of the man this report covers."

Again, Cain did not answer.

"It was because of your daughter, wasn't it, Cain?" the man with the long neck said suddenly, speaking for the first time. "Because of what happened to Doreen?"

Cain brought his eyes away from the window and let them rest on the man with the long neck. He kept his lips pressed tightly together.

"It's all there in the report," the man with the long neck said. "About how you raised the girl after your wife died twelve years ago, how you were devoted to her. And it's in there, too, about how she was run down and killed by a car on an afternoon eight months ago when she was coming home from high school; how a patrol unit nearby saw the hit-and-run and chased the car and caught it a few blocks away; how the driver pulled a gun when they approached and one of the officers was forced to shoot him in self-defense, killing him instantly; how that driver turned out to be a twenty-three-year-old drug addict and convicted felon; and how they found almost half a kilo of heroin under the dashboard of the car——"

"That's enough!" Cain was leaning forward on the bed, oblivious to the sharp pain that the sudden movement had caused in his chest; his jaw was set grimly and his eyes were flashing.

The man with the long neck seemed not to hear him. "For all intents and purposes, you went just a little crazy when you heard the news, Cain. You needed somebody to strike out at, somebody to blame for your daughter's death. The kid was dead, so it had to be somebody else. That somebody was James Agenrood, the Organization's head of narcotics distribution in this area.

"You began a one-man crusade to get Agenrood; at first, you went through official channels and the newspapers agreed to play down the investigation—which was why Agenrood never knew your name. You dug up or bought or intimidated every scrap of knowledge available on Agenrood. But at the end of it all, you hadn't uncovered a thing on him that could put him away; he was, officially, a respectable citizen, President of Consolidated Trades, Inc., and untouchable. You just couldn't let go of it, though. Getting Agenrood became an obsession; you neglected your official duties in the pursuit of it. The Commissioner had to call you in finally and order you to cease. But you refused, and he had no alternative but to suspend you. A week later, you resigned. Shortly after that, you moved to Portland to live with a married sister and everybody here was maybe a little glad to see you go because they thought that finally you were through with it.

"But you weren't through. You had to get Agenrood, one way or another. You couldn't commit murder; you'd been an honest, dedicated cop too long to resort to that. So you went up to Portland and thought it all out, looking for another way, and then you came back here last Wednesday and stole a car to make the fake attempt on Agenrood's life look professional. You knew he would never pay

the kind of money you asked him for; you knew there was only one
other thing he could do. You made sure he would be there when it
was tried, and then you contacted us. You knew we were as eager
to get something on Agenrood as you were, and you told us just
enough to get us interested—but not enough so we knew what you
were planning—so that we would agree to send a couple of men up
to that road to wait. And it worked out okay, at least to your way
of thinking. We've got Agenrood on a charge of conspiracy to commit murder, among other things; he's through with the Organization, because they won't take the chance of becoming involved by
jumping to his defense. So you got him, Cain. You got your revenge,
all right."

Cain had slumped back against the pillows. But his jaw remained
grim. He did not say anything.

"But was it worth it?" the man with the long neck went on
finally. "Was it really worth it, Cain? Was it worth the prison sentence you're facing on a list of charges that range from car theft to
carrying a concealed weapon? What the hell have you actually
gained by all this? Why didn't you let us handle it? We'd have
gotten Agenrood sooner or later. We always get them sooner or
later."

The man with the long neck stopped speaking then, and it became very quiet in the room. After a long time, Cain said, "Maybe
you would have gotten him, and maybe you wouldn't. I couldn't
take the chance, don't you see? Agenrood killed my daughter, just as
sure as if he put a gun to her head and pulled the trigger. I had to
be the one; it was up to me. I had to get him for Doreen. Don't you
understand that?"

The two men looked at Cain, and then at one another. The room
was silent again for several minutes. Then the two men stood,
walked to the door.

"Don't you?" Cain said to them, softly.

"Yes," the studious man answered, just as softly. He put his hand on the knob and opened the door. "Yes, Cain, we understand."

Cain, lying in the bed, staring at the closed door after they had gone, wondered if they really understood at all. But after a while, when he had been alone for some time, he decided that it did not matter, one way or the other.

A Lot on His Mind

Arbagast was drunk in bed when the police came.

They told the old lady who had let them in to make some coffee, and then they took Arbagast into the bathroom and put him under a cold shower. They kept him there until he started to come out of it, and by that time the coffee was ready. They fed him cup after cup, hot and black, holding him upright on a straight-backed chair.

When they were certain he was sober enough to understand, they told him they had caught the man who had run down and killed his wife four months before.

Arbagast did not say anything for a long while. When he finally spoke, the sound of his voice made one of the policemen shudder involuntarily. "Who was it?"

"A man named Philip Colineaux," the policeman who had shuddered said. "He was involved in another hit-and-run tonight, and this time we got him."

"Someone else was killed?"

"No. He sideswiped a car at an intersection and kept going. There was a patrol car in the vicinity, and they chased him a couple of blocks and flagged him over."

"Was he drinking?"

"Not this time, anyway," the other policeman said. "They took him down for the test, and he passed that all right, but he was pretty shook up. He made a few slips, and that's how we found out about the other time."

"Did he confess to it?"

"Yes," the first policeman said. "He told us he didn't see her. He's a stockbroker and had a lot on his mind. 'Preoccupied,' he called it."

"Speeding?"

"He says no. But he was punching near forty when he hit that car tonight. You can bet he wasn't crawling the other time either."

"Have you got him in jail now?"

The first policeman shook his head, watching Arbagast. There was something about the way he was sitting there, rigid, his eyes flat and unblinking, showing nothing, that made the policeman feel cold. He said, "His lawyer came down and got him out on bail."

"All right," Arbagast said. "Thank you for coming by to tell me."

The two policemen looked at each other, hesitant to leave. The first one said, "Mr. Arbagast, we know you've had a terrible loss. You're taking it pretty hard, and that's understandable. But, well . . ."

He faltered, groping for words. Arbagast looked at him steadily, his face impassive.

"What I'm trying to say, Mr. Arbagast," the policeman went on finally, "the law's going to take care of this one good and proper. We've got him on a manslaughter charge now, and he had the damage to his car fixed by some friend. That's compounding a felony."

"Yes?" Arbagast said.

"So if I were you, I'd just try to forget about the whole thing. It took some time, but we got him, and that's the end of it. Sure, it won't bring your wife back, and it's damned little consolation, but he's going to be punished for what he did. You can rest assured of that."

The policeman paused, trying to read Arbagast's eyes, but they were inscrutable. He seemed about to go on, and then changed his mind. He said only, "I guess that's about it."

"Thank you again for stopping by," Arbagast said.

The two policemen went to the door. "Well, good night," the first one said.

"Yes," Arbagast said. "Good night."

When they had gone, Arbagast lay down on the bed, his hands clasped beneath his head, and stared up at the darkened ceiling. There was a bottle of whiskey on the nightstand, but he did not touch that. He only lay thinking, staring up at the ceiling, until the first gray light of dawn began to filter through the single window.

Arbagast got up then and went to the closet and took the City Telephone Directory from a shelf there. Then he dressed slowly and shaved and went downstairs to his car. He drove across town to the address he had found in the telephone book and parked across the street. He sat there, looking over at the white frame house where Philip Colineaux lived.

It was a nice house, well kept, freshly painted. A flagstone walk led through a garden alive in color, and there was a high green hedge bordering the right side of the property, near the garage.

Arbagast sat staring across the street. Eight o'clock came, and then nine. No one ventured out. Colineaux wasn't going to work today. Not today.

Arbagast returned to the small furnished room. He made some coffee and fried two eggs, and then he took the gun from the closet and broke it down and oiled and cleaned it. He put shells in the chambers, spinning the cylinder, and, when he was satisfied, put on the safety and slipped it into the pocket of his overcoat.

That night, just after dark, he drove to Philip Colineaux's house and parked across the street, as he had done that morning. He sat there in the darkness until ten o'clock. There were lights in the front room, but the windows were curtained and he could not see inside. No one came out.

The following morning, Arbagast was there again at dawn. He waited until almost noon. There was no sign of activity from inside the house.

At dusk he set up his vigil once more. Shortly past nine, the porch light came on above the door. Arbagast sat up in the seat, his hand touching the gun in his coat pocket.

A man came out onto the porch, standing in the light. There was a women behind him, in the doorway. *Going out to get some air,* Arbagast thought. *He's been in there two days. But he won't drive.*

The woman shut the door after a moment, and the man stood alone on the porch. He was short, past forty, dressed in slacks and a light windbreaker; hatless. Even at the distance across the street, Arbagast could see that his features were nondescript; it was not the face you would expect to see on a killer.

The man came down the steps and began to walk along the flagstone walk toward the street. Arbagast got out of the car, his fingers clenching on the gun in his pocket, and walked quickly across the deserted street. The man stopped in the shadows of the green hedge as he approached, frowning slightly.

Arbagast said, "Colineaux? Philip Colineaux?"

"Yes?" the man said.

"My name is Walter Arbagast."

The name did not immediately mean anything to Colineaux. "Yes?" he said again.

Arbagast took the gun from his pocket. Colineaux made a half-step backward, his eyes bulging. "My God, what——?"

"Come with me, please," Arbagast said.

"With you?" Colineaux said blankly.

"That's my car across the street."

Colineaux shook his head, not comprehending. "Who are you?" he said. "What is it you want?"

"My name is Walter Arbagast. Surely you remember the name, Colineaux."

"No, I . . ."

"Rosa Arbagast was my wife."

Understanding, complete and instant, flooded Colineaux's eyes.

His mouth opened as if to speak, but no words came forth. His face paled. Spittle flecked his lips.

"Yes," Arbagast said. "That's right. The woman you murdered."

"Murdered?" Colineaux said. "No! No, listen, it was an accident! It was dark. She was wearing dark clothes. I was thinking about something else, and I didn't see her. She came out of nowhere. Oh, God, it was an accident!"

"You ran her down," Arbagast said. "You ran her down and then left her to die in the street."

The right side of Colineaux's face began to spasm convulsively. His eyes were black, terrified. "I was frightened!" he moaned. "I panicked! Can't you understand how it was?"

"I understand you murdered my wife," Arbagast said without rancor, without emotion.

"What . . . what are you going to do?"

"I'm going to kill you," Arbagast said simply. "I'm going to run you down with my car. The same way you ran my wife down."

"You're mad! You're insane!"

"Yes," Arbagast said. "Perhaps I am."

Colineaux began to sag. It was as if the bones in his body had suddenly liquefied. His mouth opened and a soundless scream bubbled from his throat.

Arbagast pressed the gun against his stomach. "Don't make a sound," he said. "If you do, I'll kill you right here in front of your house, where you stand."

Colineaux seemed about to crumble. Arbagast took his arm and led him across the street. He opened the rear door to the car. "Get inside and lie flat on the seat. Put your hands behind you."

Colineaux was like a child in his fear. Mutely, he obeyed. Arbagast shut the door and got into the front seat. He took the roll of adhesive tape from the glove compartment and began to tape Colineaux's hands and ankles. When he had finished, he put a strip of tape across his mouth.

"If you rise up in the seat," Arbagast said, "I'll stop the car and shoot you in the back of the head. Do you understand?"

There was a strangled whimper from the man in the back seat. Arbagast nodded. He started the car and drove away.

"We're going out to the Western Avenue Extension," he said aloud, for Colineaux to hear. "There's a side road there, leading up to the reservoir. Nobody uses it much anymore."

The quiet suburban street sang beneath the wheels of the car, and that was the only reply.

"Do you know the stretch just before you reach the reservoir?" Arbagast asked. "It's walled by bluffs on two sides. There's no way you can get off the road there."

The night was deep and black and still.

"I'm going to untie you and let you out there," Arbagast said. "I'm going to give you a chance, Colineaux. You can run for your life. That's more of a chance than you gave Rosa."

The street sang faster, faster . . .

Arbagast turned his head slightly, looking into the rear seat. "Do you hear me, Colineaux? Do you—"

He did not see the woman until it was almost too late.

The street had been empty, dark. Then, as if by some strange necromancy, she was there, directly in front of him, a shadowy blur with a grotesque white face that seemed to rush at him, hurtling through the night as he stood still, an empyreal vision captured in the yellow glare of his headlights.

Arbagast swung the wheel in terror, his foot crashing down on the brake, just as that monstrous white face seemed about to strike him head on. The car went into a vicious skid, the quiet, still night exploding into the scream of rubber against pavement. One of the wheels went up over the curb, and the rear end scraped the base of a giant eucalyptus tree that grew there, and then the car settled, and died, on the street. The black night was once again silent.

Arbagast threw open the door, leaning out. The woman stood in the middle of the street behind him, an obscure statue. Then she began to walk, moving unsteadily, coming up the street toward him, and he could see her clearly, see her white face shining in the darkness.

It was Rosa's face.

A strangled cry tore from Arbagast's throat. He slammed the door, his hand twisting the ignition key. The starter whirred, whirred, and then caught, and he fought the lever into gear, his hands trembling violently on the wheel, his heart plunging in his chest. He got the car turned, straightened, and then he was pulling away, and the woman, the apparition, grew smaller and smaller in the rearview mirror until she became a speck that was swallowed, digested, by the night.

Oh, my God! Arbagast thought. *Oh, my God in Heaven!*

He drove three blocks and turned to the right, pulling in at the curb on a poorly lighted street. He shut off the engine, the headlights.

Turning on the seat, he reached into the back and pulled Colineaux to a sitting position. His trembling hands tore the tape from Colineaux's mouth.

"What happened back there?" Colineaux gasped, his voice mirroring the fear on his face. "What happened?"

Arbagast was unable to answer. He leaned down and unwound the tape from Colineaux's legs, from his hands. He forced words to come then. "Get out," he said. "Get out now."

Colineaux sat there, immobile. He did not understand. He could not believe.

"Get out," Arbagast said again, and wrenched open the rear door.

Colineaux moved. His body came alive, and he scuttled across the seat, hands clawing, pushing himself outside. He hesitated there for a second, looking back at Arbagast, and then he began to run.

Arbagast watched him running off, spindle-legged, down the

darkened street. After a long moment, he started the car again and drove away in the opposite direction.

Slowly, carefully, keeping well within the legal speed limit, his eyes fixed on the retreating concrete no longer singing beneath his headlights, he drove back to his small furnished room.

He was drunk in bed when the police came.

THE PATTERN

At 11:23 P.M. on Saturday, the twenty-sixth of April, a small man wearing rimless glasses and a dark gray business suit walked into the detective squad room in San Francisco's Hall of Justice and confessed to the murders of three Bay Area housewives whose bodies had been found that afternoon and evening.

Inspector Glenn Rauxton, who first spoke to the small man, thought he might be a crank. Every major homicide in any large city draws its share of oddballs and mental cases, individuals who confess to crimes in order to attain public recognition in otherwise unsubstantial lives; or because of some secret desire for punishment; or for any number of reasons that can be found in the casebooks of police psychiatrists. But it wasn't up to Rauxton to make a decision either way. He left the small man in the company of his partner, Dan Tobias, and went in to talk to his immediate superior, Lieutenant Jack Sheffield.

"We've got a guy outside who says he's the killer of those three women today, Jack," Rauxton said. "Maybe a crank, maybe not."

Sheffield turned away from the portable typewriter at the side of his desk; he had been making out a report for the chief's office. "He come in of his own volition?"

Rauxton nodded. "Not three minutes ago."

"What's his name?"

"He says it's Andrew Franzen."

"And his story?"

32

"So far, just that he killed them," Rauxton said. "I didn't press him. He seems pretty calm about the whole thing."

"Well, run his name through the weirdo file, and then put him in one of the interrogation cubicles," Sheffield said. "I'll look through the reports again before we question him."

"You want me to get a stenographer?"

"It would probably be a good idea."

"Right," Rauxton said, and went out.

Sheffield rubbed his face wearily. He was a lean, sinewy man in his late forties, with thick graying hair and a falconic nose. He had dark-brown eyes that had seen most everything there was to see, and been appalled by a good deal of it; they were tired, sad eyes. He wore a plain blue suit, and his shirt was open at the throat. The tie he had worn to work when his tour started at 4:00 P.M., which had been given to him by his wife and consisted of interlocking, psychedelic-colored concentric circles, was out of sight in the bottom drawer of his desk.

He picked up the folder with the preliminary information on the three slayings and opened it. Most of it was sketchy: telephone communications from the involved police forces in the Bay Area, a precursory report from the local lab, a copy of the police Telex that he had had sent out statewide as a matter of course following the discovery of the first body, and that had later alerted the other authorities in whose areas the two subsequent corpses had been found. There was also an Inspector's Report on that first and only death in San Francisco, filled out and signed by Rauxton. The last piece of information had come in less than a half-hour earlier, and he knew the facts of the case by memory; but Sheffield was a meticulous cop and he liked to have all the details fixed in his mind.

The first body was of a woman named Janet Flanders, who had been discovered by a neighbor at 4:15 that afternoon in her small duplex on 39th Avenue, near Golden Gate Park. She had been killed by several blows about the head with an as yet unidentified blunt instrument.

The second body, of one Viola Gordon, had also been found by a neighbor—shortly before 5:00 P.M.—in her neat, white frame cottage in South San Francisco. Cause of death: several blows about the head with an unidentified blunt instrument.

The third body, Elaine Dunhill, had been discovered at 6:37 P.M. by a casual acquaintance who had stopped by to return a borrowed book. Mrs. Dunhill lived in a modest cabin-style home clinging to the wooded hillside above Sausalito Harbor, just north of San Francisco. She, too, had died as a result of several blows about the head with an unidentified blunt instrument.

There were no witnesses, or apparent clues, in any of the killings. They would have, on the surface, appeared to be unrelated if it had not been for the facts that each of the three women had died on the same day, and in the same manner. But there were other cohesive factors as well—factors, that, taken in conjunction with the surface similarities, undeniably linked the murders.

Item: each of the three women had been between the ages of thirty and thirty-five, on the plump side, and blonde.

Item: each of them had been orphaned non-natives of California, having come to the San Francisco Bay Area from different parts of the Midwest within the past six years.

Item: each of then had been married to traveling salesmen who were home only short periods each month, and who were all— according to the information garnered by investigating officers from neighbors and friends—currently somewhere on the road.

Patterns, Sheffield thought as he studied the folder's contents. Most cases had one, and this case was no exception. All you had to do was fit the scattered pieces of its particular pattern together, and you would have your answer. Yet the pieces here did not seem to join logically, unless you concluded that the killer of the women was a psychopath who murdered blonde, thirtyish, orphaned wives of traveling salesmen for some perverted reason of his own.

That was the way the news media would see it, Sheffield knew, because that kind of slant always sold copies, and attracted viewers and listeners. They would try to make the case into another Zodiac thing. The radio newscast he had heard at the cafeteria across Bryant Street, when he had gone out for supper around nine, had presaged the discovery of still more bodies of Bay Area housewives and had advised all women whose husbands were away to remain behind locked doors. The announcer had repeatedly referred to the deaths as "the bludgeon slayings."

Sheffield had kept a strictly open mind. It was, for all practical purposes, his case—the first body had been found in San Francisco, during his tour, and that gave him jurisdiction in handling the investigation. The cops in the two other involved cities would be in constant touch with him, as they already had been. He would have been foolish to have made any premature speculations not based solely on fact, and Sheffield was anything but foolish. Anyway, psychopath or not, the case still promised a hell of a lot of not very pleasant work.

Now, however, there was Andrew Franzen.

Crank? Or multiple murderer? Was this going to be one of those blessed events—a simple case? Or was Franzen only the beginning of a long series of very large headaches?

Well, Sheffield thought, *we'll find out soon enough.* He closed the folder and got to his feet and crossed to the door of his office.

In the squad room, Rauxton was just finishing a computer check. He came over to Sheffield and said, "Nothing on Franzen in the weirdo file, Jack."

Sheffield inclined his head and looked off toward the row of glass-walled interrogation cubicles at the rear of the squad room. In the second one, he could see Dan Tobias propped on a corner of the bare metal desk inside; the man who had confessed, Andrew Franzen, was sitting with his back to the squad room, stiffly erect in his chair. Also waiting inside, stoically seated in the near corner, was one of the police stenographers.

Sheffield said, "Okay, Glenn, let's hear what he has to say."

He and Rauxton went over to the interrogation cubicle and

stepped inside. Tobias stood, shook his head almost imperceptibly to let Sheffield and Rauxton know that Franzen hadn't said anything to him. Tobias was tall and muscular, with a slow smile and big hands and—like Rauxton—a strong dedication to the life's work he had chosen.

He moved to the right corner of the metal desk, and Rauxton to the left corner, assuming set positions like football halfbacks running a bread-and-butter play. Sheffield, the quarterback, walked behind the desk, cocked one hip against the edge and leaned forward slightly, so that he was looking down at the small man sitting with his hands flat on his thighs.

Franzen had a round, inoffensive pink face with tiny-shelled ears and a Cupid's-bow mouth. His hair was brown and wavy, immaculately cut and shaped, and it saved him from being nondescript; it gave him a certain boyish character, even though Sheffield placed his age at around forty. His eyes were brown and liquid, like those of a spaniel, behind his rimless glasses.

Sheffield got a ball-point pen out of his coat pocket and tapped it lightly against his front teeth; he liked to have something in his hands when he was conducting an interrogation. He broke the silence, finally, by saying, "My name is Sheffield. I'm the lieutenant in charge here. Now before you say anything, it's my duty to advise you of your rights."

He did so, quickly and tersely, concluding with, "You understand all of your rights as I've outlined them, Mr. Franzen?"

The small man sighed softly and nodded.

"Are you willing, then, to answer questions without the presence of counsel?"

"Yes, yes."

Sheffield continued to tap the ball-point pen against his front teeth. "All right," he said at length. "Let's have your full name."

"Andrew Leonard Franzen."

"Where do you live?"

"Here in San Francisco."

"At what address?"

"Nine-oh-six Greenwich."

"Is that a private residence?"

"No, it's an apartment building."

"Are you employed?"

"Yes."

"Where?"

"I'm an independent consultant."

"What sort of consultant?"

"I design languages between computers."

Rauxton said, "You want to explain that?"

"It's very simple, really," Franzen said tonelessly. "If two business firms have different types of computers, and would like to set up a communication between them so that the information stored in the memory banks of each computer can be utilized by the other, they call me. I design the linking electronic connections between the two computers, so that each can understand the other; in effect, so that they can converse."

"That sounds like a very specialized job," Sheffield said.

"Yes."

"What kind of salary do you make?"

"Around eighty thousand a year."

Two thin, horizontal frown lines appeared in Sheffield's forehead. Franzen had the kind of vocation that bespoke of intelligence and upper-class respectability; why would a man like that want to confess to the brutal murders of three simple-living housewives? Or an even more puzzling question: If his confession was genuine, what was his reason for the killings?

Sheffield said, "Why did you come here tonight, Mr. Franzen?"

"To confess." Franzen looked at Rauxton. "I told this man that when I walked in a few minutes ago."

"To confess to what?"

"The murders."

"What murders, specifically?"

Franzen sighed. "The three women in the Bay Area today."

"Just the three?"

"Yes."

"No others whose bodies maybe have not been discovered as yet?"

"No, no."

"Suppose you tell us why you decided to turn yourself in?"

"Why? Because I'm guilty. Because I killed them."

"And that's the only reason?"

Franzen was silent for a moment. Then slowly, he said, "No, I suppose not. I went walking in Aquatic Park when I came back to San Francisco this afternoon, just walking and thinking. The more I thought, the more I knew that it was hopeless. It was only a matter of time before you found out I was the one, a matter of a day or two. I guess I could have run, but I wouldn't know how to begin to do that. I've always done things on impulse, things I would never do if I stopped to think about them. That's how I killed them, on some insane impulse; if I had thought about it I never would have done it. It was so useless . . ."

Sheffield exchanged glances with the two inspectors. Then he said, "You want to tell us how you did it, Mr. Franzen?"

"What?"

"How did you kill them?" Sheffield asked. "What kind of weapon did you use?"

"A tenderizing mallet," Franzen said without hesitation.

Tobias asked, "What was that again?"

"A tenderizing mallet. One of those big wooden things with serrated ends that women keep in the kitchen to tenderize a piece of steak."

It was silent in the cubicle now. Sheffield looked at Rauxton, and then at Tobias; they were all thinking the same thing: the police had released no details to the news media as to the kind of weapon involved in the slayings, other than the general information that it was a blunt instrument. But the initial lab report on the first victim—and the preliminary observations on the other two—stated the wounds of each had been made by a roughly square-shaped instrument, which had sharp "teeth" capable of making a series of deep indentations as it bit into the flesh. A mallet such as Franzen had just described fitted those characteristics exactly.

Sheffield asked, "What did you do with this mallet, Mr. Franzen?"

"I threw it away."

"Where?"

"In Sausalito, into some bushes along the road."

"Do you remember the location?"

"I think so."

"Then you can lead us there later on?"

"I suppose so, yes."

"Was Elaine Dunhill the last woman you killed?"

"Yes."

"What room did you kill her in?"

"The bedroom."

"Where in the bedroom?"

"Beside her vanity."

"Who was your first victim?" Rauxton asked.

"Janet Flanders."

"You killed her in the bathroom, is that right?"

"No, no, in the kitchen . . ."

"What was she wearing?"

"A flowered housecoat."

"Why did you strip her body?"

"I didn't. Why would I—"

"Mrs. Gordon was the middle victim, right?" Tobias asked.

"Yes."

"Where did you kill *her?*"

"The kitchen."

"She was sewing, wasn't she?"

"No, she was canning," Franzen said. "She was canning plum

preserves. She had mason jars and boxes of plums and three big pressure cookers all over the table and the stove . . ."

There was wetness in Franzen's eyes now. He stopped talking and took his rimless glasses off and wiped at the tears with the back of his left hand. He seemed to be swaying slightly on the chair.

Sheffield, watching him, felt a curious mixture of relief and sadness. The relief was due to the fact that there was no doubt in his mind—nor in the minds of Rauxton and Tobias; he could read their eyes—that Andrew Franzen was the slayer of the three women. They had thrown detail and "trip-up" questions at him, one right after another, and he had had all the right answers; he knew particulars that had also not been given to the news media, that no crank could possibly have known, that only the murderer could have been aware of. The case had turned out to be one of the simple ones, after all, and it was all but wrapped up now; there would be no more "bludgeon slayings," no public hue and cry, no attacks on police inefficiency in the press, no pressure from the commissioners or the mayor. The sadness was the result of twenty-six years of police work, of living with death and crime every day, of looking at a man who seemed to be the essence of normalcy and yet who was a cold-blooded multiple murderer.

Why? Sheffield thought. That was the big question. *Why did he do it?*

He said, "You want to tell us the reason, Mr. Franzen? Why you killed them?"

The small man moistened his lips. "I was very happy, you see. My life had some meaning, some challenge. I was fulfilled—but they were going to destroy everything." He stared at his hands. "One of them had found out the truth—I don't know how—and tracked down the other two. I had come to Janet this morning, and she told me that they were going to expose me, and I just lost my head and picked up the mallet and killed her. Then I went to the others and killed them. I couldn't stop myself; it was as if I were moving in a nightmare."

"What are you trying to say?" Sheffield asked softly. "What was your relationship with those three women?"

The tears in Andrew Franzen's eyes shone like tiny diamonds in the light from the overhead fluorescents.

"They were my wives," he said.

I Don't Understand It

Well, I'd been on the road for two days, riding on the produce trucks from El Centro to Bakersfield, when a refrigerator van picked me up and took me straight through to the Salinas Valley. They let me out right where I was headed, too, in front of this dirt road about three miles the other side of San Sinandro.

I stood there on the side of the road, hanging onto the tan duffel with my stuff in it, and it was plenty hot all right, just past noon, and the sun all yellow and hazed over. I looked at the big wood sign that was stuck up there, and it said: JENSEN PRODUCE—PICKERS WANTED, and had a black arrow pointing off down the dirt road. That was the name of the place, sure enough.

I started up the dirt road, and it was pretty dry and dusty. Off on both sides you could see the rows and rows of lettuce shining nice and green in the sun, and the pickers hunched over in there. Most of them looked like Mex's, but here and there was some college boys that are always around to pick in the spring and summer months.

Pretty soon I come over a rise and I could see a wide clearing. There was a big white house set back a ways, and down in front an area that was all paved off. On one side was a big corrugated-iron warehouse, the sun coming off the top of that iron roof near to blinding you, it was so bright. About six flatbeds, a couple of Jimmy pickups, and a big white Lincoln was sitting beside the warehouse.

All of them had JENSEN PRODUCE done up in these big gold and blue letters on the door.

I come down there onto the asphalt part. Just to my right was four long, flat buildings made of wood, but with corrugated roofs. I knew that was where the pickers put down.

I walked across to the big warehouse. Both of the doors in front was shut, but there was a smaller one to the left and it was standing wide open.

Just as I come up to that door, this woman come out, facing inside, and sure enough she banged right into me before I could get out of the way. I stumbled back and dropped the duffel.

She come around and looked at me. She said, "Oh, I'm sorry. I didn't see you there."

Well, she was about the most beautiful woman I ever saw in my whole life. She had this long dark hair and green eyes with little gold flecks in them, and she was all brown and tan and her skin shined in the sun like she had oil rubbed on it. She had on a pair of white shorts and this white blouse with no sleeves. Her hands was in little fists on her hips, and she was smiling at me real nice and friendly. She said, "Well, I don't think I've seen you before."

I couldn't say nothing right then. I mean, I never been much good around the women anyway—I can't never think of nothing to talk to them about—and this one was so pretty she could've been in them Hollywood pictures.

My ears felt all funny and hot, with her looking right into my face like she was. But I couldn't just stand there, so I kind of coughed a little and bent down and picked up the duffel.

I said, "No, ma'am."

"I'm Mrs. Jensen. Is there something I can do for you?"

"Well, I heard you needed pickers."

"Yes, we do," she said. "The hot weather came on before we expected it. We have to harvest before the heat ruins the crop and we're awfully shorthanded."

I started to say something about being glad to help out, but just then this big good-looking fellow in a blue work shirt that had the sleeves rolled up and was unbuttoned down the front so you could see all the hair he had on his chest, he come out of the door. The woman turned and saw him and said, "Oh, this is Mr. Carbante. He's our foreman."

I said, "How are you, Mr. Carbante?"

"Okay," he said. "You looking for work?"

"Sure."

"Ever picked lettuce before?"

"No, sir. But I picked plenty of other things."

"Such as?"

"Well, citrus."

"Where?"

"Down in the Imperial Valley."

"What else?"

"Tomatoes. Grapes and apples and celery, too."

"All right," Mr. Carbante said. "You're on."

"I sure do thank you."

This Mrs. Jensen was still standing there with her hands on her hips. She looked at me. "I'm sorry again about that bump."

"Oh, it's nothing."

"Good luck."

"Thanks."

"I'll see you later, Gino," she said to Mr. Carbante.

"Okay, Mrs. Jensen."

When she was gone, around to the side, Mr. Carbante took me into the warehouse. They had a criss-cross of conveyer belts in there, and packing bins lining one wall, and there was a lot of Mex women that was sorting out the lettuce heads and putting the good ones off on one belt to where they was trimmed and graded and packed, and putting the ones that wasn't any good off on another belt.

We went into a little office they had there, and Mr. Carbante give me a little book to keep track of how many crates I was to pick, and told me what they paid for each crate. Then he said what bunkhouse I was to sleep in and the bunk number and what time they give you supper and what time you had to be up and ready for work in the morning.

He just finished telling me all that when this old bird come into the office. He had a nice head of white hair and pink cheeks, and he stopped where we was and give me a smile. He must've been close to seventy, sure enough, but his eyes was bright and he looked to get around pretty good.

Mr. Carbante said, "This is Mr. Jensen. He's the owner."

"How do you do, Mr. Jensen?"

"Glad to know you, son. You going to work for us?"

"Yes, sir."

"Well, that's fine."

"Yes, sir."

"Did you want to see me, Mr. Jensen?" Mr. Carbante asked.

"Have you seen Mrs. Jensen?"

"Not since breakfast."

"All right, Gino," Mr. Jensen said, and he went on out.

I said, "Mrs. Jensen was right here with you, Mr. Carbante."

"Never mind, boy."

"Yes, sir," I said. "Is that Mrs. Jensen's husband?"

Mr. Carbante's eyes got all narrow. "That's right. Why?"

"Well, nothing," I said, but I was wondering how come old Mr. Jensen was to have such a young wife. People sure do funny things sometimes, specially when they get old.

Mr. Carbante said, "You just mind your own business and pick your quota every day, and you'll get along fine here. You understand that, boy?"

"Sure, Mr. Carbante."

"Okay, then. You'll be down on the south side. There's a couple of Mex's out there who'll give you the hang of it."

*   *   *

Do you know how they pick lettuce?

The way you do it is, you have this long knife, real sharp, and you walk in along the rows, which are about two feet apart, and you clip off the heads in close to the ground and put them in these field crates you drag along with you. When you get a crate filled, you leave it in there between the rows and then a truck comes along and picks up the crates and takes them up to the warehouse.

Now, it don't sound like much, me telling it like that, but there's plenty of little tricks to it, all right.

These two men that Mr. Carbante had told me about give me some tips on how to tell which heads was to be cut, and how to tell which ones had been chewed up by the aphids, and which ones had got the mildew or been burnt by the sun. I took to watching this one big fellow, whose name was Haysoos. He was pretty near pure black from the sun, and had tiny little eyes and thick, bushy eyebrows. But he sure knew what he was doing in that lettuce, clipping away like nobody you ever saw.

After I watched him for a while, I got onto the knack of it and started right in myself. I had my shirt off out there, and it was plenty hot. I was burnt up pretty good from being down in the Imperial Valley, but down there you was working citrus and didn't have to pick right in under the sun like that.

Just as I got my first field crate filled up, who should come down the road but Mrs. Jensen and Mr. Carbante. They was just strolling along, side by side, her with this big floppy straw hat stuck up on her head. She was smiling, and every now and then she would wave to one of the pickers out in the lettuce. Every one of them was looking at her, sure enough.

She got up to where me and Haysoos was working and stopped and give me a nice smile. "Hello, there."

"Hello, Mrs. Jensen."

"How are you doing?"

"Just fine."

This Haysoos smiled at her with teeth that was all yellow and said something in Mex, but I guess she didn't hear him. She started off down the road again. Haysoos watched her. "*Muy bonita,* hey? Such a beautiful woman, a man's blood boils at the sight of such a beautiful woman."

"She sure is beautiful, all right," I said.

"She likes you, hey, *amigo?*"

"She's real nice and friendly."

"Haysoos she does not like. Not big ugly Haysoos."

"Oh, sure she likes you, Haysoos."

"Carbante is who she likes, hey? Carbante and a thousand others."

He turned away and started in to pick again. I didn't know what he'd meant, but I didn't want to say nothing so I just turned away too and went to work in my own row.

The next day I was pretty sore from the stooping over, but I'd had a nice sleep the night before and it didn't bother me too much. I'd got the hang of picking the lettuce now, and I was clipping along at a nice pace.

One of the trucks come around with sandwiches and milk for us at noontime, and we sat there on the side of the road to eat. Well, while we was eating, here come Mrs. Jensen down the road again.

She come right up there to where we was, smiling at everybody, and asked us if we all had enough to eat. Some of the college boys called out some things I didn't understand, and most everybody laughed, and Mrs. Jensen laughed right with them.

This Haysoos was sitting right near where I was. He kept watching Mrs. Jensen. "Everyone but Haysoos, hey?" he said.

"How was that?"

"A man's blood boils."

He sure said a lot of funny things, that Haysoos.

Saturday come around before you knew it and that was when we was to get paid. After supper we all went to the office in the big warehouse with the little books we had and old Mr. Jensen and Mr. Carbante totaled up the number of crates we had picked and give us our pay, all in cash money.

When we was all paid, old Mr. Jensen stood up and said that he was going off to Salinas for the next few days on business, and that Mr. Carbante was to be in charge and if we wanted anything we should see him. After that he went out and got into his big Lincoln and drove off down the road.

I went back to the bunks then, but most of the other pickers, they was going off into San Sinandro to drink in the bars. A couple of them asked me if I wanted to come along, but I said I wasn't much for the drinking.

I lay down on my bunk and started to read this movie magazine one of the college boys had. I sure like to read them movie magazines, all about the Hollywood people and the houses they have and the fine clothes and everything. Someday I'm going to have me all them things, too.

Well, I lay there and pretty soon it got dark outside. But it was awful hot in there and I got up and went out to get some air. It sure hadn't cooled down much.

I walked down by the other bunks and come around the south end of the second one, and I heard all this commotion inside. There was a window right there and I stopped by that and looked inside to see what it was all about.

There was this bunch of pickers in there, about six of them, and they was all pretty well oiled up. They had a couple of empty wine jugs lying around on the floor, and they was passing this other one around from one to another.

And who should be right there in the middle of all of them but Haysoos. He was sitting on one of the bunks, his eyes all glassed over. He got the jug and took a long one out of there, and passed it on to the next one. He wasn't whooping it up or nothing, like the rest of them was, but just sitting there on that bunk, kind of staring at the floor.

Well, while I watched, the rest of them started out the door and one had the wine jug. They called back to Haysoos, but he just sat there and didn't answer them at all. Then Haysoos was alone, and I heard the rest of them going off down the road singing some kind of Mex song.

Old Haysoos found another jug somewhere and had one you would hardly believe from it. He wiped off his mouth with the back of his hand and then stood up and wobbled around some. I could see his lips moving like he was talking to himself, but I couldn't hear none of it.

I got tired of watching him and went back to my bunk and lay down again, and it wasn't so hot anymore. Pretty soon I went to sleep.

I woke up right away when I heard the sirens.

I jumped off my bunk and run outside, and there was a lot of the other pickers there, too, just come back from San Sinandro. They was all running up toward the big white house.

I commenced to running up there with them, and I thought how it must be that the big white house had caught fire somehow and what a terrible thing that would be. But when I got up there, I saw that it wasn't fire engines that had made the sirens, but police cars. There was three of them there, and a big ambulance, and they all had these red lights going round and round on their tops. There was a couple of policemen, too, holding the pickers back and telling them not to come any closer.

I wedged in there, and the pickers that had been there for a while was talking pretty fast.

". . . right there in the bedroom."

"She had it coming."

"They both did."

"Yeah, but not *that* way."

"Who found them?"

"Somebody heard the screams."

"But they didn't get him?"

"Not yet."

"He must have gone through the fields."

"They've got the roads blocked."

"We'll get up a posse . . ."

I said to one of the college boys who had been talking, "What is it? What happened?"

"You don't know?"

I said, "I was sleeping. What is it?"

Just then the front door of the big white house opened and two fellows dressed in white and two policemen come out and they was carrying two stretchers. They had to pass by where I was to get to the ambulance, and I looked at the two sheet-covered stretchers and what was on them.

I just couldn't believe it at first, but the college boys was talking again, telling about it, and I knew it had to be true. I turned away, sick as anybody ever was.

The one college boy put his hand on my shoulder. "Come on," he said, "we're going after him——"

But I pulled away and run back to the bunks. I had to get away from there. I couldn't stay there no more.

You know what that crazy Haysoos had done?

He'd killed Mrs. Jensen and Mr. Carbante, that's what. He'd gone up to the big white house with that sharp, sharp lettuce knife of his and cut off both their heads.

I don't understand it, and I'm just so sick. A fine lady like Mrs. Jensen and a nice man like Mr. Carbante. Two of the swellest people you ever wanted to meet and know, and that crazy Haysoos had killed them both.

I just don't understand what could have made him do a terrible, terrible thing like that.

PROOF OF GUILT

I've been a city cop for thirty-two years now, and during that time I've heard of and been involved in some of the weirdest, most audacious crimes imaginable—on and off public record. But as far as I'm concerned, the murder of an attorney named Adam Chillingham is *the* damnedest case in my experience, if not in the entire annals of crime.

You think I'm exaggerating? Well, listen to the way it was.

My partner Jack Sherrard and I were in the Detective Squad Room one morning last summer when this call came in from a man named Charles Hearn. He said he was Adam Chillingham's law clerk, and that his employer had just been shot to death; he also said he had the killer trapped in the lawyer's private office.

It seemed like a fairly routine case at that point. Sherrard and I drove out to the Dawes Building, a skyscraper in a new business development on the city's south side, and rode the elevator up to Chillingham's suite of offices on the sixteenth floor. Hearn and a woman named Clarisse Tower, who told us she had been the dead man's secretary, were waiting in the anteroom with two uniformed patrolmen who had arrived minutes earlier.

According to Hearn, a man named George Dillon had made a ten-thirty appointment with Chillingham, had kept it punctually, and had been escorted by the attorney into the private office at that exact time. At ten-forty Hearn thought he heard a muffled explosion from inside the office, but he couldn't be sure because the walls were partially soundproofed.

Hearn got up from his desk in the anteroom and knocked on the door and there was no response; then he tried the knob and found that the door was locked from the inside. Miss Tower confirmed all this, although she said she hadn't heard any sound; her desk was farther away from the office door than was Hearn's.

A couple of minutes later the door had opened and George Dillon had looked out and calmly said that Chillingham had been murdered. He had not tried to leave the office after the announcement; instead, he'd seated himself in a chair near the desk and lighted a cigarette. Hearn satisfied himself that his employer was dead, made a hasty exit, but had the presence of mind to lock the door from the outside by the simple expediency of transferring the key from the inside to the outside—thus sealing Dillon in the office with the body. After which Hearn put in his call to Headquarters.

So Sherrard and I drew our guns, unlocked the door, and burst into the private office. This George Dillon was sitting in the chair across the desk, very casual, both his hands up in plain sight. He gave us a relieved look and said he was glad the police had arrived so quickly.

I went over and looked at the body, which was sprawled on the floor behind the desk; a pair of French windows were open in the wall just beyond, letting in a warm summer breeze. Chillingham had been shot once in the right side of the neck, with what appeared by the size of the wound to have been a small-caliber bullet; there was no exit wound, and there were no powder burns.

I straightened up, glanced around the office, and saw that the only door was the one that we had just come through. There was no balcony or ledge outside the open windows—just a sheer drop of sixteen stories to a parklike, well-landscaped lawn that stretched away for several hundred yards. The nearest building was a hundred yards distant, angled well to the right. Its roof was about on a level with Chillingham's office, it being a lower structure than the Dawes

Building; not much of the roof was visible unless you peered out and around.

Sherrard and I then questioned George Dillon—and he claimed he hadn't killed Chillingham. He said the attorney had been standing at the open windows, leaning out a little, and that all of a sudden he had cried out and fallen down with the bullet in his neck. Dillon said he'd taken a look out the windows, hadn't seen anything, checked that Chillingham was dead, then unlocked the door and summoned Hearn and Miss Tower.

When the coroner and the lab crew finally got there, and the doc had made his preliminary examination, I asked him about the wound. He confirmed my earlier guess—a small-caliber bullet, probably a .22 or .25. He couldn't be absolutely sure, of course, until he took out the slug at the post-mortem.

I talked things over with Sherrard and we both agreed that it was pretty much improbable for somebody with a .22 or .25 caliber weapon to have shot Chillingham from the roof of the nearest building; a small caliber like that just doesn't have a range of a hundred yards and the angle was almost too sharp. There was nowhere else the shot could have come from—except from inside the office. And that left us with George Dillon, whose story was obviously false and who just as obviously had killed the attorney while the two of them were locked inside this office.

You'd think it was pretty cut-and-dried then, wouldn't you? You'd think all we had to do was arrest Dillon and charge him with homicide, and our job was finished. Right?

Wrong.

Because we couldn't find the gun.

Remember, now, Dillon had been locked in that office—except for the minute or two it took Hearn to examine the body and slip out and relock the door—from the time Chillingham died until the time we came in. And both Hearn and Miss Tower swore that Dillon hadn't stepped outside the office during that minute or two. We'd already searched Dillon and he had nothing on him. We searched the office—I mean, we *searched* that office—and there was no gun there.

We sent officers over to the roof of the nearest building and down onto the landscaped lawn; they went over every square inch of ground and rooftop, and they didn't find anything. Dillon hadn't thrown the gun out the open windows then, and there was no place on the face of the sheer wall of the building where a gun could have been hidden.

So where was the murder weapon? What had Dillon done with it? Unless we found that out, we had no evidence against him that would stand up in a court of law; his word that he *hadn't* killed Chillingham, despite the circumstantial evidence of the locked room, was as good as money in the bank. It was up to us to prove him guilty, not up to him to prove himself innocent. You see the problem?

We took him into a large book-filled room that was part of the Chillingham suite—what Hearn called the "archives"—and sat him down in a chair and began to question him extensively. He was a big husky guy with blondish hair and these perfectly guileless eyes; he just sat there and looked at us and answered in a polite voice, maintaining right along that he hadn't killed the lawyer.

We made him tell his story of what had happened in the office a dozen times, and he explained it the same way each time—no variations. Chillingham had locked the door after they entered, and then they sat down and talked over some business. Pretty soon Chillingham complained that it was stuffy in the room, got up, and opened the French windows; the next thing Dillon knew, he said, the attorney collapsed with the bullet in him. He hadn't heard any shot, he said; Hearn must be mistaken about a muffled explosion.

I said finally, "All right, Dillon, suppose you tell us why you came to see Chillingham. What was this business you discussed?"

"He was my father's lawyer," Dillon said, "and the executor of my father's estate. He was also a thief. He stole three hundred and fifty thousand dollars of my father's money."

Sherrard and I stared at him. Jack said, "That gives you one hell of a motive for murder, if it's true."

"It's true," Dillon said flatly. "And yes, I suppose it does give me a strong motive for killing him. I admit I hated the man, I hated him passionately."

"You admit that, do you?"

"Why not? I have nothing to hide."

"What did you expect to gain by coming here to see Chillingham?" I asked. "Assuming you didn't come here to kill him."

"I wanted to tell him I knew what he'd done, and that I was going to expose him for the thief he was."

"You tell him that?"

"I was leading up to it when he was shot."

"Suppose you go into a little more detail about this alleged theft from your father's estate."

"All right." Dillon lit a cigarette. "My father was a hard-nosed businessman, a self-made type who acquired a considerable fortune in textiles; as far as he was concerned, all of life revolved around money. But I've never seen it that way; I've always been something of a free spirit and to hell with negotiable assets. Inevitably, my father and I had a falling-out about fifteen years ago, when I was twenty-three, and I left home with the idea of seeing some of the big wide world—which is exactly what I did.

"I traveled from one end of this country to the other, working at different jobs, and then I went to South America for a while. Some of the wanderlust finally began to wear off, and I decided to come back to this city and settle down—maybe even patch things up with my father. I arrived several days ago and learned then that he had been dead for more than two years."

"You had no contact with your father during the fifteen years you were drifting around?"

"None whatsoever. I told you, we had a falling-out. And we'd never been close to begin with."

Sherrard asked, "So what made you suspect Chillingham had stolen money from your father's estate?"

"I am the only surviving member of the Dillon family; there are no other relatives, not even a distant cousin. I knew my father wouldn't have left me a cent, not after all these years, and I didn't particularly care; but I *was* curious to find out to whom he had willed his estate."

"And what did you find out?"

"Well, I happen to know that my father had three favorite charities," Dillon said. "Before I left, he used to tell me that if I didn't 'shape-up,' as he put it, he would leave every cent of his money to those three institutions."

"He didn't, is that it?"

"Not exactly. According to the will, he left two hundred thousand dollars to each of two of them—the Cancer Society and the Children's Hospital. He also, according to the will, left three hundred and fifty thousand dollars to the Association for Medical Research."

"All right," Sherrard said, "so what does that have to do with Chillingham?"

"Everything," Dillon told him. "My father died of a heart attack—he'd had a heart condition for many years. Not severe, but he fully expected to die as a result of it one day. And so he did. And because of this heart condition, his third favorite charity—the one he felt the most strongly about—was the Heart Fund."

"Go on," I said, frowning.

Dillon put out his cigarette and gave me a humorless smile. "I looked into the Association for Medical Research and I did quite a thorough bit of checking. It doesn't exist; there *isn't* any Association for Medical Research. And the only person who could have invented it is or was my father's lawyer and executor, Adam Chillingham."

Sherrard and I thought that over and came to the same conclusion. I said, "So even though you never got along with your father, and you don't care about money for yourself, you decided to expose Chillingham."

"That's right. My father worked hard all his life to build his fortune, and admirably enough, he decided to give it to charity at his death. I believe in worthwhile causes, I believe in the work being done by the Heart Fund, and it sent me into a rage to realize they had been cheated out of a substantial fortune that could have gone toward valuable research."

"A murderous rage?" Sherrard asked softly.

Dillon showed us his humorless smile again. "I didn't kill Adam Chillingham," he said. "But you'll have to admit, he deserved killing—and that the world is better off without the likes of him."

I might have admitted that to myself, if Dillon's accusations were valid, but I didn't admit it to Dillon. I'm a cop, and my job is to uphold the law; murder is murder, whatever the reasons for it, and it can't be gotten away with.

Sherrard and I hammered at Dillon a while longer, but we couldn't shake him at all. I left Jack to continue the field questioning and took a couple of men and re-searched Chillingham's private office. No gun. I went up onto the roof of the nearest building and searched that personally. No gun. I took my men down into the lawn area and supervised another minute search. No gun.

I went back to Chillingham's suite and talked to Charles Hearn and Miss Tower again, and they had nothing to add to what they'd already told us; Hearn was "almost positive" he had heard a muffled explosion inside the office, but from the legal point of view, that was the same as not having heard anything at all.

We took Dillon down to Headquarters finally, because we knew damned well he had killed Adam Chillingham, and advised him of his rights and printed him and booked him on suspicion. He asked for counsel, and we called a public defender for him, and then we grilled him again in earnest. It got us nowhere.

The F.B.I. and state check we ran on his fingerprints got us nowhere either; he wasn't wanted, he had never been arrested, he had never even been printed before. Unless something turned up soon in the way of evidence—specifically, the missing murder weapon—we knew we couldn't hold him very long.

The next day I received the lab report and the coroner's report, and the ballistics report on the bullet taken from Chillingham's neck——.22 caliber, all right. The lab's and coroner's findings combined to tell me something I'd already guessed: the wound and the calculated angle of trajectory of the bullet did not entirely rule out the remote possibility that Chillingham had been shot from the roof of the nearest building. The ballistics report, however, told me something I hadn't guessed—something that surprised me a little.

The bullet had no rifling marks.

Sherrard blinked at this when I related the information to him. "No rifling marks?" he said. "Hell, that means the slug wasn't fired from a gun at all, at least not a lawfully manufactured one. A homemade weapon, you think, Walt?"

"That's how it figures," I agreed. "A kind of zipgun probably. Anybody can make one; all you need is a length of tubing or the like and a bullet and a grip of some sort and a detonating cap."

"But there was no zipgun, either, in or around Chillingham's office. We'd have found it if there was."

I worried my lower lip meditatively. "Well, you can make one of those zips from a dozen or more small component parts, you know; even the tubing could be soft aluminum, the kind you can break apart with your hands. When you're done using it, you can knock it down again into its components. Dillon had enough time to have done that, before opening the locked door."

"Sure," Sherrard said. "But then what? We *still* didn't find anything—not a single thing—that could have been used as part of a homemade zip."

I suggested we go back and make another search, and so we drove once more to the Dawes Building. We re-combed Chillingham's private office—we'd had a police seal on it to make sure nothing could be disturbed—and we re-combed the surrounding area. We didn't find so much as an iron filing. Then we went to the city jail and had another talk with George Dillon.

When I told him our zipgun theory, I thought I saw a light flicker in his eyes; but it was the briefest of reactions, and I couldn't be sure. We told him it was highly unlikely a zipgun using a .22-caliber bullet could kill anybody from a distance of a hundred yards, and he said he couldn't help that, *he* didn't know anything about such a weapon. Further questioning got us nowhere.

And the following day we were forced to release him, with a warning not to leave the city.

But Sherrard and I continued to work doggedly on the case; it was one of those cases that preys on your mind constantly, keeps you from sleeping well at night, because you know there has to be an answer and you just can't figure out what it is. We ran checks into Chillingham's records and found that he had made some large private investments a year ago, right after the Dillon will had been probated. And as George Dillon had claimed, there was no Association for Medical Research; it was a dummy charity, apparently set up by Chillingham for the explicit purpose of stealing old man Dillon's $350,000. But there was no definite proof of this, not enough to have convicted Chillingham of theft in a court of law; he'd covered himself pretty neatly.

As an intelligent man, George Dillon had no doubt realized that a public exposure of Chillingham would have resulted in nothing more than adverse publicity and the slim possibility of disbarment—hardly sufficient punishment in Dillon's eyes. So he had decided on what to him was a morally justifiable homicide. From the law's point of view, however, it was nonetheless Murder One.

But the law still had no idea what he'd done with the weapon, and therefore, as in the case of Chillingham's theft, the law had no proof of guilt.

As I said, though, we had our teeth into this one and we weren't about to let go. So we paid another call on Dillon, this time at the hotel where he was staying, and asked him some questions about his background. There was nothing more immediate we could investigate, and we thought that maybe there was an angle in his past that would give us a clue toward solving the riddle.

He told us, readily enough, some of what he'd done during the fifteen years since he'd left home, and it was a typical drifter's life: lobster packer in Maine, ranch hand in Montana, oil worker in Texas, road construction in South America. But there was a gap of about four years that he sort of skimmed over without saying anything specific. I jumped on that and asked him some direct questions, but he wouldn't talk about it.

His reluctance made Sherrard and me more than a little curious; we both had that cop's feeling it was important, that maybe it was the key we needed to unlock the mystery. We took the mug shots we'd made of Dillon and sent them out, along with a request for information as to his whereabouts during the four blank years, to various law-enforcement agencies in Florida—where he'd admitted to being just prior to the gap, working as a deckhand on a Key West charter-fishing boat.

Time dragged on, and nothing turned up, and we were reluctantly forced by sheer volume of other work to abandon the Chillingham case; officially, it was now buried in the Unsolved File. Then, three months later, we had a wire from the Chief of Police of a town not far from Fort Lauderdale. It said they had tentatively identified George Dillon from the pictures we'd sent and were forwarding by airmail special delivery something that might conceivably prove the nature of Dillon's activities during at least part of the specified period.

Sherrard and I fidgeted around waiting for the special delivery to arrive, and when it finally came I happened to be the only one of us in the squad room. I tore the envelope open, and what was inside was a multicolored and well-aged poster, with a picture of a man who was undeniably George Dillon depicted on it. I looked at the picture and read what was written on the poster at least a dozen times.

It told me a lot of things all right, that poster did. It told me exactly what Dillon had done with the homemade zipgun he had used to kill Adam Chillingham—an answer that was at once fantastic and yet so simple you'd never ever consider it. And it told me there wasn't a damned thing we could do about it now, that we couldn't touch him, that George Dillon actually had committed a perfect murder.

I was brooding over this when Jack Sherrard returned to the squad room. He said, "Why so glum, Walt?"

"The special delivery from Florida finally showed up," I said, and watched instant excitement animate his face. Then I saw most of it fade while I told him what I'd been brooding about, finishing with, "We simply can't arrest him now, Jack. There's no evidence, it doesn't exist any more; we can't prove a thing. And maybe it's just as well in one respect, since I kind of liked Dillon and would have hated to see him convicted for killing a crook like Chillingham. Anyway, we'll be able to sleep nights now."

"Damn it, Walt, will you tell me what you're talking about!"

"All right. Remember when we got the ballistics report and we talked over how easy it would be for Dillon to have made a zipgun? And how he could make the whole thing out of a dozen or so small component parts, so that afterward he could break it down again into those small parts?"

"Sure, sure. But I still don't care if Dillon used a hundred components, we didn't find a single one of them. Not one. So what, if that's part of the answer, did he do with them? There's not even a connecting bathroom where he could have flushed them down. What did he do with the damned zipgun?"

I sighed and slid the poster—the old carnival side-show poster— around on my desk so he could see Dillon's picture and read the

words printed below it: STEAK AND POTATOES AND APPLE PIE IS OUR
DISH; NUTS, BOLTS, PIECES OF WOOD, BITS OF METAL IS HIS! YOU HAVE
TO SEE IT TO BELIEVE IT: THE AMAZING MR. GEORGE, THE MAN WITH
THE CAST-IRON STOMACH.

Sherrard's head jerked up and he stared at me open-mouthed.
"That's right," I said wearily. "He *ate* it."

MULTIPLES
(With Barry N. Malzberg)

Kenner murdered his wife for the tenth time on the evening of July 28, in the kitchen of their New York apartment. Or perhaps it was July 29. One day is much the same as another, and I cannot seem to keep dates clearly delineated in my head. He did it for the usual reasons: because she had dominated him for fourteen years of marriage (fifteen? sixteen?), and openly and regularly ridiculed him, and sapped all his energy and drive, and, oh I simply could not stand it any more.

He did not try to be elaborately clever as to method and execution. The simpler the better—that was the way he liked to do it. So he poisoned her with ten capsules of potassium, I mean nitrous oxide, disguised as saccharine tablets, which he neatly placed in her coffee with a twist of the wrist like a kiss. Nothing amiss.

She assumed almost at once the characteristic attitude of oxide poisoning, turning a faint green as she bent into the crockery on the table. A cigarette still smoldered unevenly beside her. She drank twenty cups of coffee every day and smoked approximately four packages of cigarettes, despite repeated warnings from her doctor. Kenner found it amusing to think that her last sensations were composed of acridity, need, and lung-filling inhalation. It was even possible that she believed, as death majestically overtook her, that the *cigarette* had done her in.

Kenner, a forty-five-year-old social worker of mundane background, few friends, and full civil service tenure (but nevertheless in grave trouble with his superiors, who had recently found him to be "insufficiently motivated"), then made all efforts to arrange the scene in what he thought to be a natural manner: adjusting the corpse in a comfortable position, cleaning the unused pellets of cyanide from the table, letting the damned cat out, and so forth. Immediately afterward, he went to a movie theater; that is, he went immediately after shutting off all the lights and locking all the doors. Windows were left open in the kitchen, however, to better disperse what he thought of as "the stench of death."

What Kenner did at the movie theater was to sit through a double feature. The price he paid for admission and what films he saw or did not really see are not known at the time of this writing. Furthermore, what he hoped to gain by leaving the scene of the crime only to reenter at a "safer" time remains in doubt. I must have been crazy. Also, Kenner's usual punctiliousness and sense of order did not control his actions during this tragic series of events. I was too excited.

After emerging from the theater, Kenner purchased an ice cream cone from a nearby stand and ate it slowly while walking back to his apartment. As he turned in a westerly direction, he was accosted by two co-workers at the Welfare Unit where he was employed. They greeted him and asked the whereabouts of his wife. Kenner responded that she had had a severe headache and, since she suffered from a mild heart condition complicated by diabetes, wanted to restrain her activities to the minimum. I suppose Kenner was attempting with this tactic to lay the groundwork for a "death by natural causes" verdict, but I'm not quite sure. I do know that one of the co-workers, commenting on Kenner's appearance, said that he looked "ghastly."

Once parted from his colleagues, Kenner continued west and eventually reentered his apartment at 10:51 P.M. It was frightening in the dark. Turning on the lights, he went into the living room and found his wife waiting there for him—sitting under a small lamp, reading and drinking coffee and smoking five cigarettes in various stages of completion. Much perturbed, he was unable to account for the fact that she was still alive. I felt as if I were dreaming.

There was a brief exchange of dialogue between Kenner and his wife, the substance of which I cannot recall, and then he proceeded to his own room. He wanted to lock the door behind him but could not, owing to the fact that his wife—saying that separate bedrooms or not, she wanted to know what the "little fool" was doing at all times—had forbidden him a bolt. On the way he noticed that the plates had been removed from the kitchen table and heaped as always to fester in the sink, and that there was no sign of the violence he was *sure* had taken place earlier.

Immediately after closing his door, Kenner seized his journal and began to record the evening's curious events in his usual style. I could have been a published writer if only I had worked at it. He was hopeful that the documentation would help him to understand matters, but I was wrong, this was never the answer.

He was interrupted midway through his writing by his wife's customarily unannounced entrance into his room. She told him that his strange state of excitation this evening had upset even her, and therefore agitated her mild heart condition (she had one, all right, although she did not have diabetes). She said she thought I was "breaking down," and went on to say that she knew the "impulse to murder her" had long been uppermost in Kenner's mind but he "didn't have the guts to do it." She further stated that Kenner was no doubt "dreaming all the time of ways and means and you probably fill that damned journal of yours with all your raving imaginations; I've never cared enough to bother reading it, but it's sure to be *full* of lunatic fantasies."

Kenner responded that he was a mature person and thus not prey to hostile thoughts. He begged her to leave the room so that he could continue his entries. I told her I was writing a novel, but she didn't believe me. She knows everything.

She laughed at him and dared him to make her leave the room. Kenner stared at her mutely, whereupon she laughed again and said if looks could kill, she'd certainly be dead right now. Then she said, "But if I were dead, you'd be lost; you'd fall apart altogether. You need me and you don't *really* want me dead, you know, even though as I'm talking to you you're probably filling up pages with more vicious fantasies. I'll bet I even know what you're writing this very minute. You're imagining me dead, aren't you? You're writing down right this minute that I'm dead."

She's dead.

She's dead.

She—is—dead!

Kenner murdered his wife for the eleventh time on July 29 or July 30, in her bedroom in their New York apartment. He did it for the usual reasons, and he did not attempt to be elaborately clever as to method and execution. In fact, he chose to repeat the procedure of the previous evening. While she lounged in bed as was her custom on weekends (this was either Saturday or Sunday), I made her breakfast and poisoned her coffee with eleven capsules of nitrous oxide.

When Kenner took the tray into her bedroom, she was sitting up in bed and there were three cigarettes burning on the nightstand. She smiled at him maliciously as she lifted her cup, and asked if he had "put in a few drops of arsenic or something to sweeten the taste." After which she laughed in her diabolical way and drank some of the coffee.

With clinical curiosity, Kenner watched the cup slip from her fingers and spill the rest of the liquid over the bedclothes; watched her expression alter and her face and body once more assume the characteristic attitude of oxide poisoning as she fell back against the headboard. The faint green color looked quite well on her, he concluded.

This time Kenner did not arrange the scene in what he thought to be a natural manner. He also did not open the windows. He simply left the apartment and took a subway to Times Square, where he consumed a breakfast of indeterminate nature in a restaurant or perhaps a cafeteria. Once finished he browsed through a bookstore, purchased a candy bar, and finally took the subway home again. Upon entering his apartment, I think the time was 10:51 A.M., he proceeded directly to his wife's bedroom.

She was still lying in bed, and she was still quite surprisingly dead. The scene, however, had after all been changed in certain ways. The coffee that he was *sure* had been spilled across the bedclothes had not been spilled at all; the cup, in point of fact, rested empty on the breakfast tray. Her color was not greenish, but rather a violent purple. The three cigarettes had become four, and each had burned down to skeletal fingers of gray ash. Her hands were clutched somewhat pathetically at her breast.

Kenner stared at her for a long time, after which scrutiny he went to his room and attempted to write in his journal. I could not seem to think, I knew I would have to wait until later. Returning to his wife's bedroom once more, he paused to study the empty coffee cup and the remains of the cigarettes. It was then that he understood the truth.

The *cigarettes* and the *coffee,* not Kenner, had done her in.

What he did next is not clear. Very little is clear even now, many hours later. He does seem to have telephoned his wife's doctor, since the physician arrived eventually and pronounced her dead of a heart attack. Two or three interns also came with a stretcher and took her away. As I write this I can still smell the after-shave lotion one of them was wearing.

One thing, therefore, is quite clear: she's dead.

Damn her, she really is dead and gone forever.

What am I going to do *now?*

Kenner murdered his dead wife for the first time on August 1, or possibly August 6, in the bathroom of their New York apartment . . .

SWEET FEVER

Quarter before midnight, like on every evening except the Sabbath or when it's storming or when my rheumatism gets to paining too bad, me and Billy Bob went down to the Chigger Mountain railroad tunnel to wait for the night freight from St. Louis. This here was a fine summer evening, with a big old fat yellow moon hung above the pines on Hankers Ridge and mockingbirds and cicadas and toads making a soft ruckus. Nights like this, I have me a good feeling, hopeful, and I know Billy Bob does too.

They's a bog hollow on the near side of the tunnel opening, and beside it a woody slope, not too steep. Halfway down the slope is a big catalpa tree, and that was where we always set, side by side with our backs up against the trunk.

So we come on down to there, me hobbling some with my cane and Billy Bob holding onto my arm. That moon was so bright you could see the melons lying in Ferdie Johnson's patch over on the left, and the rail tracks had a sleek oiled look coming out of the tunnel mouth and leading off toward the Sabreville yards a mile up the line. On the far side of the tracks, the woods and the rundown shacks that used to be a hobo jungle before the county sheriff closed it off thirty years back had them a silvery cast, like they was all coated in winter frost.

We set down under the catalpa tree and I leaned my head back to catch my wind. Billy Bob said, "Granpa, you feeling right?"

"Fine, boy."

"Rheumatism ain't started paining you?"

"Not a bit."

He give me a grin. "Got a little surprise for you."

"The hell you do."

"Fresh plug of blackstrap," he said. He come out of his pocket with it. "Mr. Cotter got him in a shipment just today down at his store."

I was some pleased. But I said, "Now you hadn't ought to go spending your money on me, Billy Bob."

"Got nobody else I'd rather spend it on."

I took the plug and unwrapped it and had me a chew. Old man like me ain't got many pleasures left, but fresh blackstrap's one; good corn's another. Billy Bob gets us all the corn we need from Ben Logan's boys. They got a pretty good sized still up on Hankers Ridge, and their corn is the best in this part of the hills. Not that either of us is a drinking man, now. A little touch after supper and on special days is all. I never did hold with drinking too much, or doing anything too much, and I taught Billy Bob the same.

He's a good boy. Man couldn't ask for a better grandson. But I raised him that way—in my own image, you might say—after both my own son Rufus and Billy Bob's ma got taken from us in 1947. I reckon I done a right job of it, and I couldn't be less proud of him than I was of his pa, or love him no less, either.

Well, we set there and I worked on the chew of blackstrap and had a spit every now and then, and neither of us said much. Pretty soon the first whistle come, way off on the other side of Chigger Mountain. Billy Bob cocked his head and said, "She's right on schedule."

"Mostly is," I said, "this time of year."

That sad lonesome hungry ache started up in me again—what my daddy used to call the "sweet fever." He was a railroad man, and I grew up around trains and spent a goodly part of my early years at the roundhouse in the Sabreville yards. Once, when I was ten, he let me take the throttle of the big 2-8-0 Mogul steam locomotive on his highballing run to Eulalia, and I can't recollect no more finer experience in my whole life. Later on I worked as a callboy, and then as a fireman on a 2-10-4, and put in some time as a yard tender engineer, and I expect I'd have gone on in railroading if it hadn't been for the Depression and getting myself married and having Rufus. My daddy's short-line company folded up in 1931, and half a dozen others too, and wasn't no work for either of us in Sabreville or Eulalia or anywheres else on the iron. That squeezed the will right out of him, and he took to ailing, and I had to accept a job on Mr. John Barnett's truck farm to support him and the rest of my family. Was my intention to go back into railroading, but the Depression dragged on, and my daddy died, and a year later my wife Amanda took sick and passed on, and by the time the war come it was just too late.

But Rufus got him the sweet fever too, and took a switchman's job in the Sabreville yards, and worked there right up until the night he died. Billy Bob was only three then; his own sweet fever comes most purely from me and what I taught him. Ain't no doubt trains been a major part of all our lives, good and bad, and ain't no doubt neither they get into a man's blood and maybe change him, too, in one way and another. I reckon they do.

The whistle come again, closer now, and I judged the St. Louis freight was just about to enter the tunnel on the other side of the mountain. You could hear the big wheels singing on the track, and if you listened close you could just about hear the banging of couplings and the hiss of air brakes as the engineer throttled down for the curve. The tunnel don't run straight through Chigger Mountain; she comes in from the north and angles to the east, so that a big freight like the St. Louis got to cut back to quarter speed coming through.

When she entered the tunnel, the tracks down below seemed to shimmy, and you could feel the vibration clear up where we was sitting under the catalpa tree. Billy Bob stood himself up and peered down toward the black tunnel mouth like a bird dog on a point.

The whistle come again, and once more, from inside the tunnel, sounding hollow and miseried now. Every time I heard it like that, I thought of a body trapped and hurting and crying out for help that wouldn't come in the empty hours of the night. I swallowed and shifted the cud of blackstrap and worked up a spit to keep my mouth from drying. The sweet fever feeling was strong in my stomach.

The blackness around the tunnel opening commenced to lighten, and got brighter and brighter until the long white glow from the locomotive's headlamp spilled out onto the tracks beyond. Then she come through into my sight, her light shining like a giant's eye, and the engineer give another tug on the whistle, and the sound of her was a clattering rumble as loud to my ears as a mountain rock-slide. But she wasn't moving fast, just kind of easing along, pulling herself out of that tunnel like a night crawler out of a mound of earth.

The locomotive clacked on past, and me and Billy Bob watched her string slide along in front of us. Flats, boxcars, three tankers in a row, more flats loaded down with pine logs big around as a privy, a refrigerator car, five coal gondolas, another link of boxcars. Fifty in the string already, I thought. She won't be dragging more than sixty, sixty-five. . . .

Billy Bob said suddenly, "Granpa, look yonder!"

He had his arm up, pointing. My eyes ain't so good no more, and it took me a couple of seconds to follow his point, over on our left and down at the door of the third boxcar in the last link. It was sliding open, and clear in the moonlight I saw a man's head come out, then his shoulders.

"It's a floater, Granpa," Billy Bob said, excited. "He's gonna jump. Look at him holding there—he's gonna jump."

I spit into the grass. "Help me up, boy."

He got a hand under my arm and lifted me up and held me until I was steady on my cane. Down there at the door of the boxcar, the floater was looking both ways along the string of cars and down at the ground beside the tracks. That ground was soft loam, and the train was going slow enough that there wasn't much chance he would hurt himself jumping off. He come to that same idea, and as soon as he did he flung himself off the car with his arms spread out and his hair and coattails flying in the slipstream. I saw him land solid and go down and roll over once. Then he knelt there, shaking his head a little, looking around.

Well, he was the first floater we'd seen in seven months. The yard crews seal up the cars nowadays, and they ain't many ride the rails anyhow, even down in our part of the country. But every now and then a floater wants to ride bad enough to break a seal, or hides himself in a gondola or on a loaded flat. Kids, oldtime hoboes, wanted men. They's still a few.

And some of 'em get off right down where this one had, because they know the St. Louis freight stops in Sabreville and they's yard-men there that check the string, or because they see the rundown shacks of the old hobo jungle or Ferdie Johnson's melon patch. Man rides a freight long enough, no provisions, he gets mighty hungry; the sight of a melon patch like Ferdie's is plenty enough to make him jump off.

"Billy Bob," I said.

"Yes, Granpa. You wait easy now."

He went off along the slope, running. I watched the floater, and he come up on his feet and got himself into a clump of bushes alongside the tracks to wait for the caboose to pass so's he wouldn't be seen. Pretty soon the last of the cars left the tunnel, and then the caboose with a signalman holding a red-eye lantern out on the plat-form. When she was down the tracks and just about beyond my sight, the floater showed himself again and had him another look around. Then, sure enough, he made straight for the melon patch.

Once he got into it I couldn't see him, because he was in close to the woods at the edge of the slope. I couldn't see Billy Bob neither. The whistle sounded one final time, mournful, as the lights of the caboose disappeared, and a chill come to my neck and set there like

a cold dead hand. I closed my eyes and listened to the last singing of
the wheels fade away.

It weren't long before I heard footfalls on the slope coming near,
then the angry sound of a stranger's voice, but I kept my eyes shut
until they walked up close and Billy Bob said, "Granpa." When I
opened 'em the floater was standing three feet in front of me, white
face shining in the moonlight—scared face, angry face, evil face.

"What the hell is this?" he said. "What you want with me?"

"Give me your gun, Billy Bob," I said.

He did it, and I held her tight and lifted the barrel. The ache in
my stomach was so strong my knees felt weak and I could scarcely
breathe. But my hand was steady.

The floater's eyes come wide open and he backed off a step.
"Hey," he said, "hey, you can't—"

I shot him twice.

He fell over and rolled some and come up on his back. They
wasn't no doubt he was dead, so I give the gun back to Billy Bob
and he put it away in his belt. "All right, boy," I said.

Billy Bob nodded and went over and hoisted the dead floater
onto his shoulder. I watched him trudge off toward the bog hollow,
and in my mind I could hear the train whistle as she'd sounded
from inside the tunnel. I thought again, as I had so many times, that
it was the way my boy Rufus and Billy Bob's ma must have sounded
that night in 1947, when the two floaters from the hobo jungle
broke into their home and raped her and shot Rufus to death. She
lived just long enough to tell us about the floaters, but they was
never caught. So it was up to me, and then up to me and Billy Bob
when he come of age.

Well, it ain't like it once was, and that saddens me. But they's
still a few that ride the rails, still a few take it into their heads to
jump off down there when the St. Louis freight slows coming
through the Chigger Mountain tunnel.

Oh my yes, they'll *always* be a few for me and Billy Bob and the
sweet fever inside us both.

PUTTING THE PIECES BACK

You wouldn't think a man could change completely in four months—but when Kaprelian saw Fred DeBeque come walking into the Drop Back Inn, he had living proof that it could happen. He was so startled, in fact, that he just stood there behind the plank and stared with his mouth hanging open.

It had been a rainy off-Monday exactly like this one the last time he'd seen DeBeque, and that night the guy had been about as low as you could get and carrying a load big enough for two. Now he was dressed in a nice tailored suit, looking sober and normal as though he'd never been through any heavy personal tragedy. Kaprelian felt this funny sense of flashback come over him, like the entire last seven months hadn't even existed.

He didn't much care for feelings like that, and he shook it off. Then he smiled kind of sadly as DeBeque walked over and took his old stool, the one he'd sat on every night for the three months after he had come home from work late one afternoon and found his wife bludgeoned to death.

Actually, Kaprelian was glad to see the change in him. He hadn't known DeBeque or DeBeque's wife very well before the murder; they were just people who lived in the neighborhood and dropped in once in a while for a drink. He'd liked them both though, and he'd gotten to know Fred pretty well afterward, while he was doing all that boozing. That was why the change surprised him as much as it did. He'd been sure DeBeque would turn into a Skid Row bum or a corpse, the way he put down the sauce; a man couldn't drink like that more than maybe a year without ending up one or the other.

The thing was, DeBeque and his wife really loved each other. He'd been crazy for her, worshipped the ground she walked on— Kaprelian had never loved anybody that way, so he couldn't really understand it. Anyhow, when she'd been murdered DeBeque had gone all to pieces. Without her, he'd told Kaprelian a few times, he didn't want to go on living himself; but he didn't have the courage to kill himself either. Except with the bottle.

There was another reason why he couldn't kill himself, DeBeque said, and that was because he wanted to see the murderer punished and the police hadn't yet caught him. They'd sniffed around De-Beque himself at first, but he had an alibi and, anyway, all his and her friends told them how much the two of them were in love. So then, even though nobody had seen any suspicious types in the neighborhood the day it happened, the cops had worked around with the theory that it was either a junkie who'd forced his way into the DeBeque apartment or a sneak thief that she'd surprised. The place had been ransacked and there was some jewelry and mad money missing. Her skull had been crushed with a lamp, and the cops figured she had tried to put up a fight.

So DeBeque kept coming to the Drop Back Inn every night and getting drunk and waiting for the cops to find his wife's killer. After three months went by, they still hadn't found the guy. The way it looked to Kaprelian then—and so far that was the way it had turned out—they never would. The last night he'd seen DeBeque, Fred had admitted that same thing for the first time and then he had walked out into the rain and vanished. Until just now.

Kaprelian said, "Fred, it's good to see you. I been wondering what happened to you, you disappeared so sudden four months ago."

"I guess you never expected I'd show up again, did you, Harry?"

"You want the truth, I sure didn't. But you really look great. Where you been all this time?"

"Putting the pieces back together again," DeBeque said. "Finding new meaning in life."

Kaprelian nodded. "You know, I thought you were headed for Skid Row or an early grave, you don't mind my saying so."

"No, I don't mind. You're absolutely right, Harry."

"Well—can I get you a drink?"

"Ginger ale," DeBeque said. "I'm off alcohol now."

Kaprelian was even more surprised. There are some guys, some drinkers, you don't ever figure *can* quit, and that was how DeBeque had struck him at the tag end of those three bad months. He said, "Me being a bar owner, I shouldn't say this, but I'm glad to hear that too. If there's one thing I learned after twenty years in this business, you can't drown your troubles or your sorrows in the juice. I seen hundreds try and not one succeed."

"You tried to tell me that a dozen times, as I recall," DeBeque said. "Fortunately, I realized you were right in time to do something about it."

Kaprelian scooped ice into a glass and filled it with ginger ale from the automatic hand dispenser. When he set the glass on the bar, one of the two workers down at the other end—the only other customers in the place—called to him for another beer. He drew it and took it down and then came back to lean on the bar in front of DeBeque.

"So where'd you go after you left four months ago?" he asked. "I mean, did you stay here in the city or what? I know you moved out of the neighborhood."

"No, I didn't stay here." DeBeque sipped his ginger ale. "It's funny the way insights come to a man, Harry—and funny how long it takes sometimes. I spent three months not caring about anything, drinking myself to death, drowning in self-pity; then one morning I just woke up knowing I couldn't go on that way any longer. I wasn't sure why, but I knew I had to straighten myself out. I went upstate and dried out in a rented cabin in the mountains. The rest of the insight came there: I knew why I'd stopped drinking, what it was I had to do."

"What was that, Fred?"

"Find the man who murdered Karen."

Kaprelian had been listening with rapt attention. What DeBeque had turned into wasn't a bum or a corpse but the kind of comeback hero you see in television crime dramas and don't believe for a minute. When you heard it like this, though, in real life and straight from the gut, you knew it had to be the truth—and it made you feel good.

Still, it wasn't the most sensible decision DeBeque could have reached, not in real life, and Kaprelian said, "I don't know, Fred, if the cops couldn't find the guy—"

DeBeque nodded. "I went through all the objections myself," he said, "but I knew I still had to try. So I came back here to the city and I started looking. I spent a lot of time in the Tenderloin bars, and I got to know a few street people, got in with them, was more or less accepted by them. After a while I started asking questions and getting answers."

"You mean," Kaprelian said, astonished, "you actually got a line on the guy who did it—"

Smiling, DeBeque said, "No. All the answers I got were negative. No, Harry, I learned absolutely nothing—except that the police were wrong about the man who killed Karen. He wasn't a junkie or a sneak thief or a street criminal of any kind."

"Then who was he?"

"Someone who knew her, someone she trusted. Someone she would let in the apartment."

"Makes sense, I guess," Kaprelian said. "You have any idea who this someone could be?"

"Not at first. But after I did some discreet investigating, after I visited the neighborhood again a few times, it all came together like the answer to a mathematical equation. There was only one person it could be."

"Who?" Kaprelian asked.

"The mailman."

"The *mailman?*"

"Of course. Think about it, Harry. Who else would have easy access to our apartment? Who else could even be *seen* entering the apartment by neighbors without them thinking anything of it, or even remembering it later? The mailman."

"Well, what did you do?"

"I found out his name and I went to see him one night last week. I confronted him with knowledge of his guilt. He denied it, naturally; he kept right on denying it to the end."

"The end?"

"When I killed him," DeBeque said.

Kaprelian's neck went cold. "Killed him? Fred, you can't be serious! You didn't actually *kill* him—"

"Don't sound so shocked," DeBeque said. "What else could I do? I had no evidence, I couldn't take him to the police. But neither could I allow him to get away with what he'd done to Karen. You understand that, don't you? I had no choice. I took out the gun I'd picked up in a pawnshop, and I shot him with it—right through the heart."

"Jeez," Kaprelian said. "Jeez."

DeBeque stopped smiling then and frowned down into his ginger ale; he was silent, kind of moody all of a sudden. Kaprelian became aware of how quiet it was and flipped on the TV. While he was doing that the two workers got up from their stools at the other end of the bar, waved at him, and went on out.

DeBeque said suddenly, "Only then I realized he couldn't have been the one."

Kaprelian turned from the TV. "What?"

"It couldn't have been the mailman," DeBeque said. "He was left-handed, and the police established that the killer was probably right-handed. Something about the angle of the blow that killed Karen. So I started thinking who else it could have been, and then I knew: the grocery delivery boy. Except we used two groceries, two delivery boys, and it turned out both of them were right-handed. I talked to the first and I was sure he was the one. I shot him. Then I knew I'd been wrong, it was the other one. I shot him too."

"Hey," Kaprelian said. "Hey, Fred, what're you *saying?*"

"But it wasn't the delivery boys either." DeBeque's eyes were very bright. "Who, then? Somebody else from the neighborhood . . . and it came to me, I knew who it had to be."

Kaprelian still didn't quite grasp what he was hearing. It was all coming too fast. "Who?" he said.

"You," DeBeque said, and it wasn't until he pulled the gun that Kaprelian finally understood what was happening, what DeBeque had *really* turned into after those three grieving, alcoholic months. Only by then it was too late.

The last thing he heard was voices on the television—a crime drama, one of those where the guy's wife is murdered and he goes out and finds the real killer and ends up a hero in time for the last commercial. . . .

SMUGGLER'S ISLAND

The first I heard that somebody had bought Smuggler's Island was late on a cold, foggy morning in May. Handy Manners and Davey and I had just brought the *Jennie Too* into the Camaroon Bay wharf, loaded with the day's limit in salmon—silvers mostly, with a few big kings—and Handy had gone inside the processing shed at Bay Fisheries to call for the tally clerk and the portable scales. I was helping Davey hoist up the hatch covers, and I was thinking that he handled himself fine on the boat and what a shame it'd be if he decided eventually that he didn't want to go into commercial fishing as his livelihood. A man likes to see his only son take up his chosen profession. But Davey was always talking about traveling around Europe, seeing some of the world, maybe finding a career he liked better than fishing. Well, he was only nineteen. Decisions don't come quick or easy at that age.

Anyhow, we were working on the hatch covers when I heard somebody call my name. I glanced up, and Pa and Abner Frawley were coming toward us from down-wharf, where the café was. I was a little surprised to see Pa out on a day like this; he usually stayed home with Jennie when it was overcast and windy because the fog and cold air aggravated his lumbago.

The two of them came up and stopped, Pa puffing on one of his home-carved meerschaum pipes. They were both seventy-two and long-retired—Abner from a manager's job at the cannery a mile up the coast, Pa from running the general store in the village—and they'd been cronies for at least half their lives. But that was where all resemblance between them ended. Abner was short and round and white-haired, and always had a smile and a joke for everybody. Pa, on the other hand, was tall and thin and dour; if he'd smiled any more than four times in the forty-seven years since I was born I can't remember it. Abner had come up from San Francisco during the Depression, but Pa was a second-generation native of Camaroon Bay, his father having emigrated from Ireland during the short-lived potato boom in the early 1900s. He was a good man and a decent father, which was why I'd given him a room in our house when Ma died six years ago, but I'd never felt close to him.

He said to me, "Looks like a good catch, Verne."

"Pretty good," I said. "How come you're out in this weather?"

"Abner's idea. He dragged me out of the house."

I looked at Abner. His eyes were bright, the way they always got when he had a choice bit of news or gossip to tell. He said, "Fella from Los Angeles went and bought Smuggler's Island. Can you beat that?"

"Bought it?" I said. "You mean outright?"

"Yep. Paid the county a hundred thousand cash."

"How'd you hear about it?"

"Jack Kewin, over to the real-estate office."

"Who's the fellow who bought it?"

"Name's Roger Vauclain," Abner said. "Jack don't know any more about him. Did the buying through an agent."

Davey said, "Wonder what he wants with it?"

"Maybe he's got ideas of hunting treasure," Abner said and winked at him. "Maybe he heard about what's hidden in those caves."

Pa gave him a look. "Old fool," he said.

Davey grinned, and I smiled a little and turned to look to where Smuggler's Island sat wreathed in fog half a mile straight out across the choppy harbor. It wasn't much to look at, from a distance or up close. Just one big oblong chunk of eroded rock about an acre and a half in size, surrounded by a lot of little islets. It had a few stunted trees and shrubs, and a long headland where gulls built their nests, and a sheltered cove on the lee shore where you could put in a small boat. That was about all there was to it—except for those caves Abner had spoken of.

They were located near the lee cove and you could only get into them at low tide. Some said caves honeycombed the whole under-belly of the island, but those of us who'd ignored warnings from our parents as kids and gone exploring in them knew that this wasn't so. There were three caves and two of them had branches that led deep into the rock, but all of the tunnels were dead ends.

This business of treasure being hidden in one of those caves was just so much nonsense, of course—sort of a local legend that no-body took seriously. What the treasure was supposed to be was two million dollars in greenbacks that had been hidden by a rackets courier during Prohibition, when he'd been chased to the island by a team of Revenue agents. There was also supposed to be fifty cases of high-grade moonshine secreted there.

The bootlegging part of it had a good deal of truth though. This section of the northern California coast was a hotbed of illegal li-quor traffic in the days of the Volstead Act, and the scene of several confrontations between smugglers and Revenue agents; half a dozen men on both sides had been killed, or had turned up missing and presumed dead. The way the bootleggers worked was to bring ships down from Canada outfitted as distilleries—big stills in their holds, bottling equipment, labels for a dozen different kinds of Canadian whiskey—and anchor them twenty-five miles offshore. Then local fishermen and imported hirelings would go out in their boats and carry the liquor to places along the shore, where trucks would be waiting to pick it up and transport it down to San Francisco or east into Nevada. Smuggler's Island was supposed to have been a short-term storage point for whiskey that couldn't be trucked out right away, which may or may not have been a true fact. At any rate, that was how the island got its name.

Just as I turned back to Pa and Abner, Handy came out of the processing shed with the tally clerk and the scales. He was a big, thick-necked man, Handy, with red hair and a temper to match; he was also one of the best mates around and knew as much about salmon trolling and diesel engines as anybody in Camaroon Bay. He'd been working for me eight years, but he wouldn't be much longer. He was saving up to buy a boat of his own and only needed another thousand or so to swing the down payment.

Abner told him right away about this Roger Vauclain buying Smuggler's Island. Handy grunted and said, "Anybody that'd want those rocks out there has to have rocks in his head."

"Who do you imagine he is?" Davey asked.

"One of those damn-fool rich people probably," Pa said. "Buy something for no good reason except that it's there and they want it."

"But why Smuggler's Island in particular?"

"Got a fancy name, that's why. Now he can say to his friends, why look here, I own a place up north called Smuggler's Island, supposed to have treasure hidden on it."

I said, "Well, whoever he is and whyever he bought it, we'll find out eventually. Right now we've got a catch to unload."

"Sure is a puzzler though, ain't it, Verne?" Abner said.

"It is that," I admitted. "It's a puzzler, all right."

If you live in a small town or village, you know how it is when something happens that has no immediate explanation. Rumors start flying, based on few or no facts, and every time one of them is retold to somebody else it gets exaggerated. Nothing much goes on in a place like Camaroon Bay anyhow—conversation is pretty much limited to the weather and the actions of tourists and how the salmon are running or how the crabs seem to be thinning out a little more every year. So this Roger Vauclain buying Smuggler's Island got a lot more lip service paid to it than it would have someplace else.

Jack Kewin didn't find out much about Vauclain, just that he was some kind of wealthy resident of southern California. But that was enough for the speculations and the rumors to build on. During the next week I heard from different people that Vauclain was a real-estate speculator who was going to construct a small private club on the island; that he was a retired bootlegger who'd worked the coast during Prohibition and had bought the island for nostalgic reasons; that he was a front man for a movie company that was going to film a big spectacular in Camaroon Bay and blow up the island in the final scene. None of these rumors made much sense, but that didn't stop people from spreading them and half-believing in them.

Then, one night while we were eating supper Abner came knocking at the front door of our house on the hill above the village. Davey went and let him in, and he sat down at the table next to Pa. One look at him was enough to tell us that he'd come with news.

"Just been talking to Lloyd Simms," he said as Jennie poured him a cup of coffee. "Who do you reckon just made a reservation at the Camaroon Inn?"

"Who?" I asked.

"Roger Vauclain himself. Lloyd talked to him on the phone less than an hour ago, says he sounded pretty hard-nosed. Booked a single room for a week, be here on Thursday."

"Only a single room?" Jennie said. "Why, I'm disappointed, Abner. I expected he'd be traveling with an entourage." She's a practical woman and when it comes to things she considers nonsense, like all the hoopla over Vauclain and Smuggler's Island, her sense of humor sharpens into sarcasm.

"Might be others coming up later," Abner said seriously.

Davey said, "Week's a long time for a rich man to spend in a place like Camaroon Bay. I wonder what he figures to do all that time?"

"Tend to his island, probably," I said.

"Tend to it?" Pa said. "Tend to what? You can walk over the whole thing in two hours."

"Well, there's always the caves, Pa."

He snorted. "Grown man'd have to be a fool to go wandering in those caves. Tide comes in while he's inside, he'll drown for sure."

"What time's he due in on Thursday?" Davey asked Abner.

"Around noon, Lloyd says. Reckon we'll find out then what he's planning to do with the island."

"Not planning to do anything with it, I tell you," Pa said. "Just wants to *own* it."

"We'll see," Abner said. "We'll see."

Thursday was clear and warm, and it should have been a good day for salmon; but maybe the run had started to peter out, because it took us until almost noon to make the limit. It was after two o'clock before we got the catch unloaded and weighed in at Bay Fisheries. Davey had some errands to run and Handy had logged enough extra time, so I took the *Jennie Too* over to the commercial slips myself and stayed aboard her to hose down the decks. When I was through with that I set about replacing the port outrigger line because it had started to weaken and we'd been having trouble with it.

I was doing that when a tall man came down the ramp from the quay and stood just off the bow, watching me. I didn't pay much attention to him; tourists stop by to rubberneck now and then, and if you encourage them they sometimes hang around so you can't get any work done. But then this fellow slapped a hand against his leg, as if he were annoyed, and called out in a loud voice, "Hey, you there. Fisherman."

I looked at him then, frowning. I'd heard that tone before: sharp, full of self-granted authority. Some city people are like that; to them, anybody who lives in a rural village is a low-class hick. I didn't like it and I let him see that in my face. "You talking to me?"

"Who else would I be talking to?"

I didn't say anything. He was in his forties, smooth-looking, and dressed in white ducks and a crisp blue windbreaker. If nothing else, his eyes were enough to make you dislike him immediately; they were hard and unfriendly and said that he was used to getting his own way.

He said, "Where can I rent a boat?"

"What kind of boat? To go sport fishing?"

"No, not to go sport fishing. A small cruiser."

"There ain't any cruisers for rent here."

He made a disgusted sound, as if he'd expected that. "A big outboard then," he said. "Something seaworthy."

"It's not a good idea to take a small boat out of the harbor," I said. "The ocean along here is pretty rough——"

"I don't want advice," he said. "I want a boat big enough to get me out to Smuggler's Island and back. Now who do I see about it?"

"Smuggler's Island?" I looked at him more closely. "Your name happen to be Roger Vauclain, by any chance?"

"That's right. You heard about me buying the island, I suppose. Along with everybody else in this place."

"News gets around," I said mildly.

"About that boat," he said.

"Talk to Ed Hawkins at Bay Marine on the wharf. He'll find something for you."

Vauclain gave me a curt nod and started to turn away.

I said, "Mind if I ask *you* a question now?"

He turned back. "What is it?"

"People don't go buying islands very often," I said, "particularly one like Smuggler's. I'd be interested to know your plans for it."

"You and every other damned person in Camaroon Bay."

I held my temper. "I was just asking. You don't have to give me an answer."

He was silent for a moment. Then he said, "What the hell, it's no secret. I've always wanted to live on an island, and that one out there is the only one around I can afford."

I stared at him. "You mean you're going to *build* on it?"

"That surprises you, does it?"

"It does," I said. "There's nothing on Smuggler's Island but rocks and a few trees and a couple of thousand nesting gulls. It's fogbound most of the time, and even when it's not the wind blows at thirty knots or better."

"I like fog and wind and ocean," Vauclain said. "I like isolation. I don't like people much. That satisfy you?"

I shrugged. "To each his own."

"Exactly," he said, and went away up the ramp.

I worked on the *Jennie Too* another hour, then I went over to the Wharf Café for a cup of coffee and a piece of pie. When I came inside I saw Pa, Abner, and Handy sitting at one of the copper-topped tables. I walked over to them.

They already knew that Vauclain had arrived in Camaroon Bay. Handy was saying, "Hell, he's about as friendly as a shark. I was over to Ed Hawkins's place shooting the breeze when he came in and demanded Ed get him a boat. Threw his weight around for fifteen minutes until Ed agreed to rent him his own Chris-Craft. Then he paid for the rental in cash, slammed two fifties on Ed's desk like they were singles and Ed was a beggar."

I sat down. "He's an eccentric, all right," I said. "I talked to him for a few minutes myself about an hour ago."

"Eccentric?" Abner said, and snorted. "That's just a name they give to people who never learned manners or good sense."

Pa said to me. "He tell you what he's fixing to do with Smuggler's Island, Verne?"

"He did, yep."

"Told Abner too, over to the Inn." Pa shook his head, glowering, and lighted a pipe. "Craziest damned thing I ever heard. Build a house on that mess of rock, live out there. Crazy, that's all."

"That's a fact," Handy said. "I'd give him more credit if he was planning to hunt for that bootlegger's treasure."

"Well, I'm sure not going to relish having him for a neighbor," Abner said. "Don't guess anybody else will either."

None of us disagreed with that. A man likes to be able to get along with his neighbors, rich or poor. Getting along with Vauclain, it seemed, was going to be a chore for everybody.

In the next couple of days Vauclain didn't do much to improve his standing with the residents of Camaroon Bay. He snapped at merchants and waitresses, ignored anybody who tried to strike up a conversation with him, and complained twice to Lloyd Simms about the service at the Inn. The only good thing about him, most people were saying, was that he spent the better part of his days on Smuggler's Island—doing what, nobody knew exactly—and his nights locked in his room. Might have been he was drawing up plans there for the house he intended to build on the island.

Rumor now had it that Vauclain was an architect, one of those independents who'd built up a reputation, like Frank Lloyd Wright in the old days, and who only worked for private individuals and companies. This was probably true since it originated with Jack Kewin; he'd spent a little time with Vauclain and wasn't one to spread unfounded gossip. According to Jack, Vauclain had learned that the island was for sale more than six months ago and had been up twice before by helicopter from San Francisco to get an aerial view of it.

That was the way things stood on Sunday morning when Jennie and I left for church at 10:00. Afterward we had lunch at a place up the coast, and then, because the weather was cool but still clear, we went for a drive through the redwood country. It was almost 5:00 when we got back home.

Pa was in bed—his lumbago was bothering him, he said—and Davey was gone somewhere. I went into our bedroom to change out of my suit. While I was in there the telephone rang, and Jennie called out that it was for me.

When I picked up the receiver Lloyd Simms's voice said, "Sorry to bother you, Verne, but if you're not busy I need a favor."

"I'm not busy, Lloyd. What is it?"

"Well, it's Roger Vauclain. He went out to the island this morning like usual, and he was supposed to be back at three to take a telephone call. Told me to make sure I was around then, the call was important—you know the way he talks. The call came in right on schedule, but Vauclain didn't. He's still not back, and the party calling him has been ringing me up every half hour, demanding I get hold of him. Something about a bid that has to be delivered first thing tomorrow morning."

"You want me to go out to the island, Lloyd?"

"If you wouldn't mind," he said. "I don't much care about Vauclain, the way he's been acting, but this caller is driving me up a wall. And it could be something's the matter with Vauclain's boat; can't get it started or something. Seems kind of funny he didn't come back when he said he would."

I hesitated. I didn't much want to take the time to go out to Smuggler's Island; but then if there was a chance Vauclain was in trouble I couldn't very well refuse to help.

"All right," I said. "I'll see what I can do."

We rang off, and I explained to Jennie where I was going and why. Then I drove down to the basin where the pleasure-boat slips were and took the tarp off Davey's sixteen-foot Sportliner inboard. I'd bought it for him on his sixteenth birthday, when I figured he was old enough to handle a small boat of his own, but I used it as much as he did. We're not so well off that we can afford to keep more than one pleasure craft.

The engine started right up for a change—usually you have to choke it several times on cool days—and I took her out of the slips and into the harbor. The sun was hidden by overcast now and the wind was up, building small whitecaps, running fogbanks in from the ocean but shredding them before they reached the shore. I followed the south jetty out past the breakwater and into open sea. The water was choppier there, the color of gunmetal, and the wind was pretty cold; I pulled the collar of my jacket up and put on my gloves to keep my hands from numbing on the wheel.

When I neared the island I swung around to the north shore and into the lee cove. Ed Hawkins's Chris-Craft was tied up there, all right, bow and stern lines made fast to outcroppings on a long, natural stone dock. I took the Sportliner in behind it, climbed out onto the bare rock, and made her fast. On my right, waves broke over and into the mouths of three caves, hissing long fans of spray. Gulls wheeled screeching above the headland; farther in, scrub oak and cypress danced like bobbers in the wind. It all made you feel as though you were standing on the edge of the world.

There was no sign of Vauclain anywhere at the cove, so I went up through a tangle of artichoke plants toward the center of the island. The area there was rocky but mostly flat, dotted with under-growth and patches of sandy earth. I stopped beside a gnarled cypress and scanned from left to right. Nothing but emptiness. Then I walked out toward the headland, hunched over against the pull of the wind. But I didn't find him there either.

A sudden thought came to me as I started back and the hairs prickled on my neck. What if he'd gone into the caves and been trapped there when the tide began to flood? If that was what had happened, it was too late for me to do anything—but I started to run anyway, my eyes on the ground so I wouldn't trip over a bush or a rock.

I was almost back to the cove, coming at a different angle than before, when I saw him.

It was so unexpected that I pulled up short and almost lost my footing on loose rock. The pit of my stomach went hollow. He was lying on his back in a bed of artichokes, one arm flung out and the other wrapped across his chest. There was blood under his arm, and blood spread across the front of his windbreaker. One long look was all I needed to tell me he'd been shot and that he was dead.

Shock and an eerie sense of unreality kept me standing there another few seconds. My thoughts were jumbled; you don't think too clearly when you stumble on a dead man, a murdered man. And it *was* murder, I knew that well enough. There was no gun anywhere near the body, and no way it could have been an accident.

Then I turned, shivering, and ran down to the cove and took the Sportliner away from there at full throttle to call for the county sheriff.

Vauclain's death was the biggest event that had happened in Camaroon Bay in forty years, and Sunday night and Monday nobody talked about anything else. As soon as word got around that I was the one who'd discovered the body, the doorbell and the telephone didn't stop ringing—friends and neighbors, newspaper people, investigators. The only place I had any peace was on the *Jennie Too* Monday morning, and not much there because Davey and Handy wouldn't let the subject alone while we fished.

By late that afternoon the authorities had questioned just about everyone in the area. It didn't appear they'd found out anything though. Vauclain had been alone when he'd left for the island early Sunday; Abner had been down at the slips then and swore to the fact. A couple of tourists had rented boats from Ed Hawkins during the day, since the weather was pretty good, and a lot of locals were out in the harbor on pleasure craft. But whoever it was who had gone to Smuggler's Island after Vauclain, he hadn't been noticed.

As to a motive for the shooting, there were all sorts of wild speculations. Vauclain had wronged somebody in Los Angeles and that person had followed him here to take revenge. He'd treated a local citizen badly enough to trigger a murderous rage. He'd got in bad with organized crime and a contract had been put out on him. And the most farfetched theory of all: He'd actually uncovered some sort of treasure on Smuggler's Island and somebody'd learned about it and killed him for it. But the simple truth was, nobody had *any* idea why Vauclain was murdered. If the sheriff's department had found any clues on the island or anywhere else, they weren't talking—but they weren't making any arrests either.

There was a lot of excitement, all right. Only underneath it all people were nervous and a little scared. A killer seemed to be loose in Camaroon Bay, and if he'd murdered once, who was to say he wouldn't do it again? A mystery is all well and good when it's happening someplace else, but when it's right on your doorstep you can't help but feel threatened and apprehensive.

I'd had about all the pestering I could stand by four o'clock, so I got into the car and drove up the coast to Shelter Cove. That gave me an hour's worth of freedom. But no sooner did I get back to Camaroon Bay, with the intention of going home and locking myself in my basement workshop, than a sheriff's cruiser pulled up behind me at a stop sign and its horn started honking. I sighed and pulled over to the curb.

It was Harry Swenson, one of the deputies who'd questioned me the day before, after I'd reported finding Vauclain's body. We knew each other well enough to be on a first-name basis. He said, "Verne, the sheriff asked me to talk to you again, see if there's anything you might have overlooked yesterday. You mind?"

"No, I don't mind," I said tiredly.

We went into the Inn and took a table at the back of the dining room. A couple of people stared at us, and I could see Lloyd Simms hovering around out by the front desk. I wondered how long it would be before I'd stop being the center of attention every time I went someplace in the village.

Over coffee, I repeated everything that had happened Sunday afternoon. Harry checked what I said with the notes he'd taken; then he shook his head and closed the notebook.

"Didn't really expect you to remember anything else," he said, "but we had to make sure. Truth is, Verne, we're up against it on this thing. Damnedest case I ever saw."

"Guess that means you haven't found out anything positive."

"Not much. If we could figure a motive, we might be able to get a handle on it from that. But we just can't find one."

I decided to give voice to one of my own theories. "What about robbery, Harry?" I asked. "Seems I heard Vauclain was carrying a lot of cash with him and throwing it around pretty freely."

"We thought of that first thing," he said. "No good, though. His wallet was on the body, and there was three hundred dollars in it and a couple of blank checks."

I frowned down at my coffee. "I don't like to say this, but you don't suppose it could be one of these thrill killings we're always reading about?"

"Man, I hope not. That's the worst kind of homicide there is."

We were silent for a minute or so. Then I said, "You find anything at all on the island? Any clues?"

He hesitated. "Well," he said finally, "I probably shouldn't discuss it—but then, you're not the sort to break a confidence. We did find one thing near the body. Might not mean anything, but it's not the kind of item you'd expect to come across out there."

"What is it?"

"A cake of white beeswax," he said.

"Beeswax?"

"Right. Small cake of it. Suggest anything to you?"

"No," I said. "No, nothing."

"Not to us either. Aside from that, we haven't got a thing. Like I said, we're up against it. Unless we get a break in the next couple of days, I'm afraid the whole business will end up in the Unsolved file—That's unofficial, now."

"Sure," I said.

Harry finished his coffee. "I'd better get moving," he said. "Thanks for your time, Verne."

I nodded, and he stood up and walked out across the dining room. As soon as he was gone, Lloyd came over and wanted to know what we'd been talking about. But I'd begun to feel oddly nervous all of a sudden, and there was something tickling at the edge of my mind. I cut him off short, saying, "Let me be, will you, Lloyd? Just let me be for a minute."

When he drifted off, looking hurt, I sat there and rotated my cup on the table. Beeswax, I thought. I'd told Harry that it didn't suggest anything to me, and yet it did, vaguely. Beeswax. White beeswax . . .

It came to me then—and along with it a couple of other things, little things, like missing figures in an arithmetic problem. I went cold all over, as if somebody had opened a window and let the wind inside the room. I told myself I was wrong, that it couldn't be. But I wasn't wrong. It made me sick inside, but I wasn't wrong.

I knew who had murdered Roger Vauclain.

When I came into the house I saw him sitting out on the sun deck, just sitting there motionless with his hands flat on his knees, staring out to sea. Or out to where Smuggler's Island sat, shining hard and ugly in the glare of the dying sun.

I didn't go out there right away. First I went into the other rooms to see if anybody else was home, but nobody was. Then, when I couldn't put it off any longer, I got myself ready to face it and walked onto the deck.

He glanced at me as I leaned back against the railing. I hadn't seen much of him since finding the body, or paid much attention to him when I had; but now I saw that his eyes looked different. They didn't blink. They looked at me, they looked past me, but they didn't blink.

"Why'd you do it, Pa?" I said. "Why'd you kill Vauclain?"

I don't know what I expected his reaction to be. But there wasn't any reaction. He wasn't startled, he wasn't frightened, he wasn't anything. He just looked away from me again and sat there like a man who has expected to hear such words for a long time.

I kept waiting for him to say something, to move, to blink his eyes. For one full minute and half of another, he did nothing. Then he sighed, soft and tired, and he said, "I knew somebody'd find out this time." His voice was steady, calm. "I'm sorry it had to be you, Verne."

"So am I."

"How'd you know?"

"You left a cake of white beeswax out there," I said. "Fell out of your pocket when you pulled the gun, I guess. You're just the only person around here who'd be likely to have white beeswax in his pocket, Pa, because you're the only person who hand-carves his own meerschaum pipes. Took me a time to remember that you use wax like that to seal the bowls and give them a luster finish."

He didn't say anything.

"Couple of other things too," I said. "You were in bed yesterday when Jennie and I got home. It was a clear day, no early fog, nothing to aggravate your lumbago. Unless you'd been out some-place where you weren't protected from the wind—someplace like in a boat on open water. Then there was Davey's Sportliner starting right up for me. Almost never does that on cool days unless it's been run recently, and the only person besides Davey and me who has a key is you."

He nodded. "It's usually the little things," he said. "I always figured it'd be some little thing that'd finally do it."

"Pa," I said, "why'd you kill him?'

"He had to go and buy the island. Then he had to decide to build a house on it. I couldn't let him do that. I went out there to talk to him, try to get him to change his mind. Took my revolver along, but only just in case; wasn't intending to use it. Only he wouldn't listen to me. Called me an old fool and worse, and then he give me a shove. He was dead before I knew it, seems like."

"What'd him building a house have to do with you?"

"He'd have brought men and equipment out there, wouldn't he? They'd have dug up everything, wouldn't they? They'd have sure dug up the Revenue man."

I thought he was rambling. "Pa . . ."

"You got a right to know about that too," he said. He blinked then, four times fast. "In 1929 a fella named Frank Eberle and me went to work for the bootleggers. Hauling whiskey. We'd go out maybe once a month in Frank's boat, me acting as shotgun, and we'd bring in a load of 'shine—mostly to Shelter Cove, but some-times we'd be told to drop it off on Smuggler's for a day or two. It was easy money, and your ma and me needed it, what with you happening along; and what the hell, Frank always said, we were only helping to give the people what they wanted.

"But then one night in 1932 it all went bust. We brought a shipment to the island and just after we started unloading it this man run out of the trees waving a gun and yelling that we were under arrest. A Revenue agent, been lying up there in ambush. Lying alone because he didn't figure to have much trouble, I reckon—and I found out later the government people had bigger fish to fry up to Shelter Cove that night.

"Soon as the agent showed himself, Frank panicked and started to run. Agent put a shot over his head, and before I could think on it I cut loose with the rifle I always carried. I killed him, Verne, I shot that man dead."

He paused, his face twisting with memory. I wanted to say something—but what was there to say?

Pa said, "Frank and me buried him on the island, under a couple of rocks on the center flat. Then we got out of there. I quit the bootleggers right away, but Frank, he kept on with it and got himself killed in a big shoot-out up by Eureka just before Repeal. I knew they were going to get me too someday. Only time kept passing and somehow it never happened, and I almost had myself believing it never would. Then this Vauclain came along. You see now why I couldn't let him build his house?"

"Pa," I said thickly, "it's been forty-five years since all that happened. All anybody'd have dug up was bones. Maybe there's something there to identify the Revenue agent, but there couldn't be anything that'd point to you."

"Yes, there could," he said. "Just like there was something this time—the beeswax and all. There'd have been something, all right, and they'd have come for me."

He stopped talking then, like a machine that had been turned off, and swiveled his head away and just sat staring again. There in the sun, I still felt cold. He believed what he'd just said; he honestly believed it.

I knew now why he'd been so dour and moody for most of my life, why he almost never smiled, why he'd never let me get close to him. And I knew something else too: I wasn't going to tell the sheriff any of this. He was my father and he was seventy-two years old; and I'd see to it that he didn't hurt anybody else. But the main reason was, if I let it happen that they really did come for him he wouldn't last a month. In an awful kind of way the only thing that'd been holding him together all these years was his certainty they *would* come someday.

Besides, it didn't matter anyway. He hadn't actually got away with anything. He hadn't committed one unpunished murder, or now two unpunished murders, because there is no such thing. There's just no such thing as the perfect crime.

I walked over and took the chair beside him, and together we sat quiet and looked out at Smuggler's Island. Only I didn't see it very well because my eyes were full of tears.

UNDER THE SKIN

In the opulent lobby lounge of the St. Francis Hotel, where he and Tom Olivet had gone for a drink after the A.C.T. dramatic production was over, Walter Carpenter sipped his second Scotch-and-water and thought that he was a pretty lucky man. Good job, happy marriage, kids of whom he could be proud, and a best friend who had a similar temperament, similar attitudes, aspirations, likes and dislikes. Most people went through life claiming lots of casual friends and a few close ones, but seldom did a perfectly compatible relationship develop as it had between Tom and him. He knew brothers who were not nearly as close. Walter smiled. That's just what the two of us are like, he thought. Brothers.

Across the table Tom said, "Why the sudden smile?"

"Oh, just thinking that we're a hell of a team," Walter said.

"Sure," Tom said. "Carpenter and Olivet, the Gold Dust Twins."

Walter laughed. "No, I mean it. Did you ever stop to think how few friends get along as well as we do? I mean, we like to do the same things, go to the same places. The play tonight, for example. I couldn't get Cynthia to go, but as soon as I mentioned it to you, you were all set for it."

"Well, we've known each other for twenty years," Tom said. "Two people spend as much time together as we have, they get to thinking alike and acting alike. I guess we're one head on just about everything, all right."

"A couple of carbon copies," Walter said. "Here's to friendship."

They raised their glasses and drank, and when Walter put his down on the table he noticed the hands on his wristwatch. "Hey," he said. "It's almost eleven-thirty. We'd better hustle if we're going to catch the train. Last one for Daly City leaves at midnight."

"Right," Tom said.

They split the check down the middle, then left the hotel and walked down Powell Street to the Bay Area Rapid Transit station at Market. Ordinarily one of them would have driven in that morning from the Monterey Heights area where they lived two blocks apart; but Tom's car was in the garage for minor repairs, and Walter's wife Cynthia had needed their car for errands. So they had ridden a BART train in, and after work they'd had dinner in a restaurant near Union Square before going on to the play.

Inside the Powell station Walter called Cynthia from a pay phone and told her they were taking the next train out; she said she would pick them up at Glen Park. Then he and Tom rode the escalator down to the train platform. Some twenty people stood or sat there waiting for trains, half a dozen of them drunks and other unsavory-looking types. Subway crime had not been much of a problem since BART, which connected several San Francisco points with a number of East Bay cities, opened two years earlier. Still, there were isolated incidents. Walter began to feel vaguely nervous; it was the first time he had gone anywhere this late by train.

The nervousness eased when a westbound pulled in almost immediately and none of the unsavory-looking types followed them into a nearly empty car. They sat together, Walter next to the window. Once the train had pulled out he could see their reflections in the window glass. Hell, he thought, the two of us even *look* alike sometimes. Carbon copies, for a fact. Brothers of the spirit.

A young man in workman's garb got off at the 24th and Mission stop, leaving them alone in the car. Walter's ears popped as the train picked up speed for the run to Glen Park. He said, "These new babies really move, don't they?"

"That's for sure," Tom said.

"You ever ride a fast-express passenger train?"

"No," Tom said. "You?"

"No. Say, you know what would be fun?"

"What?"

"Taking a train trip across Canada," Walter said. "They've still got crack passenger expresses up there—they run across the whole of Canada from Vancouver to Montreal."

"Yeah, I've heard about those," Tom said.

"Maybe we could take the familes up there and ride one of them next summer," Walter said. "You know, fly to Vancouver and then fly home from Montreal."

"Sounds great to me."

"Think the wives would go for it?"

"I don't see why not."

For a couple of minutes the tunnel lights flashed by in a yellow blur; then the train began to slow and the globes steadied into a widening chain. When they slid out of the tunnel into the Glen Park station, Tom stood up and Walter followed him to the doors. They stepped out. No one was waiting to get on, and the doors hissed closed again almost immediately. The westbound rumbled ahead into the tunnel that led to Daly City.

The platform was empty except for a man in an overcoat and a baseball cap lounging against the tiled wall that sided the escalators; Walter and Tom had been the only passengers to get off. The nearest of the two electronic clock-and-message boards suspended above the platform read 12:02.

The sound of the train faded into silence as they walked toward the escalators, and their steps echoed hollowly. Midnight-empty this way, the fluorescent-lit station had an eerie quality. Walter felt the faint uneasiness return and impulsively quickened his pace.

They were ten yards from the escalators when the man in the overcoat moved away from the wall and came toward them. He had the collar pulled up around his face and his chin tucked down into it; the bill of the baseball cap hid his forehead, so that his features were shadowy. His right hand was inside a coat pocket.

The hair prickled on Walter's neck. He glanced at Tom to keep from staring at the approaching man, but Tom did not seem to have noticed him at all.

Just before they reached the escalators the man in the overcoat stepped across in front of them, blocking their way, and planted his feet. They pulled up short. Tom said, "Hey," and Walter thought in sudden alarm: Oh, my God!

The man took his hand out of his pocket and showed them the long thin blade of a knife. "Wallets," he said flatly. "Hurry it up, don't make me use this."

Walter's breath seemed to clog in his lungs; he tasted the brassiness of fear. There was a moment of tense inactivity, the three of them as motionless as wax statues in a museum exhibit. Then, jerkily, his hand trembling, Walter reached into his jacket pocket and fumbled his wallet out.

But Tom just stood staring, first at the knife and then at the man's shadowed face. He did not seem to be afraid. His lips were pinched instead with anger. "A damned mugger," he said.

Walter said, "Tom, for God's sake!" and extended his wallet. The man grabbed it out of his hand, shoved it into the other slash pocket. He moved the knife slightly in front of Tom.

"Get it out," he said.

"No," Tom said, "I'll be damned if I will."

Walter knew then, instantly, what was going to happen next. Close as the two of them were, he was sensitive to Tom's moods. He opened his mouth to shout at him, tell him not to do it; he tried to make himself grab onto Tom and stop him physically. But the muscles in his body seemed paralyzed.

Then it was too late. Tom struck the man's wrist, knocked it and the knife to one side, and lunged forward.

Walter stood there, unable to move, and watched the mugger sidestep awkwardly, pulling the knife back. The coat collar fell away, the baseball cap flew off as Tom's fist grazed the side of the man's head—and Walter could see the mugger's face clearly: beard-stubbled, jutting chin, flattened nose, wild blazing eyes.

The knife, glinting light from the overhead fluorescents, flashed between the mugger and Tom, and Tom stiffened and made a grunting, gasping noise. Walter looked on in horror as the man stepped back with the knife, blood on the blade now, blood on his hand. Tom turned and clutched at his stomach, eyes glazing, and then his knees buckled and he toppled over and lay still.

He killed him, Walter thought, he killed Tom—but he did not feel anything yet. Shock had given the whole thing a terrible dream-like aspect. The mugger turned toward him, looked at him out of those burning eyes. Walter wanted to run, but there was nowhere to go with the tracks on both sides of the platform, the electrified rails down there, and the mugger blocking the escalators. And he could not make himself move now any more than he had been able to move when he realized Tom intended to fight.

The man in the overcoat took a step toward him, and in that moment, from inside the eastbound tunnel, there was the faint rumble of an approaching train. The suspended message board flashed CONCORD, and the mugger looked up there, looked back at Walter. The eyes burned into him an instant longer, holding him transfixed. Then the man turned sharply, scooped up his baseball cap, and ran up the escalator.

Seconds later he was gone, and the train was there instead, filling the station with a rush of sound that Walter could barely hear for the thunder of his heart.

The policeman was a short thick-set man with a black mustache, and when Walter finished speaking he looked up gravely from his notebook. "And that's everything that happened, Mr. Carpenter?"

"Yes," Walter said, "that's everything."

He was sitting on one of the round tile-and-concrete benches in the center of the platform. He had been sitting there ever since it happened. When the eastbound train had braked to a halt, one of its disembarking passengers had been a BART security officer. One train too late, Walter remembered thinking dully at the time; he's one train too late. The security officer had asked a couple of terse questions, then had draped his coat over Tom and gone upstairs to call the police.

"What can you tell me about the man who did it?" the policeman asked. "Can you give me a description of him?"

Walter's eyes were wet; he took out his handkerchief and wiped them, shielding his face with the cloth, then closing his eyes behind it. When he did that he could see the face of the mugger: the stubbled cheeks, the jutting chin, the flat nose—and the eyes, above all those malignant eyes that had said as clearly as though the man had spoken the words aloud: *I've got your wallet, I know where you live. If you say anything to the cops I'll come after you and give you what I gave your friend.*

Walter shuddered, opened his eyes, lowered the handkerchief, and looked over to where the group of police and laboratory personnel were working around the body. Tom Olivet's body. Tom Olivet, lying there dead.

We were like brothers, Walter thought. We were just like brothers.

"I can't tell you anything about the mugger," he said to the policeman. "I didn't get a good look at him. I can't tell you anything at all."

CAUGHT IN THE ACT

When I drove around the bend in my driveway at four that Friday afternoon, past the screen of cypress trees, a fat little man in a gray suit was just closing the front door of my house. Surprise made me blink: he was a complete stranger.

He saw the car in that same moment, stiffened, and glanced around in a furtive way, as if looking for an avenue of escape. But there wasn't anywhere for him to go; the house is a split-level, built on the edge of a bluff and flanked by limestone outcroppings and thick vegetation. So he just stood there as I braked to a stop in front of the porch, squared his shoulders, and put on a smile that looked artificial even from a distance of thirty feet.

I got out and ran around to where he was. His smile faded, no doubt because my surprise had given way to anger and because I'm a pretty big man, three inches over six feet, weight 230; I played football for four years in college and I move like the linebacker I was. As for him, he wasn't such-a-much—just a fat little man, soft-looking, with round pink cheeks and shrewd eyes that had nervous apprehension in them now.

"Who are you?" I demanded. "What the hell were you doing in my house?"

"Your house? Ah, then you're James Loomis."

"How did you know that?"

"Your name is on your mailbox, Mr. Loomis."

"What were you doing in my house?"

He looked bewildered. "But I *wasn't* in your house"

"Don't give me that. I saw you closing the door."

"No, sir, you're mistaken. I was just coming *away* from the door. I rang the bell and there was no answer—"

"Listen, you," I said, "don't tell me what I saw or didn't see. My eyesight's just fine. Now I want an explanation."

"There's really nothing to explain," he said. "I represent the Easy-Way Vacuum Cleaner Company and I stopped by to ask if you—"

"Let's see some identification."

He rummaged around in a pocket of his suit coat, came out with a small white business card, and handed it to me. It said he was Morris Tweed, a salesman for the Easy-Way Vacuum Cleaner Company.

"I want to see your driver's license," I said.

"My, ah, driver's license?"

"You heard me. Get it out."

He grew even more nervous. "This is very embarrassing, Mr. Loomis," he said. "You see I, ah, lost my wallet this morning. A very unfortunate—"

I caught onto the front of his coat and bunched the material in my fingers; he made a funny little squeaking sound. I marched him over to the door, reached out with my free hand, and tried the knob. Locked. But that didn't mean anything one way or another; the door has a button you can turn on the inside so you don't have to use a key on your way out.

I looked over at the burglar-alarm panel, and of course the red light was off. Tweed, or whatever his name was, wouldn't have been able to walk out quietly through the front door if the system was operational. And except for my housekeeper, whom I've known for years and who is as trustworthy as they come, I was the only one who had an alarm key.

The fat little man struggled weakly to loosen my grip on his coat. "See here, Mr. Loomis," he said in a half-frightened, half-indignant voice, "you have no right to be rough with me. I haven't done anything wrong."

"We'll see about that."

I walked him back to the car, got my keys out of the ignition, returned him to the door, and keyed the alarm to the On position. The red light came on, which meant that the system was still functional. I frowned. If it was functional, how had the fat little man got in? Well, there were probably ways for a clever burglar to bypass an alarm system without damaging it; maybe that was the answer.

I shut it off again, unlocked the door, and took him inside. The house had a faint musty smell, the way houses do after they've been shut up for a time; I had been gone eight days, on a planned ten-day business trip to New York, and my housekeeper only comes in once a week. I took him into the living room, sat him down in a chair, and then went over and opened the French doors that led out to the balcony.

On the way back I glanced around the room. Everything was where it should be: the console TV set, the stereo equipment, my small collection of Oriental *objets d'art* on their divider shelves. But my main concern was what was in my study—particularly the confidential records and ledgers locked inside the wall safe.

"All right, you," I said, "take off your coat."

He blinked at me. "My coat? Really, Mr. Loomis, I don't—"

"Take off your coat."

He looked at my face, at the fist I held up in front of his nose, and took off his coat. I went through all the pockets. Sixty-five dollars in a silver money clip, a handkerchief, and a handful of business cards. But that was all; there wasn't anything of mine there, except possibly the money. I shuffled through the business cards. All of them bore the names of different companies and different people, and none of them was a duplicate of the one he had handed me outside.

"Morris Tweed, huh?" I said.

"Those cards were given to me by customers," he said. "*My* cards are in my wallet, all except the one I gave you. And I've already told you that I lost my wallet this morning."

"Sure you did. Empty out your pants pockets."

He sighed, stood up, and transferred three quarters, a dime, a penny, and a keycase to the coffee table. Then he pulled all the pockets inside out. Nothing.

"Turn around," I told him.

When he did that I patted him down the way you see cops do in the movies. Nothing.

"This is all a misunderstanding, Mr. Loomis," he said. "I'm not a thief; I'm a vacuum-cleaner salesman. You've searched me quite thoroughly, you know I don't have anything that belongs to you."

Maybe not—but I had a feeling that said otherwise. There were just too many things about him that didn't add up, and there was the plain fact that I had *seen* him coming *out* of the house. Call it intuition or whatever: I sensed this fat little man had stolen something from me. Not just come here to steal, because he had obviously been leaving when I arrived. He had something of mine, all right.

But what? And where was it?

I gave him back his coat and watched him put it on. There was a look of impending relief on his face as he scooped up his keys and change; he thought I was going to let him go. Instead I caught hold of his arm. Alarm replaced the relief and he made another of those squeaking noises as I hustled him across the room and down the hall to the smallest of the guest bathrooms, the one with a ventilator in place of a window.

When I pushed him inside he stumbled, caught his balance, and pivoted around to me. "Mr. Loomis, this is outrageous. What do you intend to do with me?"

"That depends. Turn you over to the police, maybe."

"The police? But you can't—"

I took the key out of the inside lock, shut the door on him, and locked it from the outside.

Immediately I went downstairs to my study. The Matisse print was in place and the safe door behind it was closed and locked; I worked the combination, swung the door open. And let out the breath I had been holding: the records and ledgers were there, exactly as I had left them. If those items had fallen into the wrong hands, I would be seriously embarrassed at the least and open to blackmail or possible criminal charges at the worst. Not that I was engaged in anything precisely illegal; it was just that some of the people for whom I set up accounting procedures were involved in certain extra-legal activities.

I looked through the other things in the safe—$2000 in cash, some jewelry and private papers—and they were all there, untouched. Nothing, it developed, was missing from my desk either. Or from anywhere else in the study.

Frowning, I searched the rest of the house. In the kitchen I found what might have been jimmy marks on the side door. I also found—surprisingly—electrician's tape on the burglar-alarm wires outside, tape which had not been there before I left on my trip and that might have been used to repair a cross-circuiting of the system.

What I did *not* find was anything missing. Absolutely nothing. Every item of value, every item of no value, was in its proper place.

I began to have doubts. Maybe I was wrong after all; maybe this was just a large misunderstanding. And yet, damn it, the fat little man had been in here and had lied about it, he had no identification, he was nervous and furtive, and the burglar alarm and the side door seemed to have been tampered with.

A series of improbable explanations occurred to me. He hadn't actually stolen anything because he hadn't had time; he had broken in here, cased the place, and had been on his way out with the intention of returning later in a car or van. But burglars don't operate that way; they don't make two trips to a house when they can just as easily make one, and they don't walk out the front door in broad daylight without taking *something* with them. Nor for that matter, do they take the time to repair alarm systems they've cross-circuited.

He wasn't a thief but a tramp whose sole reason for breaking in here was to spend a few days at my expense. Only tramps don't wear neat gray suits and they don't have expertise with burglar alarms. And they don't leave your larder full or clean up after themselves.

He wasn't a thief but a private detective, or an edge-of-the-law hireling, or maybe even an assassin; he hadn't come here to steal anything, he had come here to *leave* something—evidence of my extra-legal activities, a bomb or some other sort of death trap. But if there was nothing missing, there was also nothing here that shouldn't be here; I would have found it one way or another if there was, as carefully as I had searched. Besides which, there was already incriminating evidence in my safe, I was very good at my job and got along well with my clients, and I had no personal enemies who could possibly want me dead.

Nothing made sense. The one explanation I kept clinging to didn't make sense. Why would a burglar repair an alarm system before he leaves? How could a thief have stolen something if there wasn't anything missing?

Frustrated and angry, I went back to the guest bathroom and unlocked the door. The fat little man was standing by the sink, drying perspiration from his face with one of my towels. He looked less nervous and apprehensive now; there was a kind of resolve in his expression.

"All right," I said, "come out of there."

He came out, watching me warily with his shrewd eyes. "Are you finally satisfied that I'm not a thief, Mr. Loomis?"

No, I was not satisfied. I considered ordering him to take off his clothes, but that seemed pointless; I had already searched him and there just wasn't anything to look for.

"What were you doing in here?" I said.

"I was *not* in here before you arrived." The indignation was back in his voice. "Now I suggest you let me go on my way. You have no right or reason to hold me here against my will."

I made another fist and rocked it in front of his nose. "Do I have to cuff you around to get the truth?"

He flinched, but only briefly; he had had plenty of time to shore up his courage. "That wouldn't be wise, Mr. Loomis," he said. "I already have grounds for a counter-complaint against you."

"Counter-complaint?"

"For harassment and very probably for kidnaping. Physical violence would only compound a felony charge. I intend to make that counter-complaint if you call the police or if you lay a hand on me."

The anger drained out of me; I felt deflated. Advantage to the fat little man. He had grounds for a counter-complaint, okay—better grounds than I had against him. After all, I *had* forcibly brought him in here and locked him in the bathroom. And a felony charge against me would mean unfavorable publicity, not to mention police attention. In my business I definitely could not afford either of those things.

He had me then, and he knew it. He said stiffly, "May I leave or not, Mr. Loomis?"

There was nothing I could do. I let him go.

He went at a quick pace through the house, moving the way somebody does in familiar surroundings. I followed him out onto the porch and watched him hurry off down the driveway without once looking back. He was almost running by the time he disappeared behind the screen of cypress trees.

I went back inside and poured myself a double bourbon. I had never felt more frustrated in my life. The fat little man had got away with something of mine; irrationally or not, I felt it with even more conviction than before.

But what could he possibly have taken of any value?

And how could he have taken it?

I found out the next morning.

The doorbell rang at 10:45, while I was working on one of my accounts in the study. When I went out there and answered it I discovered a well-dressed elderly couple, both of whom were beaming and neither of whom I had ever seen before.

"Well," the man said cheerfully, "you must be Mr. Loomis. We're the Parmenters."

"Yes?"

"We just dropped by for another look around," he said. "When we saw your car out front we were hoping it belonged to you. We've been wanting to meet you in person."

I looked at him blankly.

"This is such a delightful place," his wife said. "We can't tell you how happy we are with it."

"Yes, sir," Parmenter agreed, "we knew it was the place for us as soon as your agent showed it to us. And such a reasonable price. Why, we could hardly believe it was only $100,000."

There was a good deal of confusion after that, followed on my part by disbelief, anger, and despair. When I finally got it all sorted out it amounted to this: the Parmenters were supposed to meet here with my "agent" yesterday afternoon, to present him with a $100,000 cashier's check, but couldn't make it at that time; so they had given him the check last night at their current residence, and he in turn had handed them copies of a notarized sales agreement carrying my signatures. The signatures were expert forgeries, of course—but would I be able to *prove* that in a court of law? Would I be able to prove I had not conspired with this bogus real estate agent to defraud the Parmenters of a six-figure sum of money?

Oh, I found out about the fat little man, all right. I found out how clever and audacious he was. And I found out just how wrong I had been—and just how right.

He hadn't stolen anything *from* my house.

He had stolen the whole damned *house*.

STRANGERS IN THE FOG

Hannigan had just finished digging the grave, down in the tule marsh where the little saltwater creek flowed toward the Pacific, when the dark shape of a man came out of the fog.

Startled, Hannigan brought the shovel up and cocked it weaponlike at his shoulder. The other man had materialized less than twenty yards away, from the direction of the beach, and had stopped the moment he saw Hannigan. The diffused light from Hannigan's lantern did not quite reach the man; he was a black silhouette against the swirling billows of mist. Beyond him the breakers lashed at the hidden shore in a steady pulse.

Hannigan said, "Who the hell are you?"

The man stood staring down at the roll of canvas near Hannigan's feet, at the hole scooped out of the sandy earth. He seemed to poise himself on the balls of his feet, body turned slightly, as though he might bolt at any second. "I'll ask you the same question," he said, and his voice was tense, low-pitched.

"I happen to live here." Hannigan made a gesture to his left with the shovel, where a suggestion of shimmery light shone high up through the fog. "This is a private beach."

"Private graveyard, too?"

"My dog died earlier this evening. I didn't want to leave him lying around the house."

"Must have been a pretty big dog."

"He was a Great Dane," Hannigan said. He wiped moisture from his face with his free hand. "You want something, or do you just like to take strolls in the fog?"

The man came forward a few steps, warily. Hannigan could see him more clearly then in the pale lantern glow: big, heavy-shouldered, damp hair flattened across his forehead, wearing a plaid lumberman's jacket, brown slacks, and loafers.

"You got a telephone I can use?"

"That would depend on why you need to use it."

"I could give you a story about my car breaking down," the big man said, "but then you'd just wonder what I'm doing down here instead of up on the Coast Highway."

"I'm wondering that anyway."

"It's safe down here, the way I figured it."

"I don't follow," Hannigan said.

"Don't you listen to your radio or TV?"

"Not if I can avoid it."

"So you don't know about the lunatic who escaped from the state asylum at Tescadero."

The back of Hannigan's neck prickled. "No," he said.

"Happened late this afternoon," the big man said. "He killed an attendant at the hospital—stabbed him with a kitchen knife. He was in there for the same kind of thing. Killed three people with a kitchen knife."

Hannigan did not say anything.

The big man said, "They think he may have headed north, because he came from a town up near the Oregon border. But they're not sure. He may have come south instead—and Tescadero is only twelve miles from here."

Hannigan gripped the handle of the shovel more tightly. "You still haven't said what *you're* doing down here in the fog."

"I came up from San Francisco with a girl for the weekend," the big man said. "Her husband was supposed to be in Los Angeles, on business, only I guess he decided to come home early. When he found her gone he must have figured she'd come up to this summer place they've got and so he drove up without calling first. We had just enough warning for her to throw me out."

"You let this woman throw you out?"

"That's right. Her husband is worth a million or so, and he's generous. You understand?"

"Maybe," Hannigan said. "What's the woman's name?"

"That's my business."

"Then how do I know you're telling me the truth?"

"Why wouldn't I be?"

"You might have reasons for lying."

"Like if I was the escaped lunatic, maybe?"

"Like that."

"If I was, would I have told you about him?"

Again Hannigan was silent.

"For all I know," the big man said, "*you* could be the lunatic. Hell, you're out here digging a grave in the middle of the night—"

"I told you, my dog died. Besides, would a lunatic dig a grave for somebody he killed? Did he dig one for that attendant you said he stabbed?"

"Okay, neither one of us is the lunatic." The big man paused and ran his hands along the side of his coat. "Look, I've had enough of this damned fog; it's starting to get to me. Can I use your phone or not?"

"Just who is it you want to call?"

"Friend of mine in San Francisco who owes me a favor. He'll drive up and get me. That is, if you wouldn't mind my hanging around your place until he shows up."

Hannigan thought things over and made up his mind. "All right. You stand over there while I finish putting Nick away. Then we'll go up."

The big man nodded and stood without moving. Hannigan knelt, still grasping the shovel, and rolled the canvas-wrapped body carefully into the grave. Then he straightened, began to scoop in sandy earth from the pile to one side. He did all of that without taking his eyes off the other man.

When he was finished he picked up the lantern, then gestured with the shovel, and the big man came around the grave. They went up along the edge of the creek, Hannigan four or five steps to the left. The big man kept his hands up and in close to his chest, and he walked with the tense springy stride of an animal prepared to attack or flee at any sudden movement. His gaze hung on Hannigan's face; Hannigan made it reciprocal.

"You have a name?" Hannigan asked him.

"Doesn't everybody?"

"Very funny. I'm asking your name."

"Art Vickery, if it matters."

"It doesn't, except that I like to know who I'm letting inside my house."

"I like to know whose house I'm going into," Vickery said.

Hannigan told him. After that neither of them had anything more to say.

The creek wound away to the right after fifty yards, into a tangle of scrubbrush, sage, and tule grass; to the left and straight ahead were low rolling sand dunes, and behind them the earth became hard-packed and rose sharply into the bluff on which the house had been built. Hannigan took Vickery onto the worn path between two of the dunes. Fog massed around them in wet gray swirls, shredding as they passed through it, reknitting again at their backs. Even with the lantern, visibility was less than thirty yards in any direction, although as they neared the bluff the house lights threw a progressively brighter illumination against the screen of mist.

They were halfway up the winding path before the house itself loomed into view—a huge redwood-and-glass structure with a wide balcony facing the sea. The path ended at a terraced patio, and there were wooden steps at the far end that led up alongside the house.

When they reached the steps Hannigan gestured for Vickery to go up first. The big man did not argue; but he ascended sideways, looking back down at Hannigan, neither of his hands touching the railing. Hannigan followed by four of the wood runners.

At the top, in front of the house, was a parking area and a small garden. The access road that came in from the Coast Highway and the highway itself were invisible in the misty darkness. The light over the door burned dully, and as Vickery moved toward it Hannigan shut off the lantern and put it and the shovel down against the wall. Then he started after the big man.

He was just about to tell Vickery that the door was unlocked and to go on in when another man came out of the fog.

Hannigan saw him immediately, over on the access road, and stopped with the back of his neck prickling again. This newcomer was about the same size as Vickery, and Hannigan himself; thick through the body, dressed in a rumpled suit but without a tie. He had wildly unkempt hair and an air of either agitation or harried intent. He hesitated briefly when he saw Hannigan and Vickery, then he came toward them holding his right hand against his hip at a spot covered by his suit jacket.

Vickery had seen him by this time and he was up on the balls of his feet again, nervously watchful. The third man halted opposite the door and looked back and forth between Hannigan and Vickery. He said, "One of you the owner of this house?"

"I am," Hannigan said. He gave his name. "Who are you?"

"Lieutenant McLain, Highway Patrol. You been here all evening, Mr. Hannigan?"

"Yes."

"No trouble of any kind?"

"No. Why?"

"We're looking for a man who escaped from the hospital at Tescadero this afternoon," McLain said. "Maybe you've heard about that?"

Hannigan nodded.

"Well, I don't want to alarm you, but we've had word that he may be in this vicinity."

Hannigan wet his lips and glanced at Vickery.

"If you're with the Highway Patrol," Vickery said to McLain, "how come you're not in uniform?"

"I'm in Investigation. Plainclothes."

"Why would you be on foot? And alone? I thought the police always traveled in pairs."

McLain frowned and studied Vickery for a long moment, penetratingly. His eyes were wide and dark and did not blink much. At length he said, "I'm alone because we've had to spread ourselves thin in order to cover this whole area, and I'm on foot because my damned car came up with a broken fanbelt. I radioed for assistance, and then I came down here because I didn't see any sense in sitting around waiting and doing nothing."

Hannigan remembered Vickery's words on the beach: *I could give you a story about my car breaking down.* He wiped again at the dampness on his face.

Vickery said, "You mind if we see some identification?"

McLain took his hand away from his hip and produced a leather folder from his inside jacket pocket. He held it out so Hannigan and Vickery could read it. "That satisfy you?"

The folder corroborated what McLain had told them about himself; but it did not contain a picture of him. Vickery said nothing.

Hannigan asked, "Have you got a photo of this lunatic?"

"None that will do us any good. He destroyed his file before he escaped from the asylum, and he's been in there sixteen years. The only pictures we could dig up are so old, and he's apparently changed so much, the people at Tescadero tell us there's almost no likeness any more."

"What about a description?"

"Big, dark-haired, regular features, no deformities or identifying marks. That could fit any one of a hundred thousand men or more in Northern California."

"It could fit any of the three of us," Vickery said.

McLain studied him again. "That's right, it could."

"Is there anything else about him?" Hannigan asked. "I mean, could he pretend to be sane and get away with it?"

"The people at the hospital say yes."

"That makes it even worse, doesn't it?"

"You bet it does," McLain said. He rubbed his hands together briskly. "Look, why don't we talk inside? It's pretty cold out here."

Hannigan hesitated. He wondered if McLain had some other reason for wanting to go inside, and when he looked at Vickery it seemed to him the other man was wondering the same thing. But he could see no way to refuse without making trouble.

He said, "No, I guess not. The door's open."

For a moment all three of them stood motionless, McLain still watching Vickery intently. Vickery had begun to fidget under the scrutiny. Finally, since he was closest to the door, he jerked his head away, opened it, and went in sideways, the same way he had climbed the steps from the patio. McLain kept on waiting, which left Hannigan no choice except to follow Vickery. When they were both inside, McLain entered and shut the door.

The three of them went down the short hallway into the big beam-ceilinged family room. McLain glanced around at the field-stone fireplace, the good reproductions on the walls, the tasteful modern furnishings. "Nice place," he said. "You live here alone, Mr. Hannigan?"

"No, with my wife."

"Is she here now?"

"She's in Vegas. She likes to gamble and I don't."

"I see."

"Can I get you something? A drink?"

"Thanks, no. Nothing while I'm on duty."

"I wouldn't mind having one," Vickery said. He was still fidgeting because McLain was still watching him and had been the entire time he was talking to Hannigan.

Near the picture window that took up the entire wall facing the ocean was a leather-topped standing bar; Hannigan crossed to it.

The drapes were open and wisps of the gray fog outside pressed against the glass like skeletal fingers. He put his back to the window and lifted a bottle of bourbon from one of the shelves inside the bar.

"I didn't get your name," McLain said to Vickery.

"Art Vickery. Look, why do you keep staring at me?"

McLain ignored that. "You a friend of Mr. Hannigan's?"

"No," Hannigan said from the bar. "I just met him tonight, a few minutes ago. He wanted to use my phone."

McLain's eyes glittered slightly. "Is that right?" he said. "Then you don't live around here, Mr. Vickery?"

"No, I don't live around here."

"Your car happened to break down too, is that it?"

"Not exactly."

"What then—exactly?"

"I was with a woman, a married woman, and her husband showed up unexpectedly." There was sweat on Vickery's face now. "You know how that is."

"No," McLain said, "I don't. Who was this woman?"

"Listen, if you're with the Highway Patrol as you say, I don't want to give you a name."

"What do you mean, *if* I'm with the Highway Patrol as I say? I told you I was, didn't I? I showed you my identification, didn't I?"

"Just because you're carrying it doesn't make it yours."

McLain's lips thinned and his eyes did not blink at all now. "You trying to get at something, mister? If so, maybe you'd better just spit it out all at once."

"I'm not trying to get at anything," Vickery said. "There's an unidentified lunatic running around loose in this damned fog."

"So you're not even trustful of a law officer."

"I'm just being careful."

"That's a good way to be," McLain said. "I'm that way myself. Where do you live, Vickery?"

"In San Francisco."

"How were you planning to get home tonight?"

"I'm going to call a friend to come pick me up."

"Another lady friend?"

"No."

"All right. Tell you what. You come with me up to where my car is, and when the tow truck shows up with a new fanbelt I'll drive you down to Bodega. You can make your call from the Patrol station there."

A muscle throbbed in Vickery's temple. He tried to match McLain's stare, but it was only seconds before he averted his eyes.

"What's the matter?" McLain said. "Something you don't like about my suggestion?"

"I can make my call from right here."

"Sure, but then you'd be inconveniencing Mr. Hannigan. You wouldn't want to do that to a total stranger, would you?"

"*You're* a total stranger," Vickery said. "I'm not going out in that fog with you, not alone and on foot."

"I think maybe you are."

"No. I don't like those eyes of yours, the way you keep staring at me."

"And I don't like the way you're acting, or your story, or the way *you* look," McLain said. His voice had got very soft, but there was a hardness underneath that made Hannigan—standing immobile now at the bar—feel ripples of cold along his back. "We'll just be going, Vickery. Right now."

Vickery took a step toward him, and Hannigan could not tell if it was involuntary or menacing. Immediately McLain swept the tail of his suit jacket back and slid a gun out of a holster on his hip, centered it on Vickery's chest. The coldness on Hannigan's back deepened; he found himself holding his breath.

"Outside, mister," McLain said.

Vickery had gone pale and the sweat had begun to run on his face. He shook his head and kept on shaking it as McLain advanced on him, as he himself started to back away. "Don't let him do it,"

Vickery said desperately. He was talking to Hannigan but looking at the gun. "Don't let him take me out of here!"

Hannigan spread his hands. "There's nothing I can do."

"That's right, Mr. Hannigan," McLain said, "you just let me handle things. Either way it goes with this one, I'll be in touch."

A little dazedly, Hannigan watched McLain prod Vickery into the hall, to the door; heard Vickery shout something. Then they were gone and the door slammed shut behind them.

Hannigan got a handkerchief out of his pocket and mopped his forehead. He poured himself a drink, swallowed it, poured and drank a second. Then he went to the door.

Outside, the night was silent except for the rhythmic hammering of the breakers in the distance. There was no sign of Vickery or McLain. Hannigan picked up the shovel and the lantern from where he had put them at the house wall and made his way down the steps to the patio, down the fogbound path toward the tule marsh.

He thought about the two men as he went. Was Vickery the lunatic? Or could it be McLain? Well, it didn't really matter; all that mattered now was that Vickery might say something to somebody about the grave. Which meant that Hannigan had to dig up the body and bury it again in some other place.

He hadn't intended the marsh to be a permanent burial spot anyway; he would find a better means of disposal later on. Once that task was taken care of, he could relax and make a few definite plans for the future. Money was made to be spent, particularly if you had a lot of it. It was too bad he had never been able to convince Karen of that.

At the gravesite Hannigan set the lantern down and began to unearth the strangled body of his wife.

And that was when the third man, a stranger carrying a long sharp kitchen knife, crept stealthily out of the fog. . . .

His Name Was Legion

His name was Legion.

No, sir, I mean that literal—Jimmy Legion, that was his name. He knew about the Biblical connection, though. Used to say, "*My name is Legion*," like he was Christ Himself quoting Scripture.

Religious man? No, sir! Furthest thing from it. Jimmy Legion was a liar, a blasphemer, a thief, a fornicator, and just about anything else you can name. A pure hellion—a devil's son if ever there was one. Some folks in Wayville said that after he ran off with Amanda Sykes that September of 1931, he sure must have crossed afoul of the law and come to a violent end. But nobody rightly knew for sure. Not about him, nor about Amanda Sykes either.

He came to Wayville in the summer of that year, 1931. Came in out of nowhere in a fancy new Ford car, seemed to have plenty of money in his pockets; claimed he was a magazine writer. Wayville wasn't much in those days—just a small farm town with a population of around five hundred. Hardly the kind of place you'd expect a man like Legion to gravitate to. Unless he was hiding out from the law right then, which is the way some folks figured it—but only after he was gone. While he lived in Wayville he was a charmer.

First day I laid eyes on him, I was riding out from town with saddlebags and a pack all loaded up with small hardware—

Yes, that's right—saddlebags. I was only nineteen that summer, and my family was too poor to afford an automobile. But my father gave me a horse of my own when I was sixteen—a fine light-colored gelding that I called Silverboy—and after I was graduated from high school I went to work for Mr. Hazlitt at Wayville Hardware.

Depression had hit everybody pretty hard in our area, and not many small farmers could afford the gasoline for truck trips into town every time they needed something. Small merchants like Mr. Hazlitt couldn't afford it either. So what I did for him, I used Silverboy to deliver small things like farm tools and plumbing supplies and carpentry items. Rode him most of the time, hitched him to a wagon once in a while when the load was too large to carry on horseback. Mr. Hazlitt called me Ben Boone the Pony Express Deliveryman, and I liked that fine. I was full of spirit and adventure back then.

Anyhow, this afternoon I'm talking about I was riding Silverboy out to the Baker farm when I heard a roar on the road behind me. Then a car shot by so fast and so close that Silverboy spooked and spilled both of us down a ten-foot embankment.

Wasn't either of us hurt, but we could have been—we could have been killed. I only got a glimpse of the car, but it was enough for me to identify it when I got back to Wayville. I went hunting for the owner and found him straightaway inside Chancellor's Cafe.

First thing he said to me was, "*My* name is Legion."

Well, we had words. Or rather, I had the words; he just stood there and grinned at me, all wise and superior, like a professor talking to a bumpkin. Handsome brute, he was, few years older than me, with slicked-down hair and big brown eyes and teeth so white they glistened like mica rocks in the sun.

He shamed me, is what he did, in front of a dozen of my friends and neighbors. Said what happened on the road was my fault, and why didn't I go somewhere and curry my horse, *he* had better things to do than argue road right-of-ways.

Every time I saw him after that he'd make some remark to me. Polite, but with brimstone in it—I guess you know what I mean. I tried to fight him once, but he wouldn't fight. Just stood grinning at me like the first time, hands down at his sides, daring me. I couldn't hit him that way, when he wouldn't defend himself. I wanted to, but I was raised better than that.

If me and some of the other young fellows disliked him, most of the girls took to him like flies to honey. All they saw were his smile and his big brown eyes and his city charm. And his lies about being a magazine writer.

Just about every day I'd see him with a different girl, some I'd dated myself on occasion, such as Bobbie Jones and Dulcea Wade. Oh, he was smooth and evil, all right. He ruined more than one of those girls, no doubt of that. Got Dulcea Wade pregnant, for one, although none of us found out about it until after he ran off with Amanda Sykes.

Falsehoods and fornication were only two of his sins. Like I said before, he was guilty of much more than that. Including plain thievery.

He wasn't in town more than a month before folks started missing things. Small amounts of cash money, valuables of one kind or another. Mrs. Cooley, who owned the boardinghouse where Legion took a room, lost a solid gold ring her late husband gave her. But she never suspected Legion, and hardly anybody else did either until it was too late.

All this went on for close to three months—the lying and the fornicating and the stealing. It couldn't have lasted much longer than that without the truth coming out, and I guess Legion knew that best of all. It was a Friday in late September that he and Amanda Sykes disappeared together. And when folks did learn the truth about him, all they could say was good riddance to him and her both—the Sykeses among them because they were decent God-fearing people.

I reckon I was one of the last to see either of them. Fact is, in a way I was responsible for them leaving as sudden as they did.

At about two o'clock that Friday afternoon I left Mr. Hazlitt's

store with a scythe and some other tools George Pickett needed on
his farm and rode out the north road. It was a burning hot day, no
wind at all—I remember that clear. When I was two miles outside
Wayville, and about two more from the Pickett farm, I took Silverboy over to a stream that meandered through a stand of cottonwoods. He was blowing pretty hard because of the heat, and I
wanted to give him a cool drink. Give myself a cool drink too.

But no sooner did I rein him up to the stream than I spied two
people lying together in the tall grass. And I mean "lying together"
in the biblical sense—no need to explain further. It was Legion and
Amanda Sykes.

Well, they were so involved in their sinning that they didn't
notice me until I was right up to them. Before I could turn Silverboy and set him running, Legion jumped up and grabbed hold of me
and dragged me down to the ground. He cursed me like a crazy
man; I never saw anybody that wild and possessed before or since.

"I'll teach you to spy on me, Ben Boone!" he shouted, and he hit
me a full right-hand wallop on the face. Knocked me down in the
grass and bloodied my nose, bloodied it so bad I couldn't stop the
flow until a long while later.

Then he jumped on me and pounded me two more blows until I
was half senseless. And after that he reached in my pocket and took
my wallet—stole my wallet and all the money I had.

Amanda Sykes just sat there covering herself with her dress and
watching. She never said a word the whole time.

It wasn't a minute later they were gone. I saw them get into this
Ford that was hidden in the cottonwoods nearby and roar away. I
couldn't have stopped them with a rifle, weak as I was.

When my strength finally came back I washed the blood off me
as best I could, and rode Silverboy straight back to Wayville to
report to the local constable. He called in the state police and they
put out a warrant for the arrest of Legion and Amanda Sykes, but
nothing came of it. Police didn't find them; nobody ever heard of
them again.

Yes, sir, I know the story doesn't seem to have much point right now. But it will in just a minute. I wanted you to hear it first the way I told it back in 1931—the way I been telling it over and over in my own mind ever since then so I could keep on living with myself.

A good part of it's lies you see. Lies worse than Jimmy Legion's.

That's why I asked you to come, Reverend. Doctors here at the hospital tell me my heart's about ready to give out. They don't figure I'll last the week. I can't die with sin on my soul. Time's long past due for me to make peace with myself and with God.

The lies? Mostly what happened on that last afternoon, after I came riding up to the stream on my way to the Pickett farm. About Legion attacking me and bloodying me and stealing my wallet. About him and Amanda Sykes running off together. About not telling of the sinkhole near the stream that was big enough and deep enough to swallow anything smaller than a house.

Those things, and the names of two of the three of us that were there.

No, I didn't mean *him*. Everything I told you about him is the truth as far as I know it, including his name.

His name was Legion.

But Amanda's name wasn't Sykes. Not anymore it wasn't, not for five months prior to that day.

Her name was Amanda Boone.

Yes, Reverend, that's right—she was my wife. I'd dated those other girls, but I'd long *courted* Amanda; we eloped over the state line before Legion arrived and got married by a justice of the peace. We did it that way because her folks and mine were dead-set against either of us marrying so young—not that they knew we were at such a stage. We kept that part of our relationship a secret too, I guess because it was an adventure for the both of us, at least in the beginning.

My name? Yes, it's really Ben Boone. Yet it *wasn't* on that afternoon. The one who chanced on Legion and Amanda out there by the stream, who caught them sinning and listened to them laugh all shameless and say they were running off together . . . he wasn't Ben Boone at all.

His name, Reverend, that one who sat grim on his pale horse with Farmer Pickett's long, new-honed scythe in one hand . . .

His name was Death.

REBOUND
(With Barry N. Malzberg)

The last time I had seen Alex Rolfe was twenty-one years ago at the old Madison Square Garden at 49th Street and Eighth Avenue, in what was once called the heart of Manhattan.

That night, with the Continental Basketball Association championship series between the New York Sabers and the Chicago Wildcats tied at three games apiece, Rolfe had come into the last quarter of the seventh game when the Wildcats' first-string center twisted an already tender ankle. And he had scored 18 points in ten minutes on a remarkable assortment of fadeaway jumpers and hook shots and reverse layups, had blocked five shots, had taken down eight rebounds, and had, unusual for a big man, twice forced turnovers on pressure defense. As a result, the Wildcats had wiped out a 13-point Sabers lead and on the strength of Rolfe's last-second tip-in sent the game into overtime.

In the five-minute extra period he had blocked two more shots, grabbed off another four rebounds, and scored all 14 of the Wildcats' points. The final score was 109-100, Chicago. His teammates had surrounded him after the buzzer and half carried him off the court, not a small accomplishment considering that Alex Rolfe was six-nine and weighed in the neighborhood of 270 pounds.

He was twenty-seven then, born on September 12, 1930, according to the program, and in his fifth season in the CBA. He had kicked around quite a bit; the Wildcats were his fourth team. He'd been a competent center in college, but the faster and more intri-

cate patterns of professional basketball seemed to have confused
him. Or they had until that one game, that one brilliant performance.

The next day all the New York papers, including the *Telegram* and
Journal-American and *Daily Mirror* of sainted memory, had been filled
with interviews and suggestions by a couple of columnists that Rolfe
might be on the verge of realizing his full potential. I remember one
particularly effusive writer suggesting that he might even become
another George Mikan. My own write-up of the game—in those
days I had covered the Sabers for the *Herald-Tribune,* also of sainted
memory—had been a bit more restrained. There was no denying
what Rolfe had accomplished, or of its impact on professional basketball in that era, but the Sabers were my team and he had almost
singlehandedly taken what would have been their first championship
away from them.

As things turned out, though, that game was to be Rolfe's last.
The day after it was over he literally disappeared from sight, never
to be heard from again. No one seemed to know where he'd gone,
or why—not even the management of the Wildcats—and he failed
to show up when training camp opened the following season. There
were a few "Whatever happened to Alex Rolfe?" stories that summer and during the next year, but after that most people forgot
about him and about that glorious night in the Garden. Yesterday's
sports heroes are always quickly forgotten. It's the heroes of today
who get the ink and the adulation.

Now, twenty-one years later, Alex Rolfe was just a name in the
yellowing pages of newspapers and sports magazines and record
books. The old CBA was gone; all its great players were retired or
coaching obscurely at the high-school or small-college level and just
as forgotten as Rolfe himself. Professional basketball had entered a
new and different age, a better age in a lot of ways. The high and
low points of its past were little more than dim memories.

But some people still remembered, and I was one of them. Even
after two decades I remembered that night in the Garden and I

remembered Alex Rolfe and what he'd done. Rolfe had become something of an obsession with me over the years. The thing was, I thought I knew why he had vanished so suddenly and so completely, and I wanted to find him and talk to him about it. And the thing was, too, that his performance against the Sabers in 1957 had marked a turning point in my own life.

I had been young and ambitious in those days, on my way to the top, I thought; but my life and my career hadn't quite worked out the way I'd always believed they would. In 1958 I had lost my job with the *Herald-Tribune,* for internal reasons that weren't my fault, and I had also lost my wife in the divorce courts for domestic reasons that may or may not have been my fault. After that, my life and my career had settled into mediocrity—a succession of jobs with minor newspapers, a few freelance articles for second-string sports magazines, two sports biographies that hadn't sold well, too many sessions with the bottle, and too many loveless affairs. My own dim memories of the past were all I had left now. Memories of the way it had been in the old days in New York, covering the Sabers and dreaming of wealth and fame. Memories of men like Alex Rolfe.

Off and on for the past twenty years I had spent time and energy trying to locate him, without success. Then, three days ago, the paper I was working for in Dayton had taken on a sports reporter whose last job was in Madison, Wisconsin. This reporter and I had gone out for a drink, and talk had turned to basketball, and Rolfe's name had come up. And it turned out that the reporter knew of Rolfe, knew where he was living—in a small village in upstate Wisconsin, where he owned a tavern. The reporter had wanted to do a feature on him a year or so ago, but Rolfe had been uncooperative, saying that he didn't want any publicity; the reporter hadn't pursued the matter.

I had gotten on the phone immediately, dug up an address and number for Rolfe in the village of Harbor Lake, and then called the number. When I got through to Rolfe I explained that I was writing a series of articles on basketball players of the fifties for a national sports magazine and did he remember my name? He was silent for several seconds; then he said yes, he remembered me, but he didn't want to be interviewed and besides, I had to be scraping the bottom of the barrel if I wanted to do a story on him. I reminded him of the championship game in the Garden and told him the magazine had given me *carte blanche,* write up anyone I cared to, not necessarily the stars but the journeymen players who had had moments of greatness in the past.

He still didn't want to see me. I said I was going to be in Wisconsin anyway to talk to another old player and that I intended to drop in on him; said I was going to write about the Sabers-Wildcats title game with or without an interview. He told me it was my privilege to write whatever I felt like writing, and hung up on me.

The next day I took a leave of absence from the paper, got into my car, and headed north to Wisconsin.

And now, two days and eight hundred miles later, I had arrived in Harbor Lake. It wasn't much of a town, just a few scattered houses along a small tree-rimmed lake and half a dozen stores along a one-block main street. Quiet, sleepy, off the beaten track. It was a little past 4:00 P.M. as I drove through it, looking for the Harbor Lake Tavern. The leaden sky forecast rain, but there was nothing on the windshield of my car except streaks of dirt that gave the buildings and the gray-looking lake water a vaguely distorted appearance.

Rolfe's tavern turned out to be on the far side of the village, tucked back near the water's edge. It was a small weathered building with a rustic façade, shaded by pines; no neon sign or electric beer advertisements, nothing to tell you it was a bar except for the neatly painted wooden sign above the door that spelled out its name. I imagined that he did most of his business at night, even during these late spring months; there was only one other car on the gravel parking lot besides mine when I shut off the engine and went inside.

The car must have belonged to Rolfe himself because he was the only one in the place. He stood behind the plank, slicing lemons and limes into wedges. A man six-nine in his twenties is imposing, but in his forties he angles toward a question mark. There were heavy lines in his cheeks and a kind of melancholy in his expression, and when he came down to the stool I had taken he walked with a pronounced limp, as if he were suffering from arthritis. He looked old and tired—the same way my reflection looked in the backbar mirror. The years hadn't been good to him either.

He asked me what I'd have, and I told him a double Scotch and soda and watched him build it. When he set the glass down in front of me I said, "You don't recognize me, do you, Rolfe?"

He stared at me, searching his memory, and after a time I saw recognition seep into his eyes. His body stiffened a little; the fingers of both hands curled into fists, relaxed, curled again, relaxed again. "Joe Brady," he said.

"That's right. Joe Brady."

"I told you I didn't want to see you."

"I'm here, Rolfe, like it or not."

"I don't want to talk about the past."

"No? Why not?"

"Because it's dead. Dead and buried. I haven't thought about basketball in years."

"Haven't you?" I said.

Emotion flickered across his face; he looked away from me, through a window at the rear that framed a view of the lake. His hands curled into fists again. "Just what do you want from me, Brady?"

"An interview. A story."

"I don't have a story for you."

"I think you do."

His eyes shifted back to mine. "It's been twenty-one years since that game in the Garden," he said. "Nobody cares any more. Nobody remembers."

"I care. I remember."

"Why?"

"You played a great game, the finest game of your career. And then you disappeared, you quit cold."

"And you want to know why."

I nodded.

He didn't say anything for a time. His eyes took on a remoteness, as if he were looking backward into the past. It was quiet in there, hushed except for the faint whirring of the refrigeration unit. From outside, over the lake, I thought I could hear the distant sheetmetal rumble of thunder.

Rolfe blinked finally and the remoteness was gone. "All right," he said. "I left basketball after that game because it *was* the finest of my career. I figured I'd never have another one like it; it was a fluke and I was a second-string center and always would be. Not many mediocre pro athletes have great games and not many have the sense to get out if they do. I had a chance to quit a hero, a champion, and I took it. That's all."

"Is it?" I drank some of my Scotch and soda. "Tell me about the game, Rolfe."

"Tell you about it? You were there."

"Sure. But I want to hear your version of it, everything you remember. The fourth quarter, coming off the bench, scoring the eighteen points—start with that."

"The shots I took went in. I was lucky."

"You weren't lucky, you were inspired. You made moves and shots you'd never even tried before. Remember the fourteen points in overtime? Remember the fadeaway jumpers you made with three men on you that hit nothing but net?"

"No," Rolfe said, "I don't remember."

"Sure you do. You remember every point of it. Every footfall on the floor, every move and rebound and blocked shot, who was guarding you each time you scored."

He shook his head. Kept on shaking it.

"There's something else you remember, too. The most important thing of all about that game."

"I don't know what you're talking about."

"I'm talking about point-shaving, Rolfe," I said. "I'm talking about criminal collusion with the gambling syndicates in New York and Chicago."

Something seemed to break deep inside him; his body lost its stiffness, seemed to shrink in on itself. His eyes turned cloudy with pain.

"Lots of point-shaving in those days," I said. "Mostly in the college ranks but there was talk that it was going on in the pros too. Vague rumors that the gamblers got to you and Donovan, the Wildcats' shooting guard; I heard them and so did a couple of other reporters, but not until weeks after the game and then we couldn't find enough proof to break the story.

"Point spread was Sabers plus five and you and Donovan were supposed to make sure the Wildcats didn't beat that spread because there was heavy syndicate money on the Sabers. Help win the game if you could but not by more than four points; if the Wildcats built up a lead of six or better, then the two of you were to purposely miss shots, make a turnover or two, do whatever you could to get the margin down to less than five.

"Donovan delivered—he tried his damnedest to keep you from scoring all those points in overtime; but you played the best basketball of your life and crossed up the gamblers and blew the spread. Isn't that the way it was?"

He turned away from me, limped over to the backbar, picked up a bottle of bourbon , came back, poured a triple shot, and drank it neat. I watched him shudder. "I knew something like this would happen," he said thickly, talking more to himself than to me. "Twenty-one years, but I knew it would come out some day."

"So you're not going to deny it."

He let out a heavy sighing breath. "Look at me," he said. "You know it's the truth, you can see that it is."

I was looking at him, all right. I'd thought that if this moment of confrontation ever came, I would feel something—hatred for him, a kind of perverse satisfaction. But I felt nothing. Too many years had passed since that night in 1957. Too many years.

"What I want to know is why," I said. "Why did you sell out to the gamblers and then double-cross them? A change of heart, is that it? They got to you in a weak moment, tempted you, and you couldn't go through with it when the time came? The honest man triumphant?"

Anguish made the lines in Rolfe's face look as deep as incisions. "I wish to God that was the way it was," he said. "I'd still be something of a hero then, wouldn't I? I'd still be able to live with myself. But it wasn't like that at all."

"How was it, then?"

No response at first. Thunder rumbled again over the lake, closer this time; a gust of wind rattled the tavern's front door and window.

"I was a wild kid in those days," Rolfe said abruptly. "I didn't give a damn about much of anything except fast cars, fast women, and big money. I got in with the gamblers and I lost six thousand to them on the horses and playing high-stakes poker, and I couldn't pay off my markers. So it was agree to shave points in the championship game or get my legs broken with a baseball bat. I agreed; I was eager as hell to agree. I went out there that night with every intention of doing what I was told to do."

"So why didn't you?"

"Because whatever else I was, I was also a basketball player. I loved the game, I'd always wanted to play it the way the best did. Only I just wasn't good enough—a big slow reserve center who was lucky to be in a professional uniform. I'd had some good games in college and in the pros, but nothing outstanding, nothing that even came close to real excellence. Except that night, that one night. I went into the game in the fourth quarter and it was all there: the moves, the shots, the *excellence*. You understand, Brady? For the first time in my life it was all there."

I felt a little shiver along the saddle of my back. "Yeah," I said, "I understand."

"I couldn't do anything wrong. I couldn't even *make* myself do anything wrong. It was like I was drunk on basketball; all I could think about was the game, making the moves, making the shots, doing all the things I'd always wanted to do but had never been able to do. Nothing else mattered; there wasn't anything else." Rolfe swallowed heavily. There was sweat on his face now. "It wasn't until the game was over that I realized I'd blown the point spread. That I realized what that one great game, those few minutes of real excellence, was going to cost me."

I let out a breath. "What happened with the gamblers?"

"What do you think happened?" he said. His mouth twisted bitterly. "They did what they'd warned me they would do. They broke both my legs with a baseball bat."

There wasn't anything to say. I picked up my drink and finished it.

"I didn't go back to Chicago after the game," Rolfe said. "I ran instead—packed up my things at the hotel and bought a cheap car and drove out here to Wisconsin. A couple of weeks later I got in touch with the Wildcats and had them send my share of the championship money to a bank in Madison; I used that and borrowed the rest to pay off the six thousand I owed the gamblers.

"But it wasn't any use and I knew it. They found me inside of a month. One of them visited me in the county hospital afterward and told me I was through playing basketball. I knew that too. But he could have saved himself the trouble because my right leg never did heal properly; that's why I walk with a limp. I've got that limp to remind me of my one great game every time I take a step. Every step for the past twenty-one years.

"But that's not the worst of it. Waiting all these years for someone like you to come along, listening for footsteps out of the past—

that's not the worst of it either. The worst of it was all the years of wondering if that game really was a fluke or if the moves and the shots and the excellence would have been there for me in other games; if I could have *been* great some day. I'll never know, Brady. I'll never know."

Outside, rain began to fall; I could hear it drumming against the roof of the tavern. The day had turned dark—but no darker than it was in here, or than it was inside Alex Rolfe.

He ran a hand across his face, as if to wipe away emotion as well as sweat. When he took the hand away his expression was weary and resigned. "So now you know the whole story," he said. "Go ahead and write it if you want. I just don't care any more."

"I'm not going to write it," I said.

He stared at me as I got off my stool. "That's why you came here, isn't it? To get the truth so you could tell the world what happened back in 1957?"

"Maybe it is. But I'm still not going to write the story. It's something that happened twenty-one years ago; nobody cares any more, nobody remembers—you were right about that. Except you and me, and we've both got to keep on living with ourselves."

I turned my back on him because I didn't want to watch his reaction, didn't want to look at him any longer, and hurried to the door and out into the warm spring rain.

But in my car, on the way back through the village, the image of Rolfe's face remained sharp in my mind. Full of guilt, that face, full of torment and loss. Full of all the same things as that other face, the familiar one in the backbar mirror.

I had come to Harbor Lake to confront Rolfe with the truth, yes; but I had not sought him out for the sake of justice, not planned to write the real story behind the CBA championship game for public-spirited reasons. I had done it instead for the sole purpose of making him pay, even after all these years, for what I'd convinced myself he had done to me.

Because I had not, as I'd told him, found out about the point-shaving weeks after the game. I had found out about it the day *before* the game, through a personal contact in the gambling syndicate. And instead of breaking the story, blowing the lid off the whole sordid affair, I had withdrawn my wife's and my entire savings of $8,000 and bet it all on the New York Sabers.

Yet it was not Rolfe who had cost me my savings, and as a result my marriage; it was me who had lost them, me who had robbed myself. I could admit that now, after all this time. I was no better than Rolfe; we were two of a kind. Just as he had had his moment of greatness in 1957, so had I had my moment. Just as he had fallen from grace because of one terrible mistake, and lost a career full of promise and a chance for fulfillment, so had I.

Alex Rolfe had lived in his own private hell for twenty-one years; he would go on living in it for the rest of his life.

And so would I in mine.

BLACK WIND

It was one of those freezing late-November nights, just before the winter snows, when a funny east wind comes howling down out of the mountains and across Woodbine Lake a quarter mile from the village. The sound that wind makes is something hellish, full of screams and wailings that can raise the hackles on your neck if you're not used to it. In the old days the Indians who used to live around here called it a "black wind"; they believed that it carried the voices of evil spirits, and that if you listened to it long enough it could drive you mad.

Well, there are a lot of superstitions in our part of upstate New York; nobody pays much mind to them in this modern age. Or if they do, they won't admit it even to themselves. The fact is, though, that when the black wind blows the local folks stay pretty close to home and the village, like as not, is deserted after dusk.

That was the way it was on this night. I hadn't had a customer in my diner in more than an hour, since just before seven o'clock, and I had about decided to close up early and go on home. To a glass of brandy and a good hot fire.

I was pouring myself a last cup of coffee when the headlights swung into the diner's parking lot.

They whipped in fast, off the county highway, and I heard the squeal of brakes on the gravel just out front. Kids, I thought, because that was the way a lot of them drove, even around here—fast and a little reckless. But it wasn't kids. It turned out instead to be a man and a woman in their late thirties, strangers, both of them bundled up in winter coats and mufflers, the woman carrying a big fancy alligator purse.

The wind came in with them, shrieking and swirling. I could feel the numbing chill of it even in the few seconds the door was open; it cuts through you like the blade of a knife, that wind, right straight to the bone.

The man clumped immediately to where I was behind the counter, letting the woman close the door. He was handsome in a suave, barbered city way; but his face was closed up into a mask of controlled rage.

"Coffee," he said. The word came out in a voice that matched his expression—hard and angry, like a threat.

"Sure thing. Two coffees."

"One coffee," he said. "Let her order her own."

The woman had come up on his left, but not close to him—one stool between them. She was nice-looking in the same kind of made-up, city way. Or she would have been if her face wasn't pinched up worse than his; the skin across her cheekbones was stretched so tight it seemed ready to split. Her eyes glistened like a pair of wet stones and didn't blink at all.

"Black coffee," she said to me.

I looked at her, at him, and I started to feel a little uneasy. There was a kind of savage tension between them, thick and crackling; I could feel it like static electricity. I wet my lips, not saying anything, and reached behind me for the coffee pot and two mugs.

The man said, "I'll have a ham-and-cheese sandwich on rye bread. No mustard, no mayonnaise; just butter. Make it to go."

"Yes, sir. How about you, ma'am?"

"Tuna fish on white," she said thinly. She had close-cropped blonde hair, wind-tangled under a loose scarf; she kept brushing at it with an agitated hand. "I'll eat it here."

"No, she won't," the man said to me. "Make it to go, just like mine."

She threw him an ugly look. "I want to eat here."

"Fine," he said—to me again; it was as if she wasn't there. "But I'm leaving in five minutes, as soon as I drink my coffee. I want that ham-and-cheese ready by then."

"Yes, sir."

I finished pouring out the coffee and set the two mugs on the counter. The man took his, swung around, and stomped over to one of the tables. He sat down and stared at the door, blowing into the mug, using it to warm his hands.

"All right," the woman said, "all right, all right. All right." Four times like that, all to herself. Her eyes had cold little lights in them now, like spots of foxfire.

I said hesitantly, "Ma'am? You still want the tuna sandwich to eat here?"

She blinked then, for the first time, and focused on me. "No. To hell with it. I don't want anything to eat." She caught up her mug and took it to another of the tables, two away from the one he was sitting at.

I went down to the sandwich board and got out two pieces of rye bread and spread them with butter. The stillness in there had a strained feel, made almost eerie by the constant wailing outside. I could feel myself getting more jittery as the seconds passed.

While I sliced ham I watched the two of them at the tables— him still staring at the door, drinking his coffee in quick angry sips; her facing the other way, her hands fisted in her lap, the steam from her cup spiraling up around her face. Well-off married couple from New York City, I thought: they were both wearing the same type of expensive wedding ring. On their way to a weekend in the moun- tains, maybe, or up to Canada for a few days. And they'd had a hell of a fight over something, the way married people do on long tiring drives; that was all there was to it.

Except that that *wasn't* all there was to it.

I've owned this diner thirty years and I've seen a lot of folks come and go in that time; a lot of tourists from the city, with all sorts of marital problems. But I'd never seen any like these two. That tension between them wasn't anything fresh-born, wasn't just the brief and meaningless aftermath of a squabble. No, there was real hatred on both sides—the kind that builds and builds, seething, over long bitter weeks or months or even years. The kind that's liable to explode some day.

Well, it wasn't really any of my business. Not unless the blowup happened in here, it wasn't, and that wasn't likely. Or so I kept telling myself. But I was a little worried just the same. On a night like this, with that damned black wind blowing and playing hell with people's nerves, anything could happen. Anything at all.

I finished making the sandwich, cut it in half, and plastic-bagged it. Just as I slid it into a paper sack, there was a loud banging noise from across the room that made me jump half a foot; it sounded like a pistol shot. But it had only been the man slamming his empty mug down on the table.

I took a breath, let it out silently. He scraped back his chair as I did that, stood up, and jammed his hands into his coat pockets. Without looking at her, he said to the woman, "You pay for the food," and started past her table toward the restrooms in the rear.

She said, "Why the hell should I pay for it?"

He paused and glared back at her. "You've got all the money."

"I've got all the money? Oh, that's a laugh. *I've* got all the money!"

"Go on, keep it up." Then in a louder voice, as if he wanted to make sure I heard, he said, "Bitch." And stalked away from her.

She watched him until he was gone inside the corridor leading to the restrooms; she was as rigid as a chunk of wood. She sat that way for another five or six seconds, until the wind gusted outside, thudded against the door and the window like something trying to break in. Jerkily she got to her feet and came over to where I was at the sandwich board. Those cold lights still glowed in her eyes.

"Is his sandwich ready?"

I nodded and made myself smile. "Will that be all, ma'am?"

"No. I've changed my mind. I want something to eat too." She leaned forward and stared at the glass pastry container on the back counter. "What kind of pie is that?"

"Cinnamon apple."

"I'll have a piece of it."

"Okay—sure. Just one?"

"Yes. Just one."

I turned back there, got the pie out, cut a slice, and wrapped it in waxed paper. When I came around with it she was rummaging in her purse, getting her wallet out. Back in the restroom area, I heard the man's hard, heavy steps; in the next second he appeared. And headed straight for the door.

The woman said, "How much do I owe you?"

I put the pie into the paper sack with the sandwich, and the sack on the counter. "That'll be three-eighty."

The man opened the door; the wind came shrieking in, eddying drafts of icy air. He went right on out, not even glancing at the woman or me, and slammed the door shut behind him.

She laid a five-dollar bill on the counter. Caught up the sack, pivoted, and started for the door.

"Ma'am?" I said. "You've got change coming."

She must have heard me, but she didn't look back and she didn't slow up. The pair of headlights came on out front, slicing pale wedges from the darkness; through the front window I could see the evergreens at the far edge of the lot, thick swaying shadows bent almost double by the wind. The shrieking rose again for two or three seconds, then fell back to a muted whine; she was gone.

I had never been gladder or more relieved to see customers go. I let out another breath, picked up the fiver, and moved over to the cash register. Outside, above the thrumming and wailing, the car engine revved up to a roar and there was the ratcheting noise of tires spinning on gravel. The headlights shot around and probed out toward the county highway.

Time now to close up and go home, all right; I wanted a glass of brandy and a good hot fire more than ever. I went around to the tables they'd used, to gather up the coffee cups. But as much as I wanted to forget the two of them, I couldn't seem to get them out of my mind. Especially the woman.

I kept seeing those eyes of hers, cold and hateful like the wind, as if there was a black wind blowing inside her, too, and she'd been listening to it too long. I kept seeing her lean forward across the counter and stare at the pastry container. And I kept seeing her rummage in that big alligator purse when I turned around with the slice of pie. Something funny about the way she'd been doing that. As if she hadn't just been getting her wallet out to pay me. As if she'd been—

Oh my God, I thought.

I ran back behind the counter. Then I ran out again to the door, threw it open, and stumbled onto the gravel lot. But they were long gone; the night was a solid ebony wall.

I didn't know what to do. What could I do? Maybe she'd done what I suspicioned, and maybe she hadn't; I couldn't be sure because I don't keep an inventory on the slots of utensils behind the sandwich board. And I didn't know who they were or where they were going. I didn't even know what kind of car they were riding in.

I kept on standing there, chills racing up and down my back, listening to that black wind scream and scream around me. Feeling the cold sharp edge of it cut into my bare flesh, cut straight to the bone.

Just like the blade of a knife . . .

A CRAVING FOR ORIGINALITY

Charlie Hackman was a professional writer. He wrote popular fiction, any kind from sexless Westerns to sexy Gothics to oversexed historical romances, whatever the current trends happened to be. He could be counted on to deliver an acceptable manuscript to order in two weeks. He had published 9,000,000 words in a fifteen-year career, under a variety of different names (Allison St. Cyr being the most prominent), and he couldn't tell you the plot of any book he'd written more than six months ago. He was what is euphemistically known in the trade as "a dependable wordsmith," or "a versatile pro," or "a steady producer of commercial commodities."

In other words, he was well-named: Hackman was a hack.

The reason he was a hack was not because he was fast and prolific, or because he contrived popular fiction on demand, or because he wrote for money. It was because he was and did all these things with no ambition and no sense of commitment. It was because he wrote without originality of any kind.

Of course, Hackman had not started out to be a hack; no writer does. But he had discovered early on, after his first two novels were rejected with printed slips by thirty-seven publishers each, that (a) he was not very good, and (b) what talent he did possess was in the form of imitations. When he tried to do imaginative, ironic, meaningful work of his own he failed miserably; but when he imitated the ideas and visions of others, the blurred carbon copies he produced were just literate enough to be publishable.

Truth to tell, this didn't bother him very much. The one thing he had always wanted to be was a professional writer; he had dreamed of nothing else since his discovery of the Hardy Boys and Tarzan books in his pre-teens. So from the time of his first sale he accepted what he was, shrugged, and told himself not to worry about it. What was wrong with being a hack, anyway? The writing business was full of them—and hacks, no less than nonhacks, offered a desirable form of escapist entertainment to the masses; the only difference was, his readership had nondiscriminating tastes. Was his product, after all, any less honorable than what television offered? Was he hurting anybody, corrupting anybody? No. Absolutely not. So what was wrong with being a hack?

For one and a half decades, operating under this cheerful set of rationalizations, Hackman was a complacent man. He wrote from ten to fifteen novels per year, all for minor and exploitative paperback houses, and earned an average annual sum of $25,000. He married an ungraceful woman named Grace and moved into a suburban house on Long Island. He went bowling once a week, played poker once a week, argued conjugal matters with his wife once a week, and took the train into Manhattan to see his agent and editors once a week. Every June he and Grace spent fourteen pleasant days at Lake George in the Adirondacks. Every Christmas Grace's mother came from Pennsylvania and spent fourteen miserable days with them.

He drank a little too much sometimes and worried about lung cancer because he smoked three packs of cigarettes a day. He cheated moderately on his income tax. He coveted one of his neighbors' wives. He read all the current paperback bestsellers, dissected them in his mind, and then reassembled them into similar plots for his own novels. When new acquaintances asked him what he did for a living he said, "I'm a writer," and seldom failed to feel a small glow of pride.

That was the way it was for fifteen years—right up until the morning of his fortieth birthday.

Hackman woke up on that morning, looked at Grace lying beside him, and realized she had put on at least forty pounds since their marriage. He listened to himself wheeze as he lighted his first cigarette of the day. He got dressed and walked downstairs to his office, where he read the half page of manuscript still in his typewriter (an occult pirate novel, the latest craze). He went outside and stood on the lawn and looked at his house. Then he sat down on the porch steps and looked at himself.

I'm not just a writer of hack stories, he thought sadly, I'm a liver of a hack life.

Fifteen years of cohabiting with trite fictional characters in hackneyed fictional situations. Fifteen years of cohabiting with an unimaginative wife in a trite suburb in a hackneyed lifestyle in a conventional world. Hackman the hack, doing the same things over and over again; Hackman the hack, grinding out books and days one by one. No uniqueness in any of it, from the typewriter to the bedroom to the Adirondacks.

No originality.

He sat there for a long while, thinking about this. No originality. Funny. It was like waking up to the fact that, after forty years, you've never tasted pineapple, that pineapple was missing from your life. All of a sudden you craved pineapple; you wanted it more than you'd ever wanted anything before. Pineapple or originality—it was the same principle.

Grace came out eventually and asked him what he was doing. "Thinking that I crave originality," he said, and she said, "Will you settle for eggs and bacon?" Trite dialogue, Hackman thought. Hackneyed humor. He told her he didn't want any breakfast and went into his office.

Originality. Well, even a hack ought to be able to create something fresh and imaginative if he applied himself; even a hack learned a few tricks in fifteen years. How about a short story? Good. He had never written a short story; he would be working in new territory already. Now how about a plot?

He sat at his typewriter. He paced the office. He lay down on the couch. He sat at the typewriter again. Finally the germ of an idea came to him and he nurtured it until it began to develop. Then he began to type.

It took him all day to write the story, which was about five thousand words long. That was his average wordage per day on a novel, but on a novel he never revised so much as a comma. After supper he went back into the office and made pen-and-ink corrections until eleven o'clock. Then he went to bed, declined Grace's reluctant offer of "a birthday present," and dreamed about the story until 6:00 A.M. At which time he got up, retyped the pages, made some more revisions in ink, and retyped the story a third time before he was satisfied. He mailed it that night to his agent.

Three days later the agent called about a new book contract. Hackman asked him, "Did you have a chance to read the short story I sent you?"

"I read it, all right. And sent it straight back to you."

"Sent it back? What's wrong with it?"

"It's old hat," the agent said. "The idea's been done to death."

Hackman went out into the back yard and lay down in the hammock. All right, so maybe he was doomed to hackdom as a writer; maybe he just wasn't capable of *writing* anything original. But that didn't mean he couldn't *do* something original, did it? He had a quick mind, a good grasp of what was going on in the world. He ought to be able to come up with at least one original idea, maybe even an idea that would not only satisfy his craving for originality but change his life, get him out of the stale rut he was in.

He closed his eyes.

He concentrated.

He thought about jogging backward from Long Island to Miami Beach and then applying for an entry in the Guinness Book of World Records.

Imitative.

He thought about marching naked through Times Square at high noon, waving a standard paperback contract and using a bullhorn to protest man's literary inhumanity to man.

Trite.

He thought about adopting a red-white-and-blue disguise and robbing a bank in each one of the original thirteen states.

Derivative.

He thought about changing his name to Holmes, finding a partner named Watson, and opening a private inquiry agency that specialized in solving the unsolved and insoluble.

Parrotry.

He thought about doing other things legal and illegal, clever and foolish, dangerous and harmless.

Unoriginal. Unoriginal. Unoriginal.

That day passed and several more just like it. Hackman became obsessed with originality—so much so that he found himself unable to write, the first serious block he had had as a professional. It was maddening, but every time he thought of a sentence and started to type it out, something would click in his mind and make him analyze it as original or banal. The verdict was always banal.

He thought about buying a small printing press, manufacturing bogus German Deutsche marks in his basement, and then flying to Munich and passing them at the Oktoberfest.

Counterfeit.

Hackman took to drinking a good deal more than his usual allotment of alcohol in the evenings. His consumption of cigarettes rose to four packs a day and climbing. His originality quotient remained at zero.

He thought about having a treasure map tattooed on his chest, claiming to be the sole survivor of a gang of armored car thieves, and conning all sorts of greedy people out of their life savings.

Trite.

The passing days turned into passing weeks. Hackman still wasn't able to write; he wasn't able to do much of anything except vainly overwork his brain cells. He knew he couldn't function again as a writer or a human being until he did something, *anything* original.

He thought about building a distillery in his garage and becoming Long Island's largest manufacturer and distributor of bootleg whiskey.

Hackneyed.

Grace had begun a daily and voluble series of complaints. Why was he moping around, drinking and smoking so much? Why didn't he go into his office and write his latest piece of trash? What were they going to do for money if he didn't fulfill his contracts? How would they pay the mortgage and the rest of their bills? What was the *matter* with him, anyway? Was he going through some kind of midlife crisis or what?

Hackman thought about strangling her, burying her body under the acacia tree in the back yard—committing the perfect crime.

Stale. Bewhiskered.

Another week disappeared. Hackman was six weeks overdue now on an occult pirate novel and two weeks overdue on a male-action novel; his publishers were upset, his agent was upset; where the hell were the manuscripts? Hackman said he was just polishing up the first one. "Sure you are," the agent said over the phone. "Well, you'd better have it with you when you come in on Friday. I mean that, Charlie. You'd better deliver."

Hackman thought about kidnapping the star of Broadway's top musical extravaganza and holding her for a ransom of $1,000,000 plus a role in her next production.

Old stuff.

He decided that things couldn't go on this way. Unless he came up with an original idea pretty soon, he might just as well shuffle off this mortal coil.

He thought about buying some rat poison and mixing himself an arsenic cocktail.

More old stuff.

Or climbing a utility pole and grabbing hold of a high-tension wire.

Prosaic. Corny.

Or hiring a private plane to fly him over the New Jersey swamps and then jumping out at two thousand feet.

Ho-hum.

Damn! He couldn't seem to go on, he couldn't seem *not* to go on. So what was he going to do?

He thought about driving over to Pennsylvania, planting certain carefully faked documents inside Grace's mother's house, and turning the old bat in to the F.B.I. as a foreign spy.

Commonplace.

On Friday morning he took his cigarettes (the second of the five packs a day he was now consuming) and his latest hangover down to the train station. There he boarded the express for Manhattan and took a seat in the club car.

He thought about hijacking the train and extorting $20,000,000 from the state of New York.

Imitative.

When the train arrived in Manhattan he trudged the six blocks to his agent's office. In the elevator on the way up an attractive young blonde gave him a friendly smile and said it was a nice day, wasn't it?

Hackman thought about making her his mistress, having a torrid affair, and then running off to Acapulco with her and living in sin in a villa high above the harbor and weaving Mexican *serapes* by day and drinking tequila by night.

Hackneyed.

The first thing his agent said to him was, "Where's the manuscript, Charlie?" Hackman said it wasn't ready yet, he was having a few personal problems. The agent said, "You think you got problems? What about *my* problems? You think I can afford to have hack writers missing deadlines and making editors unhappy? That kind of stuff reflects back on me, ruins my reputation. I'm not in this business for my health, so maybe you'd better just find yourself another agent."

Hackman thought about bashing him over the head with a paperweight, disposing of the body, and assuming his identity after first gaining sixty pounds and going through extensive plastic surgery.

Moth-eaten. Threadbare.

Out on the street again, he decided he needed a drink and turned into the first bar he came to. He ordered a triple vodka and sat brooding over it. I've come to the end of my rope, he thought. If there's one original idea in this world, I can't even imagine what it is. For that matter, I can't even imagine a partly original idea, which I'd settle for right now because maybe there *isn't* anything completely original any more.

"What am I going to do?" he asked the bartender.

"Who cares?" the bartender said. "Stay, go, drink, don't drink— it's all the same to me."

Hackman sighed and got off his stool and swayed out onto East 52nd Street. He turned west and began to walk back toward Grand Central, jostling his way through the mid-afternoon crowds. Overhead, the sun glared down at him between the buildings like a malevolent eye.

He was nearing Madison Avenue, muttering clichés to himself, when the idea struck him.

It came out of nowhere, full-born in an instant, the way most great ideas (or so he had heard) always do. He came to an abrupt standstill. Then he began to smile. Then he began to laugh. Passersby gave him odd looks and detoured around him, but Hackman didn't care. The idea was all that mattered.

It was inspired.

It was imaginative.

It was meaningful.

It was original.

Oh, not one-hundred-percent original—but that was all right. He had already decided that finding total originality was an impossi-

ble goal. This idea was close, though. It was close and it was won-
derful and he was going to do it. Of course he was going to do it;
after all these weeks of search and frustration, how could he *not* do
it?

Hackman set out walking again. His stride was almost jaunty and
he was whistling to himself. Two blocks south he entered a sporting
goods store and found what he wanted. The salesman who waited
on him asked if he was going camping. "Nope," Hackman said, and
winked. "Something *much* more original than that."

He left the store and hurried down to Madison to a bookshop
that specialized in mass-market paperbacks. Inside were several long
rows of shelving, each shelf containing different categories of fiction
and nonfiction, alphabetically arranged. Hackman stepped into the
fiction section, stopped in front of the shelf marked "Historical Romances," and squinted at the titles until he located one of his own
pseudonymous works. Then he unwrapped his parcel.

And took out the woodsman's hatchet.

And got a comfortable grip on its handle.

And raised it high over his head.

And—

Whack! Eleven copies of *Love's Tender Fury* by Allison St. Cyr were
drawn and quartered.

A male customer yelped; a female customer shrieked. Hackman
took no notice. He moved on to the shelf marked "Occult Pirate
Adventure," raised the hatchet again, and—

Whack! Nine copies of *The Devil Daughter of Jean Lafitte* by Adam
Caine were exorcised and scuttled.

On to "Adult Westerns." And—

Whack! Four copies of *Lust Rides the Outlaw Trail* by Galen McGee
bit the dust.

Behind the front counter a chubby little man was jumping up and
down, waving his arms. "What are you doing?" he kept shouting at
Hackman. "What are you doing?"

"Hackwork!" Hackman shouted back. "I'm a hack writer doing hackwork!"

He stepped smartly to "Gothic Suspense." And—

Whack! Five copies of *Mansion of Dread* by Melissa Ann Farnsworth were reduced to rubble.

On to "Male Action Series," and—

Whack! Ten copies of Max Ruffe's *The Grenade Launcher/23: Blowup at City Hall* exploded into fragments.

Hackman paused to survey the carnage. Then he nodded in satisfaction and turned toward the front door. The bookshop was empty now, but the chubby little man was visible on the sidewalk outside, jumping up and down and semaphoring his arms amid a gathering crowd. Hackman crossed to the door in purposeful strides and threw it open.

People scattered every which way when they saw him come out with the hatchet aloft. But they needn't have feared; he had no interest in people, except as bit players in this little drama. After all, what hack worth the name ever cared a hoot about his audience?

He began to run up 48th Street toward Fifth Avenue, brandishing the hatchet. Nobody tried to stop him, not even when he lopped off the umbrella shading a frankfurter vendor's cart.

"I'm a hack!" he shouted.

And shattered the display window of an exclusive boutique.

"I'm Hackman the hack!" he yelled.

And halved the product and profits of a pretzel vendor.

"I'm Hackman the hack and I'm hacking my way to glory!" he bellowed.

And sliced the antenna off an illegally parked Cadillac limousine.

He was almost to Fifth Avenue by this time. Ahead of him he could see a red signal light holding up crosstown traffic; this block of 48th Street was momentarily empty. Behind him he could hear angry shouts and what sounded like a police whistle. He looked back over his shoulder. Several people were giving pursuit, including the chubby little man from the bookshop; the leader of the pack, a blue uniform with a red face atop it, was less than fifty yards distant.

But the game was not up yet, Hackman thought. There were more bookstores along Fifth; with any luck he could hack his way through two or three before they got him. He decided south was the direction he wanted to go, pulled his head around, and started to sprint across the empty expanse of 48th.

Only the street wasn't empty any longer; the signal on Fifth had changed to green for the eastbound traffic.

He ran right out in front of an oncoming car.

He saw it too late to jump clear, and the driver saw him too late to brake or swerve. But before he and the machine joined forces, Hackman had just enough time to realize the full scope of what was happening—and to feel a sudden elation. In fact, he wished with his last wish that he'd thought of this himself. It was the crowning touch, the final fillip, the *coup de grâce*; it lent the death of Hackman, unlike the life of Hackman, a genuine originality.

Because the car that did him in was not just a car; it was a New York City taxi cab.

Otherwise known as a hack.

PEEKABOO

Roper came awake with the feeling that he wasn't alone in the house.

He sat up in bed, tense and wary, a crawling sensation on the back of his scalp. The night was dark, moonless; warm clotted black surrounded him. He rubbed sleep-mucus from his eyes, blinking, until he could make out the vague grayish outlines of the open window in one wall, the curtains fluttering in the hot summer breeze.

Ears straining, he listened. But there wasn't anything to hear. The house seemed almost graveyard still, void of even the faintest of night sounds.

What was it that had waked him up? A noise of some kind? An intuition of danger? It might only have been a bad dream, except that he couldn't remember dreaming. And it might only have been imagination, except that the feeling of not being alone was strong, urgent.

There's somebody in the house, he thought.

Or some *thing* in the house?

In spite of himself Roper remembered the story the nervous real estate agent in Whitehall had told him about this place. It had been built in the early 1900s by a local family, and when the last of them died off a generation later it was sold to a man named Lavolle who had lived in it for forty years. Lavolle had been a recluse whom the locals considered strange and probably evil; they hadn't had anything to do with him. But then he'd died five years ago, of natural causes, and evidence had been found by county officials that he'd been "some kind of devil worshiper" who had "practiced all sorts of dark rites." That was all the real estate agent would say about it.

Word had gotten out about that and a lot of people seemed to believe the house was haunted or cursed or something. For that reason, and because it was isolated and in ramshackle condition, it had stayed empty until a couple of years ago. Then a man called Garber, who was an amateur parapsychologist, leased the place and lived here for ten days. At the end of that time somebody came out from Whitehall to deliver groceries and found Garber dead. Murdered. The real estate agent wouldn't talk about how he'd been killed; nobody else would talk about it either.

Some people thought it was ghosts or demons that had murdered Garber. Others figured it was a lunatic—maybe the same one who'd killed half a dozen people in this part of New England over the past couple of years. Roper didn't believe in ghosts or demons or things that went bump in the night; that kind of supernatural stuff was for rural types like the ones in Whitehall. He believed in psychotic killers, all right, but he wasn't afraid of them; he wasn't afraid of anybody or anything. He'd made his living with a gun too long for that. And the way things were for him now, since the bank job in Boston had gone sour two weeks ago, an isolated back-country place like this was just what he needed for a few months.

So he'd leased the house under a fake name, claiming to be a writer, and he'd been here for eight days. Nothing had happened in that time: no ghosts, no demons, no strange lights or wailings or rattling chains—and no lunatics or burglars or visitors of any kind. Nothing at all.

Until now.

Well, if he *wasn't* alone in the house, it was because somebody human had come in. And he sure as hell knew how to deal with a human intruder. He pushed the blankets aside, swung his feet out of bed, and eased open the nightstand drawer. His fingers groped inside, found his .38 revolver and the flashlight he kept in there with it; he took them out. Then he stood, made his way carefully across to the bedroom door, opened it a crack, and listened again.

The same heavy silence.

Roper pulled the door wide, switched on the flash, and probed the hallway with its beam. No one there. He stepped out, moving on the balls of his bare feet. There were four other doors along the hallway: two more bedrooms, a bathroom, and an upstairs sitting room. He opened each of the doors in turn, swept the rooms with the flash, then put on the overhead lights.

Empty, all of them.

He came back to the stairs. Shadows clung to them, filled the wide foyer below. He threw the light down there from the landing. Bare mahogany walls, the lumpish shapes of furniture, more shadows crouching inside the arched entrances to the parlor and the library. But that was all: no sign of anybody, still no sounds anywhere in the warm dark.

He went down the stairs, swinging the light from side to side. At the bottom he stopped next to the newel post and used the beam to slice into the blackness in the center hall. Deserted. He arced it around into the parlor, followed it with his body turned sideways to within a pace of the archway. More furniture, the big fieldstone fireplace at the far wall, the parlor windows reflecting glints of light from the flash. He glanced back at the heavy darkness inside the library, didn't see or hear any movement over that way, and reached out with his gun hand to flick the switch on the wall inside the parlor.

Nothing happened when the electric bulbs in the old-fashioned chandelier came on; there wasn't anybody lurking in there.

Roper turned and crossed to the library arch and scanned the interior with the flash. Empty bookshelves, empty furniture. He put on the chandelier. Empty room.

He swung the cone of light past the staircase, into the center hall—and then brought it back to the stairs and held it there. The

area beneath them had been walled on both sides, as it was in a lot
of these old houses, to form a coat or storage closet; he'd found that
out when he first moved in and opened the small door that was set
into the staircase on this side. But it was just an empty space now,
full of dust . . .

The back of his scalp tingled again. And a phrase from when he
was a kid playing hide-and-seek games popped into his mind.

Peekaboo, I see you. Hiding under the stair.

His finger tightened around the butt of the .38. He padded forward cautiously, stopped in front of the door. And reached out with
the hand holding the flash, turned the knob, jerked the door open,
and aimed the light and the gun inside.

Nothing.

Roper let out a breath, backed away to where he could look
down the hall again. The house was still graveyard quiet; he couldn't
even hear the faint grumblings its old wooden joints usually made in
the night. It was as if the whole place was wrapped in a breathless
waiting hush. As if there was some kind of unnatural presence at
work here. . . .

Screw that, he told himself angrily. No such things as ghosts and
demons. There seemed to be presence here, all right—he could feel
it just as strongly as before—but it was a human presence. Maybe a
burglar, maybe a tramp, maybe even a goddamn lunatic. But *human.*

He snapped on the hall lights and went along there to the archway that led into the downstairs sitting room. First the flash and
then the electric wall lamps told him it was deserted. The dining
room off the parlor next. And the kitchen. And the rear porch.

Still nothing.

Where was he, damn it? Where was he hiding?

The cellar? Roper thought.

It didn't make sense that whoever it was would have gone down
there. The cellar was a huge room, walled and floored in stone, that
ran under most of the house; there wasn't anything in it except
spiderwebs and stains on the floor that he didn't like to think about,

not after the real estate agent's story about Lavolle and his dark rites. But it was the only place left that he hadn't searched.

In the kitchen again, Roper crossed to the cellar door. The knob turned soundlessly under his hand. With the door open a crack, he peered into the thick darkness below and listened. Still the same heavy silence.

He started to reach inside for the light switch. But then he remembered that there wasn't any bulb in the socket above the stairs; he'd explored the cellar by flashlight before, and he hadn't bothered to buy a bulb. He widened the opening and aimed the flash downward, fanning it slowly from left to right and up and down over the stone walls and floor. Shadowy shapes appeared and disappeared in the bobbing light: furnace, storage shelves, a wooden wine rack, the blackish gleaming stains at the far end, spiderwebs like tattered curtains hanging from the ceiling beams.

Roper hesitated. Nobody down there either, he thought. Nobody in the house after all? The feeling that he wasn't alone kept nagging at him—but it *could* be nothing more than imagination. All that business about devil worshiping and ghosts and demons and Garber being murdered and psychotic killers on the loose might have affected him more than he'd figured. Might have jumbled together in his subconscious all week and finally come out tonight, making him imagine menace where there wasn't any. Sure, maybe that was it.

But he had to make certain. He couldn't see all of the cellar from up here; he had to go down and give it a full search before he'd be satisfied that he really was alone. Otherwise he'd never be able to get back to sleep tonight.

Playing the light again, he descended the stairs in the same wary movements as before. The beam showed him nothing. Except for the faint whisper of his breathing, the creak of the risers when he put his weight on them, the stillness remained unbroken. The odors of dust and decaying wood and subterranean dampness dilated his nostrils; he began to breathe through his mouth.

When he came off the last of the steps he took a half-dozen

strides into the middle of the cellar. The stones were cold and clammy against the soles of his bare feet. He turned to his right, then let the beam and his body transcribe a slow circle until he was facing the stairs.

Nothing to see, nothing to hear.

But with the light on the staircase, he realized that part of the wide, dusty area beneath them was invisible from where he stood— a mass of clotted shadow. The vertical boards between the risers kept the beam from reaching all the way under there.

The phrase from when he was a kid repeated itself in his mind: *Peekaboo, I see you. Hiding under the stair.*

With the gun and the flash extended at arm's length, he went diagonally to his right. The light cut away some of the thick gloom under the staircase, letting him see naked stone draped with more gray webs. He moved closer to the stairs, ducked under them, and put the beam full on the far joining of the walls.

Empty.

For the first time Roper began to relax. Imagination, no doubt about it now. No ghosts or demons, no burglars or lunatics hiding under the stair. A thin smile curved the corners of his mouth. Hell, the only one hiding under the stair was himself—

"Peekaboo," a voice behind him said.

TWO WEEKS EVERY SUMMER

We found out how Webb Patterson spends his summer vacations when five of us regulars were jawing around the card table in the Cedarville firehouse one Saturday afternoon in early June.

We weren't firemen, at least not in the sense that we were on the town payroll. Cedarville was still too small to need or afford full-time civil employees, so resident volunteers had to supplement the services provided by the county. There were ten volunteer firemen and some of us always got together on Saturdays, mostly to play pinochle or just exercise our jaw muscles; there isn't much else to do in a small town on the weekends. Unless you've got a family, of course, but except for Ernie Boone, whose wife had a voice like a train whistle and a nosy-Parker for a mother, all of us regulars were either bachelors or widowers with grown kids.

This particular Saturday was a fine late-spring day, not too hot, not too breezy, with the scent of wildflowers and the first dusty hint of summer in the air. We had the main double doors open wide, and all the windows raised, so we could breathe that air and watch the townspeople passing by in the sunshine outside. We weren't doing much except talking; it was too nice a day to concentrate on card-playing.

The conversation got around to vacations when Aaron Cubbage, who owns the drugstore, said something about weather like this making him itch for a fishing pole and a spot under one of the oaks at Lake Keystone. He went up to the lake for a couple of weeks every summer with a crony of his from the county seat and spent the whole time fishing for blue gills and drinking wine coolers; he'd been doing that for thirty years and he'd keep on doing it until he died.

The rest of us varied our vacations, though. Ernie Boone said he and the missus planned to close up their hardware store on the Fourth of July and take a trip through the Ozark Mountains. If his mother-in-law insisted on going along, he said, he'd keep driving until he found somebody to trade her to for a jug of mountain dew—which got a pretty good laugh. Doc Pollard, Cedarville's only dentist, said he was thinking about taking one of those nostalgic paddlewheel steamboat trips down the Mississippi River to New Orleans. I said that if the town could get along without the Holloway Floral and Gardening Service for three weeks, I was going to pack up my camper and drive over and up into Colorado. I'd never seen the Sangre de Cristo range, or any other part of that state, and I like to visit new places every year.

Webb Patterson, who doubled as Cedarville's lawyer and notary public, was the only one who didn't volunteer any information about his vacation plans. Not that his reticence was surprising; Webb had been a quiet and sort of private fellow for as long as I'd known him, which was since he'd moved to Cedarville from downstate four years ago. Not secretive, just private. Like the rest of us, he seemed pretty much content with the kind of quiet small-town life he led; but unlike the rest of us, he never talked about getting away for a while in the summer, seeing other parts of the state or country. Yet he always left town for two weeks in July or August, and he'd admitted to a visit to Mexico last year.

It was Doc Pollard who asked him straight out what he was planning to do this summer. At first Webb didn't answer. But the rest of us were looking at him, waiting, and finally he said in a reluctant voice, "I'm going to New York."

"New York City, you mean?" Doc asked.

"Yes."

"Never had any urge to go to New York myself," Aaron said. "I don't like big cities—too much noise and hubbub. And too much crime. Why, I heard they mug you right on the downtown streets in Manhattan."

Webb smiled at that, a funny sort of smile. "I'm sure that's an exaggeration."

"Maybe so, but I'll take my vacation at Lake Keystone, thank you."

I said, "You going to stay in New York the whole two weeks, Webb?"

"Yes, probably."

"What's there to do all that time? I mean, you can visit the Empire State Building and the United Nations and take in all the other sights in three or four days—a week at the most."

"There are other things I plan to do."

"Mind saying what they are?"

He hesitated. "Well . . . walking in Central Park, for one."

"That doesn't sound like much of an interesting vacation," Ernie said, "walking around Central Park all day."

Webb hesitated again, longer this time. Then in an impulsive way, as if he had something inside him that needed to come out, he said, "Not all day, Ernie."

"Well, part of it, then."

"Not during the day at all. At night."

Ernie looked startled. "At night? Hey, you're not serious, are you? Central Park's supposed to be full of muggers at night."

"I'm sure it is," Webb said. "That's the idea."

"What idea?"

"The danger. Danger's the whole purpose of my vacation."

We were all staring at him—and in a different way now, like maybe we didn't know him as well as we thought we did. He was dead-serious, you could see that; he wasn't trying to pull our legs.

"Now wait a minute," I said. "You mean you're fixing to walk around Central Park at night *hoping* you'll meet up with a mugger?"

"No. Hoping I won't meet one."

Aaron said, "That doesn't make any sense."

"It does if you look at it a certain way," Webb said. "It's like a game, a dangerous game where you stack the odds against yourself and then try to beat them."

"Why in hell would you want to play such a game?"

"For the danger, the excitement."

"But you could get yourself *killed!*"

"I know. Personal risk is what the game is all about."

"This is crazy," Ernie said. He scooted his chair back a little way, as if he were afraid Webb might start foaming at the mouth and try to attack him; Ernie always did have a tendency to overreact. "This is the craziest damn thing I ever heard."

Webb sighed and seemed to stare for a time at the movement of dust motes in a shaft of sunlight. "I shouldn't have told you," he said finally. "I should have known better than to tell anyone."

"It doesn't change anything," I said. "Why should it? We're still your friends."

"But you don't understand or approve, I can see that."

"Give us a little time for it to sink in."

"And some more explanation," Doc said. "What made you all of a sudden decide on this game of yours?"

"I didn't decide all of a sudden. I decided it was how I would spend my vacations nine years ago, after my wife passed away."

"Nine years ago?" Aaron said. "My God, you mean you been going to places like New York, challenging muggers, every summer for *nine years?*"

"No, of course not. I choose a different kind of danger each year. Last summer I went backpacking alone in northern Mexico, in rugged country where there are supposed to be bandits. Two years ago I hunted wild boar with a bow and arrow up in Canada. Three years ago I rode a kayak down the Colorado River. Before it was shark-hunting in the Atlantic and some tamer things such as mountain climbing and motorcycle racing."

I said, "Each year, you do something a little more dangerous than the past year, is that it?"

"Yes."

Doc was incredulous. "And you survived all those things without getting hurt?"

"I survived them, yes," Webb said, "but I've been hurt a few times. A rattlesnake bit me on the leg in Mexico last summer; I almost drowned twice in the Colorado River; I broke an arm and fractured my pelvis mountain climbing in Arizona the year before I moved here."

"Crazy," Ernie muttered again. "Just plain crazy."

Webb gave him a tolerant glance. "Not from where I sit," he said. "Risking my life for two weeks every summer is what makes living worthwhile."

"I don't follow that," Aaron said.

"It's simple, really. I was born and raised in a town not much larger than Cedarville and I've never lived anywhere other than a small town; I like the quiet, slow-paced existence. But after my wife died, life didn't seem to mean much to me any more; for the first time I was *aware* of how dull and unexciting it was. And that feeling got even worse when the time came for me to plan my first vacation alone in twenty years. Where was I going to go? What was I going to do?

"Well, that started me thinking about the whole idea of a vacation. Most people, particularly in the big cities, lead hectic lives— exciting lives in the sense that they're always doing rush-about things, facing little dangers and crises every day that build up a considerable pressure after a while. A vacation for them is two or three quiet and unexciting weeks, a time to relax and unwind so they can go back to their normal lifestyle with recharged batteries. But for me, I realized, it was just the opposite. I lived fifty quiet and unexciting weeks and what I needed to recharge *my* batteries was two weeks of excitement and physical danger."

"So that's how it is," I said. "And it works for you, this kind of vacation?"

"Oh, yes. I've never felt more alive than I have these past nine years."

"But you keep doing more and more dangerous things every year," Aaron said. "Hell, man, the odds are bound to catch up with you sooner or later. And when they do you might not come home from one of your vacations."

Webb said quietly, "Don't you think I know that? But it doesn't matter. This is the only way I can live my life now and be happy and fulfilled. When my luck runs out and my time comes, I won't have any regrets."

None of us seemed to have anything more to say after that and there was one of those long uneasy silences where everybody is wrapped up in his own thoughts. Outside there were traffic sounds and the whoop of kids playing baseball in the park behind the firehouse; but inside the hush was so heavy the air might have been muffled in wool. You could almost hear the flies walking across the sun-streaked card table.

It was Webb who broke the silence. He scraped back his chair and stood up with a kind of rueful smile lifting the corners of his mouth. "I guess I'd best be going," he said. "I've got some law work to catch up on at home."

He didn't have any work to catch up on; he never worked on weekends, or brought business home from the office. I said, "Can't it wait, Webb? I'll walk over to Beebe's Store and buy us a six-pack—a cold beer'd go good in this weather."

"No, Roy, thanks. I'd better go."

He nodded to us, turned past old Number 4, Cedarville's lone fire engine, and went out into the sunshine. We all watched him until he was out of sight, not saying anything. But it was a different kind of silence now, no longer heavy, as if a kind of tension had been broken. At length Ernie said, "Well, what in hell do you think of that? What in *hell* do you think of that?"

"Not much," I said. "A man's entitled to do what he pleases on his vacation, isn't he?"

"But challenging muggers," Aaron said, "risking his life for kicks—"

"He doesn't do it for kicks, Ernie."

"Well, that's what I call it."

Doc said, "Maybe he doesn't do it for kicks and maybe he's got every right to do it no matter what. But I'll tell you this: I wish he hadn't told us about it."

"Why not?"

"Because I can't help but feel different towards him now. He's still my friend, I don't mean that; but I just don't feel the same, knowing about these vacations of his." Doc shook his head and smacked the card table with his palm. "Damn, it would have been better for all of us if he'd kept his mouth shut."

"You're right about that, Doc," I said with some tartness. "A man's always better off to keep his private business to himself, if he doesn't want to be misunderstood or poorly thought of."

Later that day, after I got home from the firehouse, I laid out my road maps of Kansas and Colorado and studied the route I had traced out for my own vacation next month. I still wasn't sure of where I would stop in Colorado, but I'd circled four towns near the southern section of the Sangre de Cristo range that looked to have good state and county road connections. At least one of them, I thought, would be large enough to support a bank.

That was what I'd definitely decided on for this year: a bank in Colorado.

It was a matter of progression, just as it was with Webb. I'd started with a gas station in Minnesota five years ago and worked my way up through a liquor store in Iowa, a mercantile establishment in South Dakota, a supermarket in Nebraska, and a finance company in Kansas. So this year it just *had* to be a bank in Colorado.

Of course, that made next year's vacation problematical; a bank is just about the limit one man alone can handle. But then, there was no use worrying about next summer until after this one was history. Besides which, I had a notion it was about time to shift gears anyway, to try something new. I'd been doing some reading on Yellow Kid Weil, the Sanctimonious Kid, and other legendary confidence men; maybe I'd try something in their line. Not over in Europe or any place like that, though. There were still plenty of places I'd never visited in this country, still plenty of things to do right here.

Like they say, "See America First."

I thought again about Webb—what a coincidence it was, considering the size of Cedarville, for one of my friends and neighbors to have developed a philosophy so similar to my own. Or was it really such a coincidence at that? After all, there had to be thousands of fellows living quiet, unexciting lives in hundreds of other small towns from coast to coast. Could be, couldn't it, that there were quite a few of us who spent our summer vacations doing all sorts of unconventional and dangerous things?

It was sure something to wonder about . . .

THE HANGING MAN

It was Sam McCullough who found the hanging man, down on the river bank behind his livery stable.

Straightaway he went looking for Ed Bozeman and me, being as we were the local sheriff's deputies. Tule River didn't have any full-time law officers back then, in the late 1890s; just volunteers like Boze and me to keep the peace, and a fat-bottomed sheriff who came through from the county seat two or three days a month to look things over and to stuff himself on pig's knuckles at the Germany Café.

Time was just past sunup, on one of those frosty mornings Northern California gets in late November, and Sam found Boze already to work inside his mercantile. But they had to come fetch me out of my house, where I was just sitting down to breakfast. I never did open up my place of business—Miller's Feed and Grain—until 8:30 of a weekday morning.

I had some trouble believing it when Sam first told about the hanging man. He said, "Well, how in hell do you think *I* felt." He always has been an excitable sort and he was frothed up for fair just then. "I like to had a hemorrhage when I saw him hanging there on that black oak. Damnedest sight a man ever stumbled on."

"You say he's a stranger?"

"Stranger to me. Never seen him before."

"You make sure he's dead?"

Sam made a snorting noise. "I ain't even going to answer that. You just come along and see for yourself."

I got my coat, told my wife Ginny to ring up Doc Petersen on Mr. Bell's invention, and then hustled out with Sam and Boze. It was mighty cold that morning; the sky was clear and brittle-looking, like blue-painted glass, and the sun had the look of a two-day-old egg yolk above the tule marshes east of the river. When we came in alongside the stable I saw that there was silvery frost all over the grass on the river bank. You could hear it crunch when you walked on it.

The hanging man had frost on him, too. He was strung up on a fat old oak between the stable and the river, opposite a high board fence that separated Sam's property from Joel Pennywell's fixit shop next door. Dressed mostly in black, he was—black denims, black boots, a black cutaway coat that had seen better days. He had black hair, too, long and kind of matted. And a black tongue pushed out at one corner of a black-mottled face. All that black was streaked in silver, and there was silver on the rope that stretched between his neck and the thick limb above. He was the damnedest sight a man ever stumbled on, all right. Frozen up there, silver and black, glistening in the cold sunlight, like something cast up from the Pit.

We stood looking at him for a time, not saying anything. There was a thin wind off the river and I could feel it prickling up the hair on my neck. But it didn't stir that hanging man, nor any part of him or his clothing.

Boze cleared his throat, and he did it loud enough to make me jump. He asked me, "You know him, Carl?"

"No," I said. "You?"

"No. Drifter, you think?"

"Got the look of one."

Which he did. He'd been in his thirties, smallish, with a clean-shaven fox face and pointy ears. His clothes were shabby, shirt cuffs frayed, button missing off his cutaway coat. We got us a fair number of drifters in Tule River, up from San Francisco or over from the mining country after their luck and their money ran out—men looking for farm work or such other jobs as they could find. Or sometimes looking for trouble. Boze and I had caught one just two weeks before and locked him up for chicken stealing.

"What I want to know," Sam said, "is what in the name of hell he's doing *here?*"

Boze shrugged and rubbed at his bald spot, like he always does when he's fuddled. He was the same age as me, thirty-four, but he'd been losing his hair for the past ten years. He said, "Appears he's been hanging a while. When'd you close up last evening, Sam?"

"Six, like always."

"Anybody come around afterwards?"

"No."

"Could've happened any time after six, then. It's kind of a lonely spot back here after dark. I reckon there's not much chance anybody saw what happened."

"Joel Pennywell, maybe," I said. "He stays open late some nights."

"We can ask him."

Sam said, "But why'd anybody string him up like that?"

"Maybe he wasn't strung up. Maybe he hung himself."

"Suicide?"

"It's been known to happen," Boze said.

Doc Petersen showed up just then, and a couple of other towns-folk with him; word was starting to get around. Doc, who was sixty and dyspeptic, squinted up at the hanging man, grunted, and said, "Strangulation."

"Doc?"

"Strangulation. Man strangled to death. You can see that from the way his tongue's out. Neck's not broken; you can see that too."

"Does that mean he could've killed himself?"

"All it means," Doc said, "is that he didn't jump off a high branch or get jerked hard enough off a horse to break his neck."

"Wasn't a horse involved anyway," I said. "There'd be shoe

marks in the area; ground was soft enough last night, before the freeze. Boot marks here and there, but that's all."

"I don't know anything about that," Doc said. "All I know is, that gent up there died of strangulation. You want me to tell you anything else, you'll have to cut him down first."

Sam and Boze went to the stable to fetch a ladder. While they were gone I paced around some, to see if there was anything to find in the vicinity. And I did find something, about a dozen feet from the oak where the boot tracks were heaviest in the grass. It was a circlet of bronze, about three inches in diameter, and when I picked it up, I saw that it was one of those Presidential Medals the government used to issue at the Philadelphia Mint. On one side it had a likeness of Benjamin Harrison, along with his name and the date of his inauguration, 1889, and on the other were a tomahawk, a peace pipe, and a pair of clasped hands.

There weren't many such medals in California; mostly they'd been supplied to Army officers in other parts of the West, who handed them out to Indians after peace treaties were signed. But this one struck a chord in my memory: I recollected having seen it or one like it some months back. The only thing was, I couldn't quite remember where.

Before I could think any more on it, Boze and Sam came back with the ladder, a plank board, and a horse blanket. Neither of them seemed inclined to do the job at hand, so I climbed up myself and sawed through that half-frozen rope with my pocket knife. It wasn't good work; my mouth was dry when it was done. When we had him down we covered him up and laid him on the plank. Then we carried him out to Doc's wagon and took him to the Spencer Funeral Home.

After Doc and Obe Spencer stripped the body, Boze and I went through the dead man's clothing. There was no identification of any kind; if he'd been carrying any before he died, somebody had filched it. No wallet or purse, either. All he had in his pockets was the stub of a lead pencil, a half-used book of matches, a short-six seegar, a nearly empty Bull Durham sack, three wheatstraw papers, a two-bit piece, an old Spanish *real* coin, and a dog-eared and stained copy of a Beadle dime novel called *Captain Dick Talbot, King of the Road; Or, The Black-Hoods of Shasta.*

"Drifter, all right," Boze said when we were done. "Wouldn't you say, Carl?"

"Sure seems that way."

"But even drifters have more belongings than this. Shaving gear, extra clothes—at least that much."

"You'd think so," I said. "Might be he had a carpetbag or the like and it's hidden somewhere along the river bank."

"Either that or it was stolen. But we can go take a look when Doc gets through studying on the body."

I fished out the bronze medal I'd found in the grass earlier and showed it to him. "Picked this up while you and Sam were getting the ladder," I said.

"Belonged to the hanging man, maybe."

"Maybe. But it seems familiar, somehow. I can't quite place where I've seen one like it."

Boze turned the medal over in his hand. "Doesn't ring any bells for me," he said.

"Well, you don't see many around here, and the one I recollect was also a Benjamin Harrison. Could be coincidence, I suppose. Must be if that fella died by his own hand."

"If he did."

"Boze, you think it *was* suicide?"

"I'm hoping it was," he said, but he didn't sound any more convinced than I was. "I don't like the thought of a murderer running around loose in Tule River."

"That makes two of us," I said.

Doc didn't have much to tell us when he came out. The hanging man had been shot once a long time ago—he had bullet scars on his right shoulder and back—and one foot was missing a pair of toes.

There was also a fresh bruise on the left side of his head, above the ear.

Boze asked, "Is it a big bruise, Doc?"

"Big enough."

"Could somebody have hit him hard enough to knock him out?"

"And then hung him afterward? Well, it could've happened that way. His neck's full of rope burns and lacerations, the way it would be if somebody hauled him up over that tree limb."

"Can you reckon how long he's been dead?"

"Last night some time. Best I can do."

Boze and I headed back to the livery stable. The town had come awake by this time. There were plenty of people on the boardwalks and Main Street was crowded with horses and farm wagons; any day now I expected to see somebody with one of those newfangled motor cars. The hanging man was getting plenty of lip service, on Main Street and among the crowd that had gathered back of the stable to gawk at the black oak and trample the grass.

Nothing much goes on in a small town like Tule River, and such as a hanging was bound to stir up folks' imaginations. There hadn't been a killing in the area in four or five years. And damned little mystery since the town was founded back in the days when General Vallejo owned most of the land hereabouts and it was the Mexican flag, not the Stars and Stripes, that flew over California.

None of the crowd had found anything in the way of evidence on the river bank; they would have told us if they had. None of them knew anything about the hanging man, either. That included Joel Pennywell, who had come over from his fixit shop next door. He'd closed up around 6:30 last night, he said, and gone straight on home.

After a time Boze and I moved down to the river's edge and commenced a search among the tule grass and trees that grew along there. The day had warmed some; the wind was down and the sun had melted off the last of the frost. A few of the others joined in with us, eager and boisterous, like it was an Easter egg hunt. It was too soon for the full impact of what had happened to settle in on most folks; it hadn't occurred to them yet that maybe they ought to be concerned.

A few minutes before ten o'clock, while we were combing the west-side bank up near the Main Street Basin, and still not finding anything, the Whipple youngster came running to tell us that Roberto Ortega and Sam McCullough wanted to see us at the livery stable. Roberto owned a dairy ranch just south of town and claimed to be a descendant of a Spanish conquistador. He was also an honest man, which was why he was in town that morning. He'd found a saddled horse grazing on his pastureland and figured it for a runaway from Sam's livery, so he'd brought it in. But Sam had never seen the animal, an old swaybacked roan, until Roberto showed up with it. Nor had he ever seen the battered carpetbag that was tied behind the cantle of the cheap Mexican saddle.

It figured to be the drifter's horse and carpetbag, sure enough. But whether the drifter had turned the animal loose himself, or somebody else had, we had no way of knowing. As for the carpetbag, it didn't tell us any more about the hanging man than the contents of his pockets. Inside it were some extra clothes, an old Colt Dragoon revolver, shaving tackle, a woman's garter, and nothing at all that might identify the owner.

Sam took the horse, and Boze and I took the carpetbag over to Obe Spencer's to put with the rest of the hanging man's belongings. On the way we held a conference. Fact was, a pair of grain barges were due upriver from San Francisco at eleven, for loading and return. I had three men working for me, but none of them handled the paperwork; I was going to have to spend some time at the feed mill that day, whether I wanted to or not. Which is how it is when you have part-time deputies who are also full-time businessmen. It was a fact of small-town life we'd had to learn to live with.

We worked it out so that Boze would continue making inquiries while I went to work at the mill. Then we'd switch off at one o'clock so he could give his wife Ellie, who was minding the mercantile, some help with customers and with the drummers who always flocked around with Christmas wares right after Thanksgiving.

We also decided that if neither of us turned up any new information by five o'clock—or even if we did—we would ring up the country seat and make a full report to the sheriff. Not that Joe Perkins would be able to find out anything we couldn't. He was a fat-cat political appointee, and about all he knew how to find was pig's knuckles and beer. But we were bound to do it by the oath of office we'd taken.

We split up at the funeral parlor and I went straight to the mill. My foreman, Gene Kleinschmidt, had opened up; I'd given him a set of keys and he knew to go ahead and unlock the place if I wasn't around. The barges came in twenty minutes after I did, and I had to hustle to get the paperwork ready that they would be carrying back down to San Francisco—bills of lading, requisitions for goods from three different companies.

I finished up a little past noon and went out onto the dock to watch the loading. One of the bargemen was talking to Gene. And while he was doing it, he kept flipping something up and down in his hand—a small gold nugget. It was the kind of things folks made into a watch fob, or kept as a good-luck charm.

And that was how I remembered where I'd seen the Benjamin Harrison Presidential Medal. Eight months or so back a newcomer to the area, a man named Jubal Parsons, had come in to buy some sacks of chicken feed. When he'd reached into his pocket to pay the bill he had accidentally come out with the medal. "Good-luck charm," he said, and let me glance at it before putting it away again.

Back inside my office I sat down and thought about Jubal Parsons. He was a tenant farmer—had taken over a small farm owned by the Siler brothers out near Willow Creek about nine months ago. Big fellow, over six feet tall, and upwards of 220 pounds. Married to a blonde woman named Greta, a few years younger than him and pretty as they come. Too pretty, some said; a few of the womenfolk,

Ellie Bozeman included, thought she had the look and mannerisms of a tramp.

Parsons came into Tule River two or three times a month to trade for supplies, but you seldom saw the wife. Neither of them went to church on Sunday, nor to any of the social events at the Odd Fellows Hall. Parsons kept to himself mostly, didn't seem to have any friends or any particular vices. Always civil, at least to me, but taciturn and kind of broody-looking. Not the sort of fellow you find yourself liking much.

But did the medal I'd found belong to him? And if it did, had he hung the drifter? And if he had, what was his motive?

I was still puzzling on that when Boze showed up. He was a half hour early, and he had Floyd Jones with him. Floyd looked some like Santa Claus—fat and jolly and white-haired—and he liked it when you told him so. He was the night bartender at the Elkhorn Bar and Grill.

Boze said, "Got some news, Carl. Floyd here saw the hanging man last night. Recognized the body over to Obe Spencer's just now."

Floyd bobbed his head up and down. "He came into the Elkhorn about eight o'clock, asking for work."

I said, "How long did he stay?"

"Half hour, maybe. Told him we already had a swamper and he spent five minutes trying to convince me he'd do a better job of cleaning up. Then he gave it up when he come to see I wasn't listening, and bought a beer and nursed it over by the stove. Seemed he didn't much relish going back into the cold."

"He say anything else to you?"

"Not that I can recall."

"Didn't give his name, either," Boze said. "But there's something else. Tell him, Floyd."

"Well, there was another fella came in just after the drifter," Floyd said. "Ordered a beer and sat watching him. Never took his eyes off that drifter once. I wouldn't have noticed except for that and because we were near empty. Cold kept most everybody to home last night."

"You know this second man?" I asked.

"Sure do. Local farmer. Newcomer to the area, only been around for—"

"Jubal Parsons?"

Floyd blinked at me. "Now how in thunder did you know that?"

"Lucky guess. Parsons leave right after the drifter?"

"He did. Not more than ten seconds afterward."

"You see which direction they went?"

"Downstreet, I think. Toward Sam McCullough's livery."

I thanked Floyd for his help and shooed him on his way. When he was gone Boze asked me, "Just how did you know it was Jubal Parsons?"

"I finally remembered where I'd seen that Presidential Medal I found. Parsons showed it when he was here one day several months ago. Said it was his good-luck charm."

Boze rubbed at his bald spot. "That and Floyd's testimony make a pretty good case against him, don't they?"

"They do. Reckon I'll go out and have a talk with him."

"We'll both go," Boze said. "Ellie can mind the store the rest of the day. This is more important. Besides, if Parsons *is* a killer, it'll be safer if there are two of us."

I didn't argue; a hero is something I never was nor wanted to be. We left the mill and went and picked up Boze's buckboard from behind the mercantile. On the way out of town we stopped by his house and mine long enough to fetch our rifles. Then we headed west on Willow Creek Road.

It was a long cool ride out to Jubal Parsons' tenant farm, through a lot of rich farmland and stands of willows and evergreens. Neither of us said much. There wasn't much to say. But I was tensed up and I could see that Boze was, too.

A rutted trail hooked up to the farm from Willow Creek Road, and Boze jounced the buckboard along there some past three o'clock. It was pretty modest acreage. Just a few fields of corn and alfalfa, with a cluster of ramshackle buildings set near where Willow Creek cut through the northwest corner. There was a one-room farmhouse, a chicken coop, a barn, a couple of lean-tos, and a pole corral. That was all except for a small windmill—a Fairbanks, Morse Eclipse—that the Siler brothers had put up because the creek was dry more than half the year.

When we came in sight of the buildings I could tell that Jubal Parsons had done work on the place. The farmhouse had a fresh coat of whitewash, as did the chicken coop, and the barn had a new roof.

There was nobody in the farmyard, just half a dozen squawking leghorns, when we pulled in and Boze drew rein. But as soon as we stepped down, the front door of the house opened and Greta Parsons came out on the porch. She was wearing a calico dress and high-button shoes, but her head was bare; that butter-yellow hair of hers hung down to her hips, glistening like the bargeman's gold nugget in the sun. She was some pretty woman, for a fact. It made your throat thicken up just to look at her, and funny ideas start to stir around in your head. If ever there was a woman to tempt a man to sin, I thought, it was this one.

Boze stayed near the buckboard, with his rifle held loose in one hand, while I went over to the porch steps and took off my hat. "I'm Carl Miller, Mrs. Parsons," I said. "That's Ed Bozeman back there. We're from Tule River. Maybe you remember seeing us?"

"Yes, Mr. Miller. I remember you."

"We'd like a few words with your husband. Would he be somewhere nearby?"

"He's in the barn," she said. There was something odd about her voice—a kind of dullness, as if she was fatigued. She moved that way, too, loose and jerky. She didn't seem to notice Boze's rifle, or to care if she did.

I said, "Do you want to call him out for us?"

"No, you go on in. It's all right."

I nodded to her and rejoined Boze, and we walked on over to the barn. Alongside it was a McCormick & Deering binder-harvester, and further down, under a lean-to, was an old buggy with its storm curtains buttoned up. A big gray horse stood in the corral, nuzzling a pile of hay. The smell of dust and earth and manure was ripe on the cool air.

The barn doors were shut. I opened one half, stood aside from the opening, and called out, "Mr. Parsons? You in there?"

No answer.

I looked at Boze. He said, "We'll go in together," and I nodded. Then we shouldered up and I pulled the other door half open. And we went inside.

It was shadowed in there, even with the doors open; those parts of the interior I could make out were empty. I eased away from Boze, toward where the corn crib was. There was sweat on me; I wished I'd taken my own rifle out of the buckboard.

"Mr. Parsons?"

Still no answer. I would have tried a third time, but right then Boze said, "Never mind, Carl," in a way that made me turn around and face him.

He was a dozen paces away, staring down at something under the hayloft. I frowned and moved over to him. Then I saw too, and my mouth came open and there was a slithery feeling on my back.

Jubal Parsons was lying there dead on the sod floor, with blood all over his shirtfront and the side of his face. He'd been shot. There was a .45-70 Springfield rifle beside the body, and when Boze bent down and struck a match, you could see the black-powder marks mixed up with the blood.

"My God," I said, soft.

"Shot twice," Boze said. "Head and chest."

"Twice rules out suicide."

"Yeah," he said.

We traded looks in the dim light. Then we turned and crossed back to the doors. When we came out Mrs. Parsons was sitting on the front steps of the house, looking past the windmill at the alfalfa fields. We went over and stopped in front of her. The sun was at our backs, and the way we stood put her in our shadow. That was what made her look up; she hadn't seen us coming, or heard us crossing the yard.

She said, "Did you find him?"

"We found him," Boze said. He took out his badge and showed it to her. "We're county sheriff's deputies, Mrs. Parsons. You'd best tell us what happened in there."

"I shot him," she said. Matter-of-fact, like she was telling you the time of day. "This morning, just after breakfast. Ever since I've wanted to hitch up the buggy and drive in and tell about it, but I couldn't seem to find the courage. It took all the courage I had to fire the rifle."

"But why'd you do a thing like that?"

"Because of what he did in Tule River last night."

"You mean the hanging man?"

"Yes. Jubal killed him."

"Did he tell you that?"

"Yes. Not long before I shot him."

"Why did he do it—hang that fellow?"

"He was crazy jealous, that's why."

I asked her, "Who was the dead man?"

"I don't know."

"You mean to say he was a stranger?"

"Yes," she said. "I only saw him once. Yesterday afternoon. He rode in looking for work. I told him we didn't have any, that we were tenant farmers, but he wouldn't leave. He kept following me around, saying things. He thought I was alone here—a woman alone."

"Did he—make trouble for you?"

"Just with words. He kept saying things, ugly things. Men like that—I don't know why, but they think I'm a woman of easy virtue. It has always been that way, no matter where we've lived."

"What did you do?" Boze asked.

"Ignored him at first. Then I begged him to go away. I told him my husband was wild jealous, but he didn't believe me. I thought I was alone too, you see; I thought Jubal had gone off to work in the fields."

"But he hadn't?"

"Oh, he had. But he came back while the drifter was here and he overheard part of what was said."

"Did he show himself to the man?"

"No. He would have if matters had gone beyond words, but that didn't happen. After a while he got tired of tormenting me and went away. The drifter, I mean."

"Then what happened?"

"Jubal saddled his horse and followed him. He followed that man into Tule River and when he caught up with him he knocked him on the head and he hung him."

Boze and I traded another look. I said what both of us were thinking: "Just for deviling you? He hung a man for that?"

"I told you, Jubal was crazy jealous. You didn't know him. You just—you don't know how he was. He said that if a man thought evil, and spoke evil, it was the same as doing evil. He said if a man was wicked, he deserved to be hung for his wickedness and the world would be a better place for his leaving it."

She paused, and then made a gesture with one hand at her bosom. It was a meaningless kind of gesture, but you could see where a man might take it the wrong way. Might take *her* the wrong way, just like she'd said. And not just a man, either; women, too. Everybody that didn't keep their minds open and went rooting around after sin in other folks.

"Besides," she went on, "he worshipped the ground I stand on. He truly did, you know. He couldn't bear the thought of anyone sullying me."

I cleared my throat. The sweat on me had dried and I felt cold now. "Did you hate him, Mrs. Parsons?"

"Yes, I hated him. Oh, yes. I feared him, too—for a long time I feared him more than anything else. He was so big. And so strong-willed. I used to tremble sometimes, just to look at him."

"Was he cruel to you?" Boze asked. "Did he hurt you?"

"He was and he did. But not the way you mean; he didn't beat me, or once lay a hand to me the whole nine years we were married. It was his vengeance that hurt me. I couldn't stand it, I couldn't take any more of it."

She looked away from us again, out over the alfalfa fields—and a long ways beyond them, at something only she could see. "No roots," she said, "that was part of it, too. No roots. Moving here, moving there, always moving—three states and five homesteads in less than ten years. And the fear. And the waiting. This was the last time, I couldn't take it ever again. Not one more minute of his jealousy, his cruelty . . . *his* wickedness."

"Ma'am, you're not making sense—"

"But I am," she said. "Don't you see? He was Jubal Parsons, the Hanging Man."

I started to say something, but she shifted position on the steps just then—and when she did that her face came out of shadow and into the sunlight, and I saw in her eyes a kind of terrible knowledge. It put a chill on my neck like the night wind does when it blows across a graveyard.

"That drifter in Tule River wasn't the first man Jubal hung on account of me," she said. "Not even the first in California. That drifter was the Hanging Man's eighth."

CHANGES

The big flat-faced stranger came into the Elite Barber Shop just before closing that Wednesday afternoon.

Asa was stropping his old Spartacus straight razor, humming to himself and thinking how good a cold lemonade was going to taste. Over at the shoeshine stand Leroy Heavens sat on a three-legged stool, working on his own pair of brogans with a stained cloth; sweat lacquered his face and made it glisten like black onyx. The mercury in the courthouse thermometer had been up to 97 at high noon and Asa judged it wasn't much cooler than that right now: the summer flies were still heat-drugged, floating in circles on such breeze as the ceiling fan stirred up.

In the long mirror across the rear wall Asa watched the stranger shut the door and stand looking around. Leroy and the shoeshine stand got a passing glance; so did the three 1920s Otis barber chairs, the waiting-area furniture, the open door to Asa's living quarters in back, the counter full of clippers and combs and other tonsorial tools, and the display shelves of both modern and old-fashioned grooming supplies.

When the eyes flicked over him Asa said, "Sure is a hot one," by way of greeting. "That sun'll raise blisters, a person stands under it too long."

The big man didn't say anything. Just headed across to where Asa was standing behind the number one chair. He wore a loose-fitting summer shirt and a pair of spiffy cream-colored slacks; dark green-tinted sunglasses hid his eyes. Asa took him to be somewhere in his middle fifties, reckoning from the lines in his face. Some face it was, too: looked as though somebody had beat on it with a mallet to flatten it that way, to get the nose and lips all spread out and shapeless.

The display shelves were to the left of the number one chair; the stranger stopped there and peered down at the old-fashioned supplies. He picked up and inspected a silvertip-badger shaving brush, an ironstone mug, a block of crystal alum, a bottle of imported English lavender water. The left corner of his mouth bent upward in a sort of smile.

"Nice stuff you got here," he said, and Asa knew right off that he was from up North. New York, maybe; he had that kind of damn-Yankee accent you kept hearing on the TV. "Not too many places stock it nowadays."

"That's a fact," Asa agreed. "I'm just about the only barber in Hallam County that does."

"Sell much of it?"

"Nope, not much. Had that silvertip brush two years now; got a genuine tortoiseshell handle, too. Kind of a shame nobody wants it."

The stranger made a noise through his flattened nose. "Doesn't surprise me. All anybody wants these days is modern junk, modern ideas. People'd be a lot better off if they stuck to the old ways."

"Well," Asa said philosophically, "things change."

"Not for the better."

"Oh, I dunno. Sometimes I reckon they do." Asa laid the Spartacus razor down. "But sure not in the art of shaving. Now that silvertip there—a real fine piece of craftsmanship, handmade over in France. Make you a nice price on it if you're interested."

"Maybe," the big man said. He edged away from the shelves and went over by the open inner door. When he got there he paused and seemed to take inventory of the room beyond. "You live back there, old-timer?"

"I do."

"Alone?"

"Yep. You a census-taker, maybe?"

The stranger barked once, like a hound on a possum hunt; then he came back to where Asa was and looked up at the clock above the mirror. "Almost five," he said. "Sign out front says that's when you close up."

"Most days the sign's right."

"How about today?"

"If you're asking will I still barber you, the answer's yes. Ain't my policy to turn a customer away if he's here before closing."

"Any after-hours appointments?"

Asa's brows pulled down. "I don't take after-hours appointments," he said. "Haircut what you're after, is it? Looks a mite long over the collar."

No answer. The big man turned his head and looked over at the front window, where the shade was three-quarters drawn against the glare of the afternoon sun. About all you could see below it was half of the empty sidewalk outside.

Asa ran a hand through his sparse white hair. Seemed pretty quiet in there, all of a sudden, except for the whisper of the push-broom Leroy had fetched and was sweeping up with in front of the shoeshine stand. There was hardly a sound out on Willow Street, either. Folks kept to home and indoors in this heat; hadn't been much foot or machine traffic all day, and no business to speak of.

"Don't recall seeing you around Wayville before," Asa said to the stranger. "Just passing through, are you?"

"You might say that."

"Come far?"

"Far enough. The state capital."

"Nice place, the capital."

"Sure. Lots of things happening there, right? Compared to a one-horse town like this, I mean."

"Depends on how you look at it."

"For instance," the big man said, "I heard there was some real excitement over there just last week. And I heard this barber named Asa Bedloe, from Wayville here, was mixed up in it."

Asa hesitated. Then, "Now where'd a Yankee like you hear that?"

The stranger's lip bent upward at the corner again. "The way I got it, Asa was in the capital visiting his nephew. While the nephew was at work, Asa wandered downtown to look through some sec-ondhand bookstores because he likes to read. He took a short cut through an alley, heard two guys arguing inside an open doorway, and the next thing he knew, there was a shot and one guy came running out with a gun in his hand. Asa'd already ducked out of sight, so the guy didn't see him. But Asa, he got a good look at the guy's face. He went straight to the cops and picked him out of a mug book—and what do you know, the guy's name is Rawles and he's a medium bigshot in the local rackets. So the cops are happy because they've got a tight eyewitness murder rap against Rawles, and Asa's happy because he's a ten-cent hero. The only one who isn't happy is Rawles."

Asa wet his lips. His eyes stayed fixed on the stranger's face.

"What I can't figure out," the big man went on, "is why old Asa went to the cops in the first place. I mean, why didn't he just keep his mouth shut and forget the whole thing?"

"Maybe he reckoned it was his duty," Asa said.

"Duty." The stranger shook his head. "That's another modern idea: instead of staying the hell out of things that don't concern them, everybody wants to do his duty, wants to get involved. Like I said before, people'd be better off if they stuck to the old ways."

"The old ways ain't always the right ways."

"Too bad you feel that way, old-timer," the stranger said. He glanced up at the clock again. "After five now. Time to close up."

"I ain't ready to close up just yet."

"Sure you are. Go on over and lock the front door."

"Now you listen here—"

The sly humor disappeared from the big man's face like some-body had wiped it off with an eraser. His eyes said he was through playing games. And his actions said it even plainer: he reached down, hiked up the front of his loose-fitting shirt, and closed his big paw around the butt of a handgun stuck inside his belt.

"Lock the front door," he said again. "Then go over with the shoeshine boy—"

That was as far as he got.

Because by this time Leroy had come catfooting up behind him. And in the next second Leroy had one arm curled around his neck, his head jerked back, and the muzzle of a .44 Magnum pressed against his temple.

"Take the gun out and drop it," Leroy said. "Slow and careful, just use your thumb and forefinger."

The big man didn't have much choice. Asa watched him do what he'd been told. The look on his face was something to see—all popeyed and scrunched up with disbelief. He hadn't hardly paid any mind to Leroy since he walked in, and sure never once considered him to be listening and watching, much less to be a threat.

Leroy backed the two of them up a few paces. Then he said, "Asa, take charge of his gun. And then go ring up my office."

"Yes, sir, you bet."

The stranger said, "Office?"

"Why, sure. This fella's been pretending to work here for the past couple days, bodyguarding me ever since the capital police got wind Rawles had hired himself a professional gunman. Name's Leroy Heavens—*Sheriff* Leroy Heavens. First black sheriff in the history of Hallam County."

The big man just gawped at him.

Asa grinned as he bent to pick up the gun. "Looks like I was right and you were wrong, mister," he said. "Sometimes things change for the better, all right. Sometimes they surely do."

CAT'S-PAW
A "Nameless Detective" Story

There are two places that are ordinary enough during the daylight hours but that become downright eerie after dark, particularly if you go wandering around in them by yourself. One is a graveyard; the other is a public zoo. And that goes double for San Francisco's Fleishhacker Zoological Gardens on a blustery winter night when the fog comes swirling in and makes everything look like capering phantoms or two-dimensional cutouts.

Fleishhacker Zoo was where I was on this foggy winter night— alone, for the most part—and I wished I was somewhere else in- stead. *Anywhere* else, as long as it had a heater or a log fire and offered something hot to drink.

I was on my third tour of the grounds, headed past the sea-lion tank to make another check of the aviary, when I paused to squint at the luminous dial of my watch. Eleven forty-five. Less than three hours down and better than six left to go. I was already half frozen, even though I was wearing long johns, two sweaters, two pairs of socks, heavy gloves, a woolen cap, and a long fur-lined overcoat. The ocean was only a thousand yards away, and the icy wind that blew in off of it sliced through you to the marrow. If I got through this job without contracting either frostbite or pneumonia, I would consider myself lucky.

Somewhere in the fog, one of the animals made a sudden roaring noise; I couldn't tell what kind of animal or where the noise came from. The first time that sort of thing had happened, two nights ago, I'd jumped a little. Now I was used to it, or as used to it as I would ever get. How guys like Dettlinger and Hammond could work here night after night, month after month, was beyond my simple comprehension.

I went ahead toward the aviary. The big wind-sculpted cypress trees that grew on my left made looming, swaying shadows, like giant black dancers with rustling headdresses wreathed in mist. Back beyond them, fuzzy yellow blobs of light marked the location of the zoo's cafe. More nightlights burned on the aviary, although the massive fenced-in wing on the near side was dark.

Most of the birds were asleep or nesting or whatever the hell it is birds do at night. But you could hear some of them stirring around, making noise. There were a couple of dozen different varieties in there, including such esoteric types as the crested screamer, the purple gallinule, and the black crake. One esoteric type that used to be in there but wasn't any longer was something called a bunting, a brilliantly colored migratory bird. Three of them had been swiped four days ago, the latest in a rash of thefts the zoological gardens had suffered.

The thief or thieves had also got two South American Harris hawks, a bird of prey similar to a falcon; three crab-eating macaques, whatever they were; and half a dozen rare Chiricahua rattlesnakes known as *Crotalus pricei.* He or they had picked the locks on buildings and cages, and got away clean each time. Sam Dettlinger, one of the two regular watchmen, had spotted somebody running the night the rattlers were stolen, and given chase, but he hadn't got close enough for much of a description, or even to tell for sure if it was a man or a woman.

The police had been notified, of course, but there was not much they could do. There wasn't much the Zoo Commission could do either, beyond beefing up security—and all that had amounted to was adding one extra night watchman, Al Kirby, on a temporary

basis; he was all they could afford. The problem was, Fleishhacker
Zoo covers some seventy acres. Long sections of its perimeter fenc-
ing are secluded; you couldn't stop somebody determined to climb
the fence and sneak in at night if you surrounded the place with a
hundred men. Nor could you effectively police the grounds with any
less than a hundred men; much of those seventy acres is heavily
wooded, and there are dozens of grottos, brushy fields and slopes,
rush-rimmed ponds, and other areas simulating natural habitats for
some of the zoo's fourteen hundred animals and birds. Kids, and an
occasional grownup, have gotten lost in there in broad daylight. A
thief who knew his way around could hide out on the grounds for
weeks without being spotted.

I got involved in the case because I was acquainted with one of
the commission members, a guy named Lawrence Factor. He was an
attorney, and I had done some investigating for him in the past, and
he thought I was the cat's nuts when it came to detective work. So
he'd come to see me, not as an official emissary of the commission
but on his own; the commission had no money left in its small
budget for such as the hiring of a private detective. But Factor had
made a million bucks or so in the practice of criminal law, and as a
passionate animal lover, he was willing to foot the bill himself. What
he wanted me to do was sign on as another night watchman, plus
nose around among my contacts to find out if there was any word
on the street about the thefts.

It seemed like an odd sort of case, and I told him so. "Why
would anybody steal hawks and small animals and rattlesnakes?" I
asked. "Doesn't make much sense to me."

"It would if you understood how valuable those creatures are to
some people."

"What people?"

"Private collectors, for one." he said. "Unscrupulous individuals
who run small independent zoos, for another. They've been known
to pay exorbitantly high prices for rare specimens they can't obtain

through normal channels—usually because of state or federal laws protecting endangered species."

"You mean there's a thriving black market in animals?"

"You bet there is. Animals, reptiles, birds—you name it. Take the *pricei,* the Southwestern rattler, for instance. Several years ago, the Arizona Game and Fish Department placed it on a special permit list; people who want the snake first have to obtain a permit from the Game and Fish authority before they can go out into the Chiricahua Mountains and hunt one. Legitimate researchers have no trouble getting a permit, but hobbyists and private collectors are turned down. Before the permit list, you could get a *pricei* for twenty-five dollars; now, some snake collectors will pay two hundred and fifty dollars and up for one."

"The same high prices apply on the other stolen specimens?"

"Yes," Factor said. "Much higher, in the case of the Harris hawk, because it is a strongly prohibited species."

"How much higher?"

"From three to five thousand dollars, after it has been trained for falconry."

I let out a soft whistle. "You have any idea who might be pulling the thefts?"

"Not specifically, no. It could be anybody with a working knowledge of zoology and the right—or wrong—contracts for disposal of the specimens."

"Someone connected with Fleishhacker, maybe?"

"That's possible. But I damned well hope not."

"So your best guess is what?"

"A professional at this sort of thing," Factor said. "They don't usually rob large zoos like ours—there's too much risk and too much publicity; mostly they hit small zoos or private collectors, and do some poaching on the side. But it *has* been known to happen when they hook up with buyers who are willing to pay premium prices."

"What makes you think it's a pro in this case? Why not an amateur? Or even kids out on some kind of crazy lark?"

"Well, for one thing, the thief seemed to know exactly what he was after each time. Only expensive and endangered specimens were taken. For another thing, the locks on the building and cage doors were picked by an expert—and that's not my theory, it's the police's."

"You figure he'll try it again?"

"Well, he's four-for-four so far, with no hassle except for the minor scare Sam Dettlinger gave him; that has to make him feel pretty secure. And there are dozens more valuable, prohibited specimens in the gardens. I like the odds that he'll push his luck and go for five straight."

But so far the thief hadn't pushed his luck. This was the third night I'd been on the job and nothing had happened. Nothing had happened during my daylight investigation either; I had put out feelers all over the city, but nobody admitted to knowing anything about the zoo thefts. Nor had I been able to find out anything from any of the Fleishhacker employees I'd talked to. All the information I had on the case, in fact, had been furnished by Lawrence Factor in my office three days ago.

If the thief was going to make another hit, I wished he would do it pretty soon and get it over with. Prowling around here in the dark and the fog and that damned icy wind, waiting for something to happen, was starting to get on my nerves. Even if I was being well paid, there were better ways to spend long, cold winter nights. Like curled up in bed with a copy of *Black Mask* or *Detective Tales* or one of the other pulps in my collection. Like curled up in bed with my lady love, Kerry Wade . . .

I moved ahead to the near doors of the aviary and tried them to make sure they were still locked. They were. But I shone my flash on them anyway, just to be certain that they hadn't been tampered with since the last time one of us had been by. No problem there, either.

There were four of us on the grounds—Dettlinger, Hammond, Kirby, and me—and the way we'd been working it was to spread out to four corners and then start moving counterclockwise in a set but irregular pattern; that way, we could cover the grounds thoroughly without all of us congregating in one area, and without more than fifteen minutes or so going by from one building check to another. We each had a walkie-talkie clipped to our belts so one could summon the others if anything went down. We also used the things to radio our positions periodically, so we'd be sure to stay spread out from each other.

I went around on the other side of the aviary, to the entrance that faced the long, shallow pond where the bigger tropical birds had their sanctuary. The doors there were also secure. The wind gusted in over the pond as I was checking the doors, like a williwaw off the frozen Arctic tundra; it made the cypress trees genuflect, shredded the fog for an instant so that I could see all the way across to the construction site of the new Primate Discovery Center, and clacked my teeth together with a sound like rattling bones. I flexed the cramped fingers of my left hand, the one that had suffered some nerve damage in a shooting scrape a few months back; extreme cold aggravated the chronic stiffness. I thought longingly of the hot coffee in my thermos. But the thermos was over at the zoo office behind the carousel, along with my brown-bag supper, and I was not due for a break until one o'clock.

The path that led to Monkey Island was on my left; I took it, hunching forward against the wind. Ahead, I could make out the high dark mass of man-made rocks that comprised the island home of sixty or seventy spider monkeys. But the mist was closing in again, like wind-driven skeins of shiny gray cloth being woven together magically; the building that housed the elephants and pachyderms, only a short distance away, was invisible.

One of the male peacocks that roam the grounds let loose with its weird cry somewhere behind me. The damned things were always doing that, showing off even in the middle of the night. I had never cared for peacocks much, and I liked them even less now. I wondered how one of them would taste roasted with garlic and anchovies. The thought warmed me a little as I moved along the path between the hippo pen and the brown bear grottos, turned onto the wide concourse that led past the front of the Lion House.

In the middle of the concourse was an extended oblong pond, with a little center island overgrown with yucca trees and pampas grass. The vegetation had an eerie look in the fog, like fantastic creatures waving their appendages in a low-budget science fiction film. I veered away from them, over toward the glass-and-wire cages that had been built onto the Lion House's stucco facade. The cages were for show: inside was the Zoological Society's current pride and joy, a year-old white tiger named Prince Charles, one of only fifty known white tigers in the world. Young Charley was the zoo's rarest and most valuable possession, but the thief hadn't attempted to steal *him*. Nobody in his right mind would try to make off with a frisky, five-hundred-pound tiger in the middle of the night.

Charley was asleep; so was his sister, a normally marked Bengal tiger named Whiskers. I looked at them for a few seconds, decided I wouldn't like to have to pay their food bill, and started to turn away.

Somebody was hurrying toward me, from over where the otter pool was located.

I could barely see him in the mist; he was just a moving black shape. I tensed a little, taking the flashlight out of my pocket, putting my cramped left hand on the walkie-talkie so I could use the thing if it looked like trouble. But it wasn't trouble. The figure called my name in a familiar voice, and when I put my flash on for a couple of seconds I saw that it was Sam Dettlinger.

"What's up?" I said when he got to me. "You're supposed to be over by the gorillas about now."

"Yeah," he said, "but I thought I saw something about fifteen minutes ago, out back by the cat grottos."

"Saw what?"

"Somebody moving around in the bushes," he said. He tipped back his uniform cap, ran a gloved hand over his face to wipe away the thin film of moisture the fog had put there. He was in his forties, heavyset, owl-eyed, with carrot-colored hair and a mustache that looked like a dead caterpillar draped across his upper lip.

"Why didn't you put out a call?"

"I couldn't be sure I actually saw somebody and I didn't want to sound a false alarm; this damn fog distorts everything, makes you see things that aren't there. Wasn't anybody in the bushes when I went to check. It might have been a squirrel or something. Or just the fog. But I figured I'd better search the area to make sure."

"Anything?"

"No. Zip."

"Well, I'll make another check just in case."

"You want me to come with you?"

"No need. It's about time for your break, isn't it?"

He shot the sleeve of his coat and peered at his watch. "You're right, it's almost midnight—"

And something exploded inside the Lion House—a flat, cracking noise that sounded like a gunshot.

Both Dettlinger and I jumped. He said, "What the hell was that?"

"I don't know. Come on!"

We ran the twenty yards or so to the front entrance. The noise had awakened Prince Charles and his sister; they were up and starting to prowl their cage as we rushed past. I caught hold of the door handle and tugged on it, but the lock was secure.

I snapped at Dettlinger, "Have you got a key?"

"Yeah, to all the buildings . . ."

He fumbled his key ring out, and I switched on my flash to help him find the right key. From inside, there was cold dead silence; I couldn't hear anything anywhere else in the vicinity either, except for faint animal sounds lost in the mist. Dettlinger got the door unlocked, dragged it open. I crowded in ahead of him, across a short foyer and through another door that wasn't locked, into the building's cavernous main room.

A couple of the ceiling lights were on; we hadn't been able to tell from outside because the Lion House had no windows. The interior was a long rectangle with a terra cotta tile floor, now-empty feeding cages along the entire facing wall and the near side wall, another set of entrance doors in the far side wall, and a kind of indoor garden full of tropical plants flanking the main entrance to the left. You could see all of the enclosure from two steps inside, and there wasn't anybody in it. Except—

"Jesus!" Dettlinger said. "Look!"

I was looking, all right. And having trouble accepting what I saw. A man was lying sprawled on his back inside one of the cages diagonally to our right; there was a small glistening stain of blood on the front of his heavy coat and a revolver of some kind in one of his outflung hands. The small access door at the front of the cage was shut, and so was the sliding panel at the rear that let the big cats in and out at feeding time. In the pale light, I could see the man's face clearly: his teeth were bared in the rictus of death.

"It's Kirby," Dettlinger said in a hushed voice. "Sweet Christ, what—?"

I brushed past him and ran over and climbed the brass railing that fronted all the cages. The access door, a four-by-two-foot barred inset, was locked tight. I poked my nose between two of the bars, peering in at the dead man. Kirby, Al Kirby. The temporary night watchman the Zoo Commission had hired a couple of weeks ago. It looked as though he had been shot in the chest at close range; I could see where the upper middle of his coat had been scorched by the powder discharge.

My stomach jumped a little, the way it always does when I come face to face with violent death. The faint, gamy, big-cat smell that hung in the air didn't help it any. I turned toward Dettlinger, who had come up beside me.

"You have a key to this access door?" I asked him.

"No. There's never been a reason to carry one. Only the cat handlers have them." He shook his head in an awed way. "How'd Kirby get in there? What *happened?*"

"I wish I knew. Stay put for a minute."

I left him and ran down to the doors in the far side wall. They were locked. Could somebody have had time to shoot Kirby, get out through these doors, then relock them before Dettlinger and I busted in? It didn't seem likely. We'd been inside less than thirty seconds after we'd heard the shot.

I hustled back to the cage where Kirby's body lay. Dettlinger had backed away from it, around in front of the side-wall cages; he looked a little queasy now himself, as if the implications of violent death had finally registered on him. He had a pack of cigarettes in one hand, getting ready to soothe his nerves with some nicotine. But this wasn't the time or the place for a smoke; I yelled at him to put the things away, and he complied.

When I reached him I said, "What's behind these cages? Some sort of rooms back there, aren't there?"

"Yeah. Where the handlers store equipment and meat for the cats. Chutes, too, that lead out to the grottos."

"How do you get to them?"

He pointed over at the rear side wall. "That door next to the last cage."

"Any other way in or out of those rooms?"

"No. Except through the grottos, but the cats are out there."

I went around to the interior door he'd indicated. Like all the others, it was locked. I said to Dettlinger, "You do have a key to this door?"

He nodded, got it out, and unlocked the door. I told him to keep watch out here, switched on my flashlight, and went on through. The flash beam showed me where the light switches were; I flicked them on and began a quick, cautious search. The door to one of the meat lockers was open, but nobody was hiding inside. Or anywhere else back there.

When I came out I shook my head in answer to Dettlinger's silent question. Then I asked him, "Where's the nearest phone?"

"Out past the grottos, by the popcorn stand."

"Hustle out there and call the police. And while you're at it, radio Hammond to get over here on the double——"

"No need for that," a new voice said from the main entrance. "I'm already here."

I glanced in that direction and saw Gene Hammond, the other regular night watchman. You couldn't miss him; he was six-five, weighed in at a good two-fifty, and had a face like the back end of a bus. Disbelief was written on it now as he stared across at Kirby's body.

"Go," I told Dettlinger. "I'll watch things here."

"Right."

He hurried out past Hammond, who was on his way toward where I stood in front of the cage. Hammond said as he came up, "God—what happened?"

"We don't know yet."

"How'd Kirby get in there?"

"We don't know that either." I told him what we did know, which was not much. "When did you last see Kirby?"

"Not since the shift started at nine."

"Any idea why he'd have come in here?"

"No. Unless he heard something and came in to investigate. But he shouldn't have been in this area, should he?"

"Not for another half-hour, no."

"Christ, you don't think that he——"

"What?"

"Killed himself," Hammond said.

"It's possible. Was he despondent for any reason?"

"Not that I know about. But it sure looks like suicide. I mean, he's got that gun in his hand, he's all alone in the building, all the doors were locked. What else could it be?"

"Murder," I said.

"How? Where's the person who killed him, then?"

"Got out through one of the grottos, maybe."

"No way," Hammond said. "Those cats would maul anybody who went out among 'em—and I mean anybody; not even any of the handlers would try a stunt like that. Besides, even if somebody made it down into the moat, how would he scale that twenty-foot back wall to get out of it?"

I didn't say anything.

Hammond said, "And another thing: why would Kirby be locked in this cage if it was murder?"

"Why would he lock himself in to commit suicide?"

He made a bewildered gesture with one of his big hands.

"Crazy," he said. "The whole thing's crazy."

He was right. None of it seemed to make any sense at all.

I knew one of the homicide inspectors who responded to Dettlinger's call. His name was Branislaus and he was a pretty decent guy, so the preliminary questions-and-answers went fast and hassle-free. After which he packed Dettlinger and Hammond and me off to the zoo office while he and the lab crew went to work inside the Lion House.

I poured some hot coffee from my thermos, to help me thaw out a little, and then used one of the phones to get Lawrence Factor out of bed. He was paying my fee and I figured he had a right to know what had happened as soon as possible. He made shocked noises when I told him, asked a couple of pertinent questions, said he'd get out to Fleishhacker right away, and rang off.

An hour crept away. Dettlinger sat at one of the desks with a pad of paper and a pencil and challenged himself in a string of tic-tac-toe games. Hammond chain-smoked cigarettes until the air in there was blue with smoke. I paced around for the most part, now and then stepping out into the chill night to get some fresh air: all that cigarette smoke was playing merry hell with my lungs. None of us had much to say. We were all waiting to see what Branislaus and the rest of the cops turned up.

Factor arrived at one-thirty, looking harried and upset. It was the first time I had ever seen him without a tie and with his usually immaculate Robert Redford hairdo in some disarray. A patrolman accompanied him into the office, and judging from the way Factor glared at him, he had had some difficulty getting past the front gate. When the patrolman left I gave Factor a detailed account of what had taken place as far as I knew it, with embellishments from Dettlinger. I was just finishing when Branislaus came in.

Branny spent a couple of minutes discussing matters with Factor. Then he said he wanted to talk to the rest of us one at a time, picked me to go first, and herded me into another room.

The first thing he said was, "This is the screwiest shooting case I've come up against in twenty years on the force. What in bloody hell is going on here?"

"I was hoping maybe you could tell me."

"Well, I can't—yet. So far it looks like a suicide, but if that's it, it's a candidate for Ripley. Whoever heard of anybody blowing himself away in a lion cage at the zoo?"

"Any indication he locked himself in there?"

"We found a key next to his body that fits the little access door in front."

"Just one loose key?"

"That's right."

"So it could have been dropped in there by somebody else after Kirby was dead and after the door was locked. Or thrown in through the bars from outside."

"Granted."

"And suicides don't usually shoot themselves in the chest," I said.

"Also granted, although it's been known to happen."

"What kind of weapon was he shot with? I couldn't see it too well from outside the cage, the way he was lying."

"Thirty-two Iver Johnson."

"Too soon to tell yet if it was his, I guess."

"Uh-huh. Did he come on the job armed?"

"Not that I know about. The rest of us weren't, or weren't supposed to be."

"Well, we'll know more when R and I finishes running a check on the serial number," Branislaus said. "It was intact, so the thirty-two doesn't figure to be a Saturday Night Special."

"Was there anything in Kirby's pockets?"

"The usual stuff. And no sign of a suicide note. But you don't think it was suicide anyway, right?"

"No, I don't."

"Why not?"

"No specific reason. It's just that a suicide under those circumstances rings false. And so does a suicide on the heels of the thefts the zoo's been having lately."

"So you figure there's a connection between Kirby's death and the thefts?"

"Don't you?"

"The thought crossed my mind," Branislaus said dryly. "Could be the thief slipped back onto the grounds tonight, something happened before he had a chance to steal something, and he did for Kirby—I'll admit the possibility. But what were the two of them doing in the Lion House? Doesn't add up that Kirby caught the guy in there. Why would the thief enter it in the first place? Not be-cause he was trying to steal a lion or a tiger, that's for sure."

"Maybe Kirby stumbled on him somewhere else, somewhere nearby. Maybe there was a struggle; the thief got the drop on Kirby, then forced him to let both of them into the Lion House with his key."

"Why?"

"To get rid of him where it was private."

"I don't buy it," Branny said. "Why wouldn't he just knock Kirby over the head and run for it?"

"Well, it could be he's somebody Kirby knew."

"Okay. But the Lion House angle is still too much trouble for him to go through. It would've been much easier to shove the gun into Kirby's belly and shoot him on the spot. Kirby's clothing would have muffled the sound of the shot; it wouldn't have been audible more than fifty feet away."

"I guess you're right," I said.

"But even supposing it happened the way you suggest, it *still* doesn't add up. You and Dettlinger were inside the Lion House thirty seconds after the shot, by your own testimony. You checked the side entrance doors almost immediately and they were locked; you looked around behind the cages and nobody was there. So how did the alleged killer get out of the building?"

"The only way he could have got out was through one of the grottos in back.

"Only he *couldn't* have, according to what both Dettlinger and Hammond say."

I paced over to one of the windows—nervous energy—and looked out at the fog-wrapped construction site for the new monkey exhibit. Then I turned and said, "I don't suppose your men found anything in the way of evidence inside the Lion House?"

"Not so you could tell it with the naked eye."

"Or anywhere else in the vicinity?"

"No."

"Any sign of tampering on any of the doors?"

"None. Kirby used his key to get in, evidently."

I came back to where Branislaus was leaning hipshot against somebody's desk. "Listen, Branny," I said, "this whole thing is *too* screwball. You know that as well as I do. Somebody's playing games here, trying to muddle our thinking—and that means murder."

"Maybe," he said. "Hell, probably. But how was it done? I can't come up with an answer, not even one that's believably farfetched. Can you?"

"Not yet."

"Does that mean you've got an idea?"

"Not an idea; just a bunch of little pieces looking for a pattern."

He sighed. "Well, if they find it, let me know."

When I went back into the other room I told Dettlinger that he was next on the grill. Factor wanted to talk some more, but I put him off. Hammond was still polluting the air with his damned cigarettes, and I needed another shot of fresh air; I also needed to be alone for a while. I could almost feel those little random fragments bobbing around in there like flotsam on a heavy sea.

I put my overcoat on and went out and wandered past the cages where the smaller cats were kept, past the big open fields that the giraffes and rhinos called home. The wind was stronger and colder than it had been earlier; heavy gusts swept dust and twigs along the ground, broke the fog up into scudding wisps. I pulled my cap down over my ears to keep them from numbing.

The path led along to the concourse at the rear of the Lion House, where the open cat-grottos were. Big, portable electric lights had been set up there and around the front so the police could search the area. A couple of patrolmen glanced at me as I approached, but they must have recognized me because neither of them came over to ask what I was doing there.

I went to the low, shrubberied wall that edged the middle cat-grotto. Whatever was in there, lions or tigers, had no doubt been aroused by all the activity; but they were hidden inside the dens at the rear. These grottos had been newly renovated—lawns, jungly vegetation, small trees, everything to give the cats the illusion of their native habitat. The side walls separating this grotto from the other two were man-made rocks, high and unscalable. The moat below was fifty feet wide, too far for either a big cat or a man to jump; and the near moat wall was sheer and also unscalable from below, just as Hammond and Dettlinger had said.

No way anybody could have got out of the Lion House through the grottos, I thought. Just no way.

No way it could have been murder then. Unless—

I stood there for a couple of minutes, with my mind beginning, finally, to open up. Then I hurried around to the front of the Lion House and looked at the main entrance for a time, remembering things.

And then I knew.

Branislaus was in the zoo office, saying something to Factor, when I came back inside. He glanced over at me as I shut the door.

"Branny," I said, "those little pieces I told you about a while ago finally found their pattern."

He straightened. "Oh? Some of it or all of it?"

"All of it, I think."

Factor said, "What's this about?"

"I figured out what happened at the Lion House tonight," I said. "Al Kirby didn't commit suicide: he was murdered. And I can name the man who killed him."

I expected a reaction, but I didn't get one beyond some widened eyes and opened mouths. Nobody said anything and nobody moved much. But you could feel the sudden tension in the room, as thick in its own intangible way as the layers of smoke from Hammond's cigarettes.

"Name him," Branislaus said.

But I didn't, not just yet. A good portion of what I was going to say was guesswork—built on deduction and logic, but still guess-work—and I wanted to choose my words carefully. I took off my cap, unbuttoned my coat, and moved away from the door, over near where Branny was standing.

He said, "Well? Who do you say killed Kirby?"

"The same person who stole the birds and other specimens. And I don't mean a professional animal thief, as Mr. Factor suggested when he hired me. He isn't an outsider at all; and he didn't climb the fence to get onto the grounds."

"No?"

"No. He was *already* in here on those nights and on this one, because he works here as a night watchman. The man I'm talking about is Sam Dettlinger."

That got some reaction. Hammond said, "I don't believe it," and Factor said, "My God!" Branislaus looked at me, looked at Dettlinger, looked at me again—moving his head like a spectator at a tennis match.

The only one who didn't move was Dettlinger. He sat still at one of the desks, his hands resting easily on its blotter; his face betrayed nothing.

He said, "You're a liar," in a thin, hard voice.

"Am I? You've been working here for some time; you know the animals and which ones are both endangered and valuable. It was easy for you to get into the buildings during your round: just use your key and walk right in. When you had the specimens you took them to some prearranged spot along the outside fence and passed them over to an accomplice."

"What accomplice?" Branislaus asked.

"I don't know. You'll get it out of him, Branny; or you'll find out some other way. But that's how he had to have worked it."

"What about the scratches on the locks?" Hammond asked. "The police told us the locks were picked—"

"Red herring," I said. "Just like Dettlinger's claim that he chased a stranger on the grounds the night the rattlers were stolen. Designed to cover up the fact that it was an inside job." I looked back at Branislaus. "Five'll get you ten Dettlinger's had some sort of locksmithing experience. It shouldn't take much digging to find out."

Dettlinger started to get out of his chair, thought better of it, and sat down again. We were all staring at him, but it did not seem to bother him much; his owl eyes were on my neck, and if they'd been hands I would have been dead of strangulation.

Without shifting his gaze, he said to Factor, "I'm going to sue this son of a bitch for slander. I can do that, can't I, Mr. Factor?"

"If what he says isn't true, you can," Factor said.

"Well, it isn't true. It's all a bunch of lies. I never stole anything. And I sure never killed Al Kirby. How the hell could I? I was with this guy, *outside* the Lion House, when Al died inside."

"No, you weren't," I said.

"What kind of crap is that? I was standing right next to you, we both heard the shot—"

"That's right, we both heard the shot. And that's the first thing that put me onto you, Sam. Because we damned well *shouldn't* have heard it"

"No? Why not?"

"Kirby was shot with a thirty-two caliber revolver. A thirty-two is a small gun; it doesn't make much of a bang. Branny, you remember saying to me a little while ago that if somebody had shoved that thirty-two into Kirby's middle, you wouldn't have been able to hear the pop more than fifty feet away? Well, that's right. But Dettlinger and I were a lot more than fifty feet from the cage where we found Kirby—twenty yards from the front entrance, thick stucco walls, a ten-foot foyer, and another forty feet or so of floor space to the cage. Yet we not only heard a shot, we heard it loud and clear."

Branislaus said, "So how is that possible?"

I didn't answer him. Instead I looked at Dettlinger and I said, "Do you smoke?"

That got a reaction out of him. The one I wanted: confusion. "What?"

"Do you smoke?"

"What kind of question is that?"

"Gene must have smoked half a pack since we've been in here, but I haven't seen you light up once. In fact, I haven't seen you light up the whole time I've been working here. So answer me, Sam—do you smoke or not?"

"No, I don't smoke. You satisfied?"

"I'm satisfied," I said. "Now suppose you tell me what it was you had in your hand in the Lion House, when I came back from checking the side doors?"

He got it, then—the way I'd trapped him. But he clamped his lips together and sat still.

"What are you getting at?" Branislaus asked me. "What *did* he have in his hand?"

"At the time I thought it was a pack of cigarettes; that's what it looked like from a distance. I took him to be a little queasy, a delayed reaction to finding the body, and I figured he wanted some nicotine to calm his nerves. But that wasn't it at all; he wasn't queasy, he was scared—because I'd seen what he had in his hand before he could hide it in his pocket."

"So what was it?"

"A tape recorder," I said. "One of those small battery-operated jobs they make nowadays, a white one that fits in the palm of the hand. He'd just picked it up from wherever he'd stashed it earlier—behind the bars in one of the other cages, probably. I didn't notice it there because it was so small and because my attention was all on Kirby's body."

"You're saying the shot you heard was on tape?"

"Yes. My guess is, he recorded it right after he shot Kirby. Fifteen minutes or so earlier."

"Why did he shoot Kirby? And why in the Lion House?"

"Well, he and Kirby could have been in on the thefts together; they could have had some kind of falling out, and Dettlinger decided to get rid of him. But I don't like that much. As a premeditated murder, it's too elaborate. No, I think the recorder was a spur-of-the-moment idea; I doubt if it belonged to Dettlinger, in fact. Ditto the thirty-two. He's clever, but he's not a planner, he's an improviser."

"If the recorder and the gun weren't his, whose were they? Kirby's?"

I nodded. "The way I see it, Kirby found out about Dettlinger pulling the thefts; saw him do the last one, maybe. Instead of reporting it, he did some brooding and then decided tonight to try a little shakedown. But Dettlinger's bigger and tougher than he was, so he brought the thirty-two along for protection. He also brought the recorder, the idea probably being to tape his conversation with Dettlinger, without Dettlinger's knowledge, for further blackmail leverage.

"He buttonholed Dettlinger in the vicinity of the Lion House, and the two of them went inside to talk it over in private. Then something happened. Dettlinger tumbled to the recorder, got rough, Kirby pulled the gun, they struggled for it, Kirby got shot dead—that sort of scenario.

"So then Dettlinger had a corpse on his hands. What was he going to do? He could drag it outside, leave it somewhere, make it look like the mythical fence-climbing thief killed him; but if he did that he'd be running the risk of me or Hammond appearing suddenly and spotting him. Instead he got what he thought was a bright idea: he'd create a big mystery and confuse hell out of everybody, plus give himself a dandy alibi for the apparent time of Kirby's death.

"He took the gun and the recorder to the storage area behind the cages. Erased what was on the tape, used the fast-forward and the timer to run off fifteen minutes of tape, then switched to record and fired a second shot to get the sound of it on tape. I don't know for sure what he fired the bullet into; but I found one of the meat-locker doors open when I searched back there, so maybe he used a slab of meat for a target. And then piled a bunch of other slabs on top to hide it until he could get rid of it later on. The police wouldn't be looking for a second bullet, he thought, so there wasn't any reason for them to rummage around in the meat.

"His next moves were to rewind the tape, go back out front, and stash the recorder—turned on, with the volume all the way up. That gave him fifteen minutes. He picked up Kirby's body . . . most of the blood from the wound had been absorbed by the heavy coat Kirby was wearing, which was why there wasn't any blood on the floor and why Dettlinger didn't get any on him. And why I didn't notice, fifteen minutes later, that it was starting to coagulate. He carried the body to the cage, put it inside with the thirty-two in Kirby's hand, relocked the access door—he told me he didn't have a key, but that was a lie—and then threw the key in with the body. But putting Kirby in the cage was his big mistake. By doing that he made the whole thing too bizarre. If he'd left the body where it was, he'd have had a better chance of getting away with it.

"Anyhow, he slipped out of the building without being seen and hid over by the otter pool. He knew I was due there at midnight, because of the schedule we'd set up; and he wanted to be with me when that recorded gunshot went off. Make me the cat's-paw, if you don't mind a little grim humor, for what he figured would be his perfect alibi.

"Later on, when I sent him to report Kirby's death, he disposed of the recorder. He couldn't have gone far from the Lion House to get rid of it; he did make the call, and he was back within fifteen minutes. With any luck, his fingerprints will be on the recorder when your men turn it up.

"And if you want any more proof that I'm on the right track, I'll swear in court I didn't smell cordite when we entered the Lion

House; all I smelled was the gamy odor of jungle cats. I should have smelled cordite if that thirty-two had just been discharged. But it hadn't, and the cordite smell from the earlier discharges had already faded."

That was a pretty long speech and it left me dry-mouthed. But it had made its impression on the others in the room, Branislaus in particular.

He asked Dettlinger, "Well? You have anything to say for yourself?"

"I never did any of those things he said—none of 'em, you hear?"

"I hear."

"And that's all I'm saying until I see a lawyer."

"You've got one of the best sitting next to you. How about it, Mr. Factor? You want to represent Dettlinger?"

"Pass," Factor said thinly. "This is one case where I'll be glad to plead bias."

Dettlinger was still strangling me with his eyes. I wondered if he would keep on proclaiming his innocence even in the face of stronger evidence than what I'd just presented. Or if he'd crack under the pressure, as most amateurs do.

I decided he was the kind who'd crack eventually, and I quit looking at him and at the death in his eyes.

"Well, I was wrong about that much," I said to Kerry the following night. We were sitting in front of a log fire in her Diamond Heights apartment, me with a beer and her with a glass of wine, and I had just finished telling her all about it. "Dettlinger hasn't cracked and it doesn't look as if he's going to. The D.A.'ll have to work for his conviction."

"But you *were* right about the rest of it?"

"Pretty much. I probably missed on a few details; with Kirby dead, and unless Dettlinger talks, we may never know some of them for sure. But for the most part I think I got it straight."

"My hero," she said, and gave me an adoring look.

She does that sometimes—puts me on like that. I don't understand women, so I don't know why. But it doesn't matter. She has auburn hair and green eyes and a fine body; she's also smarter than I am—she works as an advertising copywriter—and she's stimulating to be around. I love her to pieces, as the boys in the back room used to say.

"The police found the tape recorder," I said. "Took them until late this morning, because Dettlinger was clever about hiding it. He'd buried it in some rushes inside the hippo pen, probably with the idea of digging it up again later on and getting rid of it permanently. There was one clear print on the fast-forward button—Dettlinger's"

"Did they also find the second bullet he fired?"

"Yep. Where I guessed it was: in one of the slabs of fresh meat in the open storage locker."

"And did Dettlinger have locksmithing experience?"

"Uh-huh. He worked for a locksmith for a year in his mid-twenties. The case against him, even without a confession, is pretty solid."

"What about his accomplice?"

"Branislaus thinks he's got a line on the guy," I said. "From some things he found in Dettlinger's apartment. Man named Gerber—got a record of animal poaching and theft. I talked to Larry Factor this afternoon and he's heard of Gerber. The way he figures it, Dettlinger and Gerber had a deal for the specimens they stole with some collectors in Florida. That seems to be Gerber's usual pattern of operation, anyway."

"I hope they get him too," Kerry said. "I don't like the idea of stealing birds and animals out of the zoo. It's . . . obscene, somehow."

"So is murder."

We didn't say anything for a time, looking into the fire, working on our drinks.

"You know," I said finally, "I have a lot of sympathy for animals myself. Take gorillas, for instance."

"Why gorillas?"

"Because of their mating habits."

"What *are* their mating habits?"

I had no idea, but I made up something interesting. Then I gave her a practical demonstration.

No gorilla ever had it so good.

SKELETON RATTLE YOUR MOULDY LEG
A "Nameless Detective" Story

He was one of the oddest people I had ever met. Sixty years old, under five and a half feet tall, slight, with great bony knobs for elbows and knees, with bat-winged ears and a bent nose and eyes that danced left and right, left and right, and had sparkly little lights in them. He wore baggy clothes—sweaters and jeans, mostly, crusted with patches—and a baseball cap turned around so that the bill poked out from the back of his head. In his back pocket he carried a whisk broom, and if he knew you, or wanted to, he would come up and say, "I know you—you've got a speck on your coat," and he would brush it off with the broom. Then he would talk, or maybe recite or even sing a little: a gnarled old harlequin cast up from another age.

These things were odd enough, but the oddest of all was his obsession with skeletons.

His name was Nick Damiano and he lived in the building adjacent to the one where Eberhardt and I had our new office—lived in a little room in the basement. Worked there, too, as a janitor and general handyman; the place was a small residence hotel for senior citizens, mostly male, called the Medford. So it didn't take long for our paths to cross. A week or so after Eb and I moved in, I was coming up the street one morning and Nick popped out of the alley that separated our two buildings.

He said, "I know you—you've got a speck on your coat," and out came the whisk broom. Industriously he brushed away the

216

imaginary speck. Then he grinned and said, "Skeleton rattle your mouldy leg."

"Huh?"

That's poetry," he said. "From *archy and mehitabel.* You know archy and mehitabel?"

"No," I said, "I don't."

"They're lower case; they don't have capitals like we do. Archy's a cockroach and mehitabel's a cat and they were both poets in another life. A fellow named don marquis created them a long time ago. He's lowercase too."

"Uh . . . I see."

"One time mehitabel went to Paris," he said, "and took up with a tom cat named francy who was once the poet Francois Villon, and they used to go to the catacombs late at night. They'd caper and dance and sing among those old bones."

And he began to recite:

> *"prince if you pipe and plead and beg*
> *you may yet be crowned with a grisly kiss*
> *skeleton rattle your mouldy leg*
> *all men's lovers come to this"*

That was my first meeting with Nick Damiano; there were others over the next four months, none of which lasted more than five minutes. Skeletons came into all of them, in one way or another. Once he sang half a dozen verses of the old spiritual, "Dry Bones," in a pretty good baritone. Another time he quoted, "'The Knight's bones are dust/And his good sword rust—/ His Soul is with the saints, I trust.'" Later I looked it up and it was a rhyme from an obscure work by Coleridge. On the other days he made sly little comments: "Why hello there, I knew it was you coming—I heard your bones chattering and clacking all the way down the street." And "Cleaned out your closet lately? Might be skeletons hiding in there." And "Sure is hot today. Sure would be fine to take off our skins and just sit around in our bones."

I asked one of the Medford's other residents, a guy named Irv Feinberg, why Nick seemed to have such a passion for skeletons. Feinberg didn't know, nobody knew, he said, because Nick wouldn't discuss it. He told me that Nick even owned a genuine skeleton, liberated from some medical facility, and that he kept it wired to the wall of his room and burned candles in its skull.

A screwball, this Nick Damiano—sure. But he did his work and did it well, and he was always cheerful and friendly, and he never gave anybody any trouble. Harmless old Nick. A happy whack, marching to the rhythm of dry old bones chattering and clacking together inside his head. Everybody in the neighborhood found him amusing, including me: San Francisco has always been proud of its characters, its kooks. Yeah, everyone liked old Nick.

Except that somebody *didn't* like him, after all.

Somebody took hold of a blunt instrument one raw November night, in that little basement room with the skeleton leering on from the wall, and beat Nick Damiano to death.

It was four days after the murder that Irv Feinberg came to see me. He was a rotund little guy in his sixties, very energetic, a retired plumber who wore loud sports coats and spent most of his time doping out the races at Golden Gate Fields and a variety of other tracks. He had known Nick as well as anyone could, had called him his friend.

I was alone in the office when Feinberg walked in; Eberhardt was down at the Hall of Justice, trying to coerce some of his former cop pals into giving him background information on a missing-person case he was working. Feinberg said by way of greeting, "Nice office you got here," which was a lie, and came over and plopped himself into one of the clients' chairs. "You busy? Or you got a few minutes we can talk?"

"What can I do for you, Mr. Feinberg?"

"The cops have quit on Nick's murder," he said. "They don't come around anymore, they don't talk to anybody in the hotel. I called down to the Hall of Justice. I wanted to know what's happening. I got the big runaround."

"The police don't quit a homicide investigation——"

"The hell they don't. A guy like Nick Damiano? It's no big deal to them. They figure it was somebody looking for easy money, a drug addict from over in the Tenderloin. On account of Dan Cady, he's the night clerk, found the door to the alley unlocked just after he found Nick's body."

"That sounds like a reasonable theory," I said.

"Reasonable, hell. The door wasn't tampered with or anything; it was just unlocked. So how'd the drug addict get in? Nick wouldn't have left that door unlocked; he was real careful about things like that. And he wouldn't have let a stranger in, not at that time of night."

"Well, maybe the assailant came in through the front entrance and went out through the alley door. . . ."

"No way," Feinberg said. "Front door's on a night security lock from eight o'clock on; you got to buzz the desk from outside and Dan Cady'll come see who you are. If he don't know you, you don't get in."

"All right, maybe the assailant wasn't a stranger. Maybe he's somebody Nick knew."

"Sure, that's what I think. But not somebody outside the hotel. Nick never let people in at night, not anybody, not even somebody lives here; you had to go around to the front door and buzz the desk. Besides, he didn't have any outside friends that came to see him. He didn't go out himself either. He had to tend to the heat, for one thing, do other chores, so he stayed put. I know all that because I spent plenty of evenings with him, shooting craps for pennies . . . Nick liked to shoot craps, he called it 'rolling dem bones.'"

Skeletons, I thought. I said, "What do you think then, Mr. Feinberg? That somebody from the hotel killed Nick?"

"That's what I think," he said. "I don't like it, most of those people are my friends, but that's how it looks to me."

"You have anybody specific in mind?"

"No. Whoever it was, he was in there arguing with Nick before he killed him."

"Oh? How do you know that?"

"George Weaver heard them. He's our newest tenant, George is, moved in three weeks ago. Used to be a bricklayer in Chicago, came out here to be with his daughter when he retired, only she had a heart attack and died last month. His other daughter died young and his wife died of cancer; now he's all alone." Feinberg shook his head. "It's a hell of a thing to be old and alone."

I agreed that it must be.

"Anyhow, George was in the basement getting something out of his storage bin and he heard the argument. Told Charley Slattery a while later that it didn't sound violent or he'd have gone over and banged on Nick's door. As it was, he just went back upstairs."

"Who's Charley Slattery?"

"Charley lives at the Medford and works over at Monahan's Gym on Turk Street. Used to be a small-time fighter; now he just hangs around doing odd jobs. Not too bright, but he's okay."

"Weaver didn't recognize the other voice in the argument?"

"No. Couldn't make out what it was all about either."

"What time was that?"

"Few minutes before eleven, George says."

"Did anyone else overhear the argument?"

"Nobody else around at the time."

"When was the last anybody saw Nick alive?"

"Eight o'clock. Nick came up to the lobby to fix one of the lamps wasn't working. Dan Cady talked to him a while when he was done."

"Cady found Nick's body around two A.M.?"

"Two-fifteen."

"How did he happen to find it? That wasn't in the papers."

"Well, the furnace was still on. Nick always shuts it off by midnight or it got to be too hot upstairs. So Dan went down to find out why and there was Nick lying on the floor of his room with his head all beat in."

"What kind of guy is Cady?"

"Quiet, keeps to himself, spends most of his free time reading library books. He was a college history teacher once, up in Oregon. But he got in some kind of trouble with a woman—this was back in the forties, teachers had to watch their morals—and the college fired him and he couldn't get another teaching job. He fell into the booze for a lot of years afterward. But he's all right now. Belongs to AA."

I was silent for a time. Then I asked, "The police didn't find anything that made them suspect one of the other residents?"

"No, but that don't mean much." Feinberg made a disgusted noise through his nose. "Cops. They don't even know what it was bashed in Nick's skull, what kind of weapon. Couldn't find it anywhere. They figure the killer took it away through that unlocked alley door and got rid of it. *I* figure the killer unlocked the door to make it look like an outside job, then went upstairs and hid the weapon somewhere till next day."

"Let's suppose you're right. Who might have a motive to've killed Nick?"

"Well . . . nobody, far as I know. But *somebody's* got one, you can bet on that."

"Did Nick get along with everybody at the Medford?"

"Sure," Feinberg said. Then he frowned a little and said, "Except Wesley Thane, I guess. But I can't see Wes beating anybody's head in. He pretends to be tough but he's a wimp. And a goddamn snob."

"Oh?"

"He's an actor. Little theater stuff these days, but once he was a bit player down in Hollywood, made a lot of crappy B movies where he was one of the minor bad guys. Hear him tell it, he was Clark

Gable's best friend back in the forties. A windbag who thinks he's better than the rest of us. He treated Nick like a freak."

"Was there ever any trouble between them?"

"Well, he hit Nick once, just after he moved in five years ago and Nick tried to brush off his coat. I was there and I saw it."

"Hit him with what?"

"His hand. A kind of slap. Nick shied away from him after that."

"How about recent trouble?"

"Not that I know about. I didn't even have to noodge him into kicking in twenty bucks to the fund. But hell, everybody in the building kicked in something except old lady Howsam; she's bedridden and can barely make ends meet on her pension, so I didn't even ask her."

I said, "Fund?"

Feinberg reached inside his gaudy sport jacket and produced a bulky envelope. He put the envelope on my desk and pushed it toward me with the tips of his fingers. "There's two hundred bucks in there," he said. "What'll that hire you for? Three-four days?"

I stared at him. "Wait a minute, Mr. Feinberg. Hire me to do what?"

"Find out who killed Nick. What do you think we been talking about here?"

"I thought it was only talk you came for. A private detective can't investigate a homicide in this state, not without police permission. . . ."

"So get permission," Feinberg said. "I told you, the cops have quit on it. Why should they try to keep you from investigating?"

"Even if I did get permission, I doubt if there's much I could do that the police haven't already—"

"Listen, don't go modest on me. You're a good detective, I see your name in the papers all the time. I got confidence in you; we all do. Except maybe the guy who killed Nick."

There was no arguing him out of it; his mind was made up, and he'd convinced the others in the Medford to go along with him. So I quit trying finally and said all right, I would call the Hall of Justice and see if I could get clearance to conduct a private investigation. And if I could, then I'd come over later and see him and take a look around and start talking to people. That satisfied him. But when I pushed the envelope back across the desk, he wouldn't take it.

"No," he said, "that's yours, you just go ahead and earn it." And he was on his feet and gone before I could do anything more than make a verbal protest.

I put the money away in the lock-box in my desk and telephoned the Hall. Eberhardt was still hanging around, talking to one of his old cronies in General Works, and I told him about Feinberg and what he wanted. Eb said he'd talk to the homicide inspector in charge of the Nick Damiano case and see what was what; he didn't seem to think there'd be any problem getting clearance. There were problems, he said, only when private eyes tried to horn in on big-money and/or VIP cases, the kind that got heavy media attention.

He used to be a homicide lieutenant so he knew what he was talking about. When he called back a half hour later he said, "You got your clearance. Feinberg had it pegged: the case is already in the Inactive File for lack of leads and evidence. I'll see if I can finagle a copy of the report for you."

Some case, I thought as I hung up. In a way it was ghoulish, like poking around in a fresh grave. And wasn't that an appropriate image; I could almost hear Nick's sly laughter.

Skeleton rattle your mouldy leg.

The basement of the Medford Hotel was dimly lighted and too warm: a big, old-fashioned oil furnace rattled and roared in one corner, giving off shimmers of heat. Much of the floor space was taken up with fifty-gallon trash receptacles, some full and some empty and one each under a pair of garbage chutes from the upper floor. Over against the far wall, and throughout a small connecting room beyond, were rows of narrow storage cubicles made out of wood and heavy wire, with padlocks on each of the doors.

Nick's room was at the rear, opposite the furnace and alongside the room that housed the hot-water heaters. But Feinberg didn't take me there directly; he said something I didn't catch, mopping his face with a big green handkerchief, and detoured over to the furnace and fiddled with the controls and got it shut down.

"Damn thing," he said. "Owner's too cheap to replace it with a modern unit that runs off a thermostat. Now we got some young snot he hired to take Nick's job, don't live here and don't stick around all day and leaves the furnace turned on too long. It's like a goddamn sauna in here."

There had been a police seal on the door to Nick's room, but it had been offically removed. Feinberg had the key; he was a sort of building mayor, by virtue of seniority—he'd lived at the Medford for more than fifteen years—and he had got custody of the key from the owner. He opened the lock, swung the thick metal door open, and clicked on the lights.

The first thing I saw was the skeleton. It hung from several pieces of shiny wire on the wall opposite the door, and it was a grisly damned thing streaked with blobs of red and green and orange candle wax. The top of the skull had been cut off and a fat red candle jutted up from the hollow inside, like some sort of ugly growth. Melted wax rimmed and dribbled from the grinning mouth, giving it a bloody look.

"Cute, ain't it?" Feinberg said. "Nick and his frigging skeletons."

I moved inside. It was just a single room with a bathroom alcove, not more than fifteen feet square. Cluttered, but in a way that suggested everything had been assigned a place. Army cot against one wall, a small table, two chairs, one of those little waist-high refrigerators with a hot plate on top, a standing cupboard full of pots and dishes; stacks of newspapers and magazines, some well-used books—volumes of poetry, an anatomical text, two popular histories about ghouls and grave-robbers, a dozen novels with either "skeleton" or "bones" in the title; a broken wooden wagon, a Victrola without its ear-trumpet amplifier, an ancient Olivetti typewriter, a collection of oddball tools, a scabrous iron-bound steamer trunk, an open box full of assorted pairs of dice, and a lot of other stuff, most of which appeared to be junk.

A thick fiber mat covered the floor. On it, next to the table, was the chalked outline of Nick's body and some dark stains. My stomach kicked a little when I looked at the stains; I had seen corpses of bludgeon victims and I knew what those stains looked like when they were fresh. I went around the table on the other side and took a closer look at the wax-caked skeleton. Feinberg tagged along at my heels.

"Nick used to talk to that thing," he said. "Ask it questions, how it was feeling, could he get it anything to eat or drink. Gave me the willies at first. He even put his arm around it once and kissed it, I swear to God. I can still see him do it."

"He got it from a medical facility?"

"One that was part of some small college he worked at before he came to San Francisco. He mentioned that once."

"Did he say where the college was?"

"No."

"Where did Nick come from? Around here?"

Feinberg shook his head. "Midwest somewhere, that's all I could get out of him."

"How long had he been in San Francisco?"

"Ten years. Worked here the last eight; before that, he helped out at a big apartment house over on Geary."

"Why did he come to the city? Did he have relatives here or what?"

"No, no relatives, he was all alone. Just him and his bones—he said that once."

I poked around among the clutter of things in the room, but if there had been anything here relevant to the murder, the police would have found it and probably removed it and it would be mentioned in their report. So would anything found among Nick's effects that determined his background. Eberhardt would have a copy of the report for me to look at later; when he said he'd try to do something he usually did it.

When I finished with the room we went out and Feinberg locked the door. We took the elevator up to the lobby. It was dim up there, too—and a little depressing. There was a lot of plaster and wood and imitation marble, and some antique furniture and dusty potted plants, and it smelled of dust and faintly of decay. A sense of age permeated the place: you felt it and you smelled it and you saw it in the surroundings, in the half-dozen men and one woman sitting on the sagging chairs, reading or staring out through the windows at O'Farrell Street, people with nothing to do and nobody to do it with, waiting like doomed prisoners for the sentence of death to be carried out. Dry witherings and an aura of hopelessness—that was the impression I would carry away with me and that would linger in my mind.

I thought: I'm fifty-four, another few years and I could be stuck in here too. But that wouldn't happen. I had work I could do pretty much to the end and I had Kerry—Kerry Wade, my lady—and I had some money in the bank and a collection of 6500 pulp magazines that were worth plenty on the collectors' market. No, this kind of place wouldn't happen to me. In a society that ignored and showed little respect for its elderly, I was one of the lucky ones.

Feinberg led me to the desk and introduced me to the day clerk, a sixtyish barrel of a man named Bert Norris. If there was anything he could do to help, Norris said, he'd be glad to oblige; he sounded eager, as if nobody had needed his help in a long time. The fact that Feinberg had primed everyone here about my investigation made things easier in one respect and more difficult in another. If the person who had killed Nick Damiano *was* a resident of the Medford, I was not likely to catch him off guard.

When Norris moved away to answer a switchboard call, Feinberg asked me, "Who're you planning to talk to now?"

"Whoever's available," I said.

"Dan Cady? He lives here—two-eighteen. Goes to the library

every morning after he gets off, but he's always back by noon. You can probably catch him before he turns in."

"All right, good."

"You want me to come along?"

"That's not necessary, Mr. Feinberg."

"Yeah, I get it. I used to hate that kind of thing too when I was out on a plumbing job."

"What kind of thing?"

"Somebody hanging over my shoulder, watching me work. Who needs crap like that? You want me, I'll be in my room with the scratch sheets for today's races."

Dan Cady was a thin, sandy-haired man in his mid-sixties, with cheeks and nose road-mapped by ruptured blood vessels—the badge of the alcoholic, practicing or reformed. He wore thick glasses, and behind them his eyes had a strained, tired look, as if from too much reading.

"Well, I'll be glad to talk to you," he said, "but I'm afraid I'm not very clear-headed right now. I was just getting ready for bed."

"I won't take up much of your time, Mr. Cady."

He let me in. His room was small and strewn with library books, most of which appeared to deal with American history; a couple of big maps, an old one of the United States and an even older parchment map of Asia, adorned the walls, and there were plaster busts of historical figures I didn't recognize, and a huge globe on a wooden stand. There was only one chair; he let me have that and perched himself on the bed.

I asked him about Sunday night, and his account of how he'd come to find Nick Damiano's body coincided with what Feinberg had told me. "It was a frightening experience," he said. "I'd never seen anyone dead by violence before. His head . . . well, it was awful."

"Were there signs of a struggle in the room?"

"Yes, some things were knocked about. But I'd say it was a brief struggle—there wasn't much damage."

"Is there anything unusual you noticed? Something that should have been there but wasn't, for instance?"

"No. I was too shaken to notice anything like that."

"Was Nick's door open when you got there?"

"Wide open."

"How about the door to the alley?"

"No. Closed."

"How did you happen to check it, then?"

"Well, I'm not sure," Cady said. He seemed faintly embarrassed; his eyes didn't quite meet mine. "I was stunned and frightened; it occurred to me that the murderer might still be around somewhere. I took a quick look around the basement and then opened the alley door and looked out there . . . I wasn't thinking very clearly. It was only when I shut the door again that I realized it had been unlocked."

"Did you see or hear anything inside or out?"

"Nothing. I left the door unlocked and went back to the lobby to call the police."

"When you saw Nick earlier that night, Mr. Cady, how did he seem to you?"

"Seem? Well, he was cheerful; he usually was. He said he'd have come up sooner to fix the lamp but his old bones wouldn't allow it. That was the way he talked. . . ."

"Yes, I know. Do you have any idea who he might have argued with that night, who might have killed him?"

"None," Cady said. "He was such a gentle soul . . . I still can't believe a thing like that could happen to him."

Down in the lobby again, I asked Bert Norris if Wesley Thane, George Weaver, and Charley Slattery were on the premises. Thane was, he said, Room 315; Slattery was at Monahan's Gym and would be until six o'clock. He started to tell me that Weaver was out, but then his eyes shifted past me and he said, "No, there he is now. Just coming in."

I turned. A heavyset, stooped man of about seventy had just entered from the street, walking with the aid of a hickory cane; but he seemed to get along pretty good. He was carrying a grocery sack in his free hand and a folded newspaper under his arm.

I intercepted him halfway to the elevator and told him who I was. He looked me over for about ten seconds, out of alert blue eyes that had gone a little rheumy, before he said, "Irv Feinberg said you'd be around." His voice was surprisingly strong and clear for a man his age. "But I can't help you much. Don't know much."

"Should we talk down here or in your room?"

"Down here's all right with me."

We crossed to a deserted corner of the lobby and took chairs in front of a fireplace that had been boarded up and painted over. Weaver got a stubby little pipe out of his coat pocket and began to load up.

I said, "About Sunday night, Mr. Weaver. I understand you went down to the basement to get something out of your storage locker. . . ."

"My old radio," he said. "New one I bought a while back quit playing and I like to listen to the eleven o'clock news before I go to sleep. When I got down there I heard Damiano and some fella arguing."

"Just Nick and one other man?"

"Sounded that way."

"Was the voice familiar to you?"

"Didn't sound familiar. But I couldn't hear it too well; I was over by the lockers. Couldn't make out what they were saying either."

"How long were you in the basement?"

"Three or four minutes, is all."

"Did the argument get louder, more violent, while you were there?"

"Didn't seem to. No." He struck a kitchen match and put the

flame to the bowl of his pipe. "If it had I guess I'd've gone over and banged on the door, announced myself. I'm as curious as the next man when it comes to that."

"But as it was you went straight back to your room?"

"That's right. Ran into Charley Slattery when I got out of the elevator; his room's just down from mine on the third floor."

"What was his reaction when you told him what you'd heard?"

"Didn't seem to worry him much," Weaver said. "So I figured it was nothing for me to worry about either."

"Slattery didn't happen to go down to the basement himself, did he?"

"Never said anything about it if he did."

I don't know what I expected Wesley Thane to be like—the Raymond Massey or John Carradine type, maybe, something along those shabbily aristocratic and vaguely sinister lines—but the man who opened the door to Room 315 looked about as much like an actor as I do. He was a smallish guy in his late sixties, he was bald, and he had a nondescript face except for mean little eyes under thick black brows that had no doubt contributed to his career as a B-movie villain. He looked somewhat familiar, but even though I like old movies and watch them whenever I can, I couldn't have named a single film he had appeared in.

He said, "Yes? What is it?" in a gravelly, staccato voice. That was familiar, too, but again I couldn't place it in any particular context.

I identified myself and asked if I could talk to him about Nick Damiano. "That cretin," he said, and for a moment I thought he was going to shut the door in my face. But then he said, "Oh, all right, come in. If I don't talk to you, you'll probably think I had something to do with the poor fool's murder."

He turned and moved off into the room, leaving me to shut the door. The room was larger than Dan Cady's and jammed with stage and screen memorabilia: framed photographs, playbills, film posters, blown-up black-and-white stills; and a variety of salvaged props, among them the plumed helmet off a suit of armor and a Napoleonic uniform displayed on a dressmaker's dummy.

Thane stopped near a lumpy-looking couch and did a theatrical about-face. The scowl he wore had a practiced look, and it occurred to me that under it he might be enjoying himself. "Well?" he said.

I said, "You didn't like Nick Damiano, did you, Mr. Thane," making it a statement instead of a question.

"No, I didn't like him. And no, I didn't kill him, if that's your next question."

"Why didn't you like him?"

"He was a cretin. A gibbering moron. All that nonsense about skeletons—he ought to have been locked up long ago."

"You have any idea who did kill him?"

"No. The police seem to think it was a drug addict."

"That's one theory," I said. "Irv Feinberg has another: he thinks the killer is a resident of this hotel."

"I know what Irv Feinberg thinks. He's a damned meddler who doesn't know when to keep his mouth shut."

"You don't agree with him then?"

"I don't care one way or another."

Thane sat down and crossed his legs and adopted a sufferer's pose; now he was playing the martyr. I grinned at him, because it was something he wasn't expecting, and went to look at some of the stuff on the walls. One of the black-and-white stills depicted Thane in Western garb, with a smoking six-gun in his hand. The largest of the photographs was of Clark Gable, with an ink inscription that read, "For my good friend, Wes."

Behind me Thane said impatiently, "I'm waiting."

I let him wait a while longer. Then I moved back near the couch and grinned at him again and said, "Did you see Nick Damiano the night he was murdered?"

"I did not."

"Talk to him at all that day?"

"No."

"When was the last you had trouble with him?"

"Trouble? What do you mean, trouble?"

"Irv Feinberg told me you hit Nick once, when he tried to brush off your coat."

"My God," Thane said, "that was years ago. And it was only a slap. I had no problems with him after that. He avoided me and I ignored him; we spoke only when necessary." He paused, and his eyes got bright with something that might have been malice. "If you're looking for someone who had trouble with Damiano recently, talk to Charley Slattery."

"What kind of trouble did Slattery have with Nick?"

"Ask him. It's none of my business."

"Why did you bring it up then?"

He didn't say anything. His eyes were still bright.

"All right, I'll ask Slattery," I said. "Tell me, what did you think when you heard about Nick? Were you pleased?"

"Of course not. I was shocked. I've played many violent roles in my career, but violence in real life always shocks me."

"The shock must have worn off pretty fast. You told me a couple of minutes ago you don't care who killed him."

"Why should I, as long as no one else is harmed?"

"So why did you kick in the twenty dollars?"

"What?"

"Feinberg's fund to hire me. Why did you contribute?"

"If I hadn't it would have made me look suspicious to the others. I have to live with these people; I don't need that sort of stigma." He gave me a smug look. "And if you repeat that to anyone, I'll deny it."

"Must be tough on you," I said.

"I beg your pardon?"

"Having to live in a place like this, with a bunch of broken-down old nobodies who don't have your intelligence or compassion or great professional skill."

That got to him; he winced, and for a moment the actor's mask slipped and I had a glimpse of the real Wesley Thane—a defeated old man with faded dreams of glory, a never-was with a small and mediocre talent, clinging to the tattered fringes of a business that couldn't care less. Then he got the mask in place again and said with genuine anger, "Get out of here. I don't have to take abuse from a cheap gumshoe."

"You're dating yourself, Mr Thane; nobody uses the word 'gumshoe' any more. It's forties B-movie dialogue."

He bounced up off the couch, pinch-faced and glaring. "Get out, I said. Get out!"

I got out. And I was on my way to the elevator when I realized why Thane hadn't liked Nick Damiano. It was because Nick had taken attention away from him—upstaged him. Thane was an actor, but there wasn't any act he could put on more compelling than the real-life performance of Nick and his skeletons.

Monahan's Gym was one of those tough, men-only places that catered to ex-pugs and oldtimers in the fight game, the kind of place you used to see a lot of in the forties and fifties but that have become an anachronism in this day of chic health clubs, fancy spas, and dwindling interest in the art of prizefighting. It smelled of sweat and steam and old leather, and it resonated with the grunts of weightlifters, the smack and thud of gloves against leather bags, the profane talk of men at liberty from a more or less polite society.

I found Charley Slattery in the locker room, working there as an attendant. He was a short, beefy guy, probably a light-heavyweight in his boxing days, gone to fat around the middle in his old age; white-haired, with a face as seamed and time-eroded as a chunk of desert sandstone. One of his eyes had a glassy look; his nose and mouth were lumpy with scar tissue. A game fighter in his day, I thought, but not a very good one. A guy who had never quite learned how to cover up against the big punches, the hammerblows that put you down and out.

"Sure, I been expectin you," he said when I told him who I was. "Irv Feinberg, he said you'd be around. You findin out anything the cops dint?"

"It's too soon to tell, Mr. Slattery."

"Charley," he said, "I hate that Mr. Slattery crap."

"All right, Charley."

"Well, I wish I could tell you somethin would help you, but I can't think of nothin. I dint even see Nick for two-three days before he was murdered."

"Any idea who might have killed him?"

"Well, some punk off the street, I guess. Guy Nick was arguin with that night—George Weaver, he told you about that, dint he? What he heard?"

"Yes. He also said he met you upstairs just afterward."

Slattery nodded. "I was headin down the lobby for a Coke, they got a machine down there, and George, he come out of the elevator with his cane and this little radio unner his arm. He looked kind of funny and I ast him what's the matter and that's when he told me about the argument."

"What did you do then?"

"What'd I do? Went down to get my Coke."

"You didn't go to the basement?"

"Nah, damn it. George, he said it was just a argument Nick was havin with somebody. I never figured it was nothin, you know, violent. If I had—Yeah, Eddie? You need somethin?"

A muscular black man in his mid-thirties, naked except for a pair of silver-blue boxing trunks, had come up. He said, "Towel and some soap, Charley. No soap in the showers again."

"Goddamn. I catch the guy keeps swipin it," Slattery said, "I'll kick his ass." He went and got a clean towel and a bar of soap, and the black man moved off with them to a back row of lockers. Slattery watched him go; then he said to me, "That's Eddie Jordan. Pretty fair welterweight once, but he never trained right, never had the right manager. He could of been good, that boy, if—" He broke off, frowning. "I shouldn't ought to call him that, I guess. 'Boy.' Blacks, they don't like to be called that nowadays."

"No," I said, "they don't."

"But I don't mean nothin by it. I mean, we always called em 'boy,' it was just somethin we called em. 'Nigger,' too, same thing. It wasn't nothin personal, you know?"

I knew, all right, but it was not something I wanted to or ever could explain to Charley Slattery. Race relations, the whole question of race, was too complex an issue. In his simple world, "nigger" and "boy" were just words, meaningless words without a couple of centuries of hatred and malice behind them, and it really wasn't anything personal.

"Let's get back to Nick," I said. "You liked him, didn't you, Charley?"

"Sure I did. He was goofy, him and his skeletons, but he worked hard and he never bothered nobody."

"I had a talk with Wesley Thane a while ago. He told me you had some trouble with Nick not long ago."

Slattery's eroded face arranged itself into a scowl. "That damn actor, he don't know what he's talkin about. Why don't he mind his own damn business? I never had no trouble with Nick."

"Not even a little? A disagreement of some kind, maybe?"

He hesitated. Then he shrugged and said, "Well, yeah, I guess we had that. A kind of disagreement."

"When was this?'

"I dunno. Couple of weeks ago."

"What was it about?"

"Garbage," Slattery said.

"Garbage?"

"Nick, he dint like nobody touching the cans in the basement. But hell, I was down there one night and the cans unner the chutes was full, so I switched em for empties. Well, Nick come around and yelled at me, and I wasn't feelin too good so I yelled back at him. Next thing, I got sore and kicked over one of the cans and spilled out some garbage. Dan Cady, he heard the noise clear up in the lobby and come down and that son of a bitch Wes Thane was with him. Dan, he got Nick and me calmed down. That's all there was to it."

"How were things between you and Nick after that?"

"Okay. He forgot it and so did I. It dint mean nothin. It was just one of them things."

"Did Nick have problems with any other people in the hotel?" I asked.

"Nah. I don't think so."

"What about Wes Thane? He admitted he and Nick didn't get along very well."

"I never heard about them havin no fight or anythin like that."

"How about trouble Nick might have had with somebody outside the Medford?"

"Nah," Slattery said. "Nick, he got along with everybody, you know? Everybody liked Nick, even if he was goofy."

Yeah, I thought, everybody liked Nick, even if he was goofy. Then why is he dead? *Why?*

I went back to the Medford and talked with three more residents, none of whom could offer any new information or any possible answers to that question of motive. It was almost five when I gave it up for the day and went next door to the office.

Eberhardt was there, but I didn't see him at first because he was on his hands and knees behind his desk. He poked his head up as I came inside and shut the door.

"Fine thing," I said, "you down on your knees like that. What if I'd been a prospective client?"

"So? I wouldn't let somebody like you hire me."

"What're you doing down there anyway?"

"I was cleaning my pipe and I dropped the damn bit." He disappeared again for a few seconds, muttered, "Here it is," reappeared, and hoisted himself to his feet.

There were pipe ashes all over the front of his tie and his white shirt; he'd even managed to get a smear of ash across his jowly chin. He was something of a slob, Eberhardt was, which gave us one of several common bonds: I was something of a slob myself. We had been friends for more than thirty years, and we'd been through some hard times together—some very hard times in the recent past. I hadn't been sure at first that taking him in as a partner after his retirement was a good idea, for a variety of reasons; but it had worked out so far. Much better than I'd expected, in fact.

He sat down and began brushing pipe dottle off his desk; he must have dropped a bowlful on it as well as on himself. He said as I hung up my coat, "How goes the Nick Damiano investigation?"

"Not too good. Did you manage to get a copy of the police report?"

"On your desk. But I don't think it'll tell you much."

The report was in an unmarked manila envelope; I read it standing up. Eberhardt was right that it didn't enlighten me much. Nick Damiano had been struck on the head at least three times by a heavy blunt instrument and had died of a brain hemorrhage, probably within seconds of the first blow. The wounds were "consistent with" a length of three-quarter-inch steel pipe, but the weapon hadn't been positively identified because no trace of it had been found. As for Nick's background, nothing had been found there either. No items of personal history among his effects, no hint of relatives or even of his city of origin. They'd run a check on his fingerprints through the FBI computer, with negative results: he had never been arrested on a felony charge, never been in military service or applied for a civil service job, never been fingerprinted at all.

When I put the report down Eberhardt said, "Anything?"

"Doesn't look like it." I sat in my chair and looked out the window for a time, at heavy rainclouds massing above the Federal Building down the hill. "There's just nothing to go on in this thing, Eb—no real leads or suspects, no apparent motive."

"So maybe it's random. A street-killing, drug-related, like the report speculates."

"Maybe."

"You don't think so?"

"Our client doesn't think so."

"You want to talk over the details?"

"Sure. But let's do it over a couple of beers and some food."

"I thought you were on a diet."

"I am. Whenever Kerry's around. But she's working late tonight—new ad campaign she's writing. A couple of beers won't hurt me. And we'll have something non-fattening to eat."

"Sure we will," Eberhardt said.

We went to an Italian place out on Clement at 25th Avenue and had four beers apiece and plates of fettucine Alfredo and half a loaf of garlic bread. But the talking we did got us nowhere. If one of the residents of the Medford had killed Nick Damiano, what was the damn motive? A broken-down old actor's petulant jealousy? A mindless dispute over garbage cans? Just what *was* the argument all about that George Weaver had overheard?

Eberhardt and I split up early and I drove home to my flat on Pacific Heights. The place had a lonely feel; after spending most of the day in and around the Medford, I needed some laughter and *bonhomie* to cheer me up—I needed Kerry. I thought about calling her at Bates and Carpenter, her ad agency, but she didn't like to be disturbed while she was working. And she'd said she expected to be there most of the evening.

I settled instead for cuddling up to my collection of pulp magazines—browsing here and there, finding something to read. On nights like this the pulps weren't much of a substitute for human companionship in general and Kerry in particular, but at least they kept my mind occupied. I found a 1943 issue of *Dime Detective* that looked interesting, took it into the bathtub, and lingered there reading until I got drowsy. Then I went to bed, went right to sleep for a change—

—and woke up at 3:00 A.M. by the luminous dial of the night-stand clock, because the clouds had finally opened up and unleashed a wailing torrent of wind-blown rain; the sound of it on the roof and on the rainspouts outside the window was loud enough to wake up a deaf man. I lay there half groggy, listening to the storm and thinking about how the weather had gone all screwy lately and maybe it was time somebody started making plans for another ark.

And then all of a sudden I was thinking about something else, and I wasn't groggy anymore. I sat up in bed, wide awake. And inside of five minutes, without much effort now that I had been primed, I knew what it was the police had overlooked and I was reasonably sure I knew who had murdered Nick Damiano.

But I still didn't know why; I didn't even have an inkling of why. That was what kept me awake until dawn—that, and the unceasing racket of the storm.

The Medford's front door was still on its night security lock when I got there at a quarter to eight. Dan Cady let me in. I asked him a couple of questions about Nick's janitorial habits, and the answers he gave me pretty much confirmed my suspicions. To make absolutely sure, I went down to the basement and spent ten minutes poking around in its hot and noisy gloom.

Now the hard part, the part I never liked. I took the elevator to the third floor and knocked on the door to Room 304. He was there; not more than five seconds passed before he called out, "Door's not locked." I opened it and stepped inside.

He was sitting in a faded armchair near the window, staring out at the rain and the wet streets below. He turned his head briefly to look at me, then turned it back again to the window. The stubby little pipe was between his teeth and the overheated air smelled of his tobacco, a kind of dry, sweet scent, like withered roses.

"More questions?" he said.

"Not exactly, Mr. Weaver. You mind if I sit down?"

"Bed's all there is."

I sat on the bottom edge of the bed, a few feet away from him. The room was small, neat—not much furniture, not much of anything; old patterned wallpaper and a threadbare carpet, both of which had a patina of gray. Maybe it was my mood and the rain-dull day outside, but the entire room seemed gray, full of that aura of age and hopelessness.

"Hot in here," I said. "Furnace is going full blast down in the basement."

"I don't mind it hot."

"Nick Damiano did a better job of regulating the heat, I understand. He'd turn it on for a few hours in the morning, leave it off most of the day, turn it back on in the evenings, and then shut it down again by midnight. The night he died, though, he didn't have time to shut it down."

Weaver didn't say anything.

"It's pretty noisy in the basement when that furnace is on," I said. "You can hardly hold a normal conversation with somebody standing right next to you. It'd be almost impossible to hear anything, even raised voices, from a distance. So you couldn't have heard an argument inside Nick's room, not from back by the storage lockers. And probably not even if you stood right next to the door, because the door's thick and made of metal."

He still didn't stir, didn't speak.

"You made up the argument because you ran into Charley Slattery, didn't you? He might have told the police he saw you come out of the elevator around the time Nick was killed, and that you seemed upset; so you had to protect yourself. Just like you protected yourself by unlocking the alley door after the murder."

More silence.

"You murdered Nick, all right. Beat him to death with your cane—hickory like that is as thick and hard as three-quarter-inch steel pipe. Charley told me you had it under your arm when you got off the elevator. Why under your arm? Why weren't you walking with it like you usually do? Has to be that you didn't want your fingers around the handle, the part you must have clubbed Nick with, even if you did wipe off most of the blood and gore."

He was looking at me now, without expression—just a dull steady waiting look.

"How did you clean the cane once you were here in your room? Soap and water? Cleaning fluid of some kind? It doesn't matter, you know. There'll still be minute traces of blood on it that the police lab can match up to Nick's."

He put an end to his silence then; he said in a clear, toneless voice, "All right. I done it," and that made it a little easier on both of us. The truth is always easier, no matter how painful it might be.

I said, "Do you want to tell me about it, Mr. Weaver?"

"Not much to tell," he said. "I went to the basement to get my other radio, like I told you before. He was fixing the door to one of the storage bins near mine. I looked at him up close, and I knew he was the one. I'd had a feeling he was ever since I moved in, but that night, up close like that, I knew it for sure."

He paused to take the pipe out of his mouth and lay it carefully on the table next to his chair. Then he said, "I accused him point blank. He put his hands over his ears like a woman, like he couldn't stand to hear it, and ran to his room. I went after him. Got inside before he could shut the door. He started babbling, crazy things about skeletons, and I saw that skeleton of his grinning across the room, and I . . . I don't know, I don't remember that part too good. He pushed me, I think, and I hit him with my cane . . . I kept hitting him . . ."

His voice trailed off and he sat there stiffly, with his big gnarled hands clenched in his lap.

"*Why,* Mr. Weaver? You said he was the one, that you accused him—accused him of what?"

He didn't seem to hear me. He said, "After I come to my senses, I couldn't breathe. Thought I was having a heart attack. God, it was hot in there . . . hot as hell. I opened the alley door to get some air and I guess I must have left it unlocked. I never did that on purpose. Only the story about the argument."

"Why did you kill Nick Damiano?"

No answer for a few seconds; I thought he still wasn't listening and I was about to ask the question again. But then he said, "My Bible's over on the desk. Look inside the front cover."

The Bible was a well-used Gideon and inside the front cover was a yellowed newspaper clipping. I opened the clipping. It was from the Chicago *Sun-Times,* dated June 23, 1957—a news story, with an accompanying photograph, that bore the headline: FLOWER SHOP BOMBER IDENTIFIED.

I took it back to the bed and sat again to read it. It said that the person responsible for a homemade bomb that had exploded in a crowded florist shop the day before, killing seven people, was a handyman named Nicholas Donato. One of the dead was Marjorie Donato, the bomber's estranged wife and an employee of the shop; another victim was the shop's owner, Arthur Cullen, with whom Mrs. Donato had apparently been having an affair. According to friends, Nicholas Donato had been despondent over the estrangement and the affair, had taken to drinking heavily, and had threatened "to do something drastic" if his wife didn't move back in with him. He had disappeared the morning of the explosion and had not been apprehended at the time the news story was printed. His evident intention had been to blow up only his wife and her lover; but Mrs. Donato had opened the package containing the bomb immediately after it was brought by messenger, in the presence of several customers, and the result had been mass slaughter.

I studied the photograph of Nicholas Donato. It was a head-and-shoulders shot, of not very good quality, and I had to look at it closely for a time to see the likeness. But it was there: Nicholas Donato and Nick Damiano had been the same man.

Weaver had been watching me read. When I looked up from the clipping he said, "They never caught him. Traced him to Indianapolis, but then he disappeared for good. All these years, twenty-seven years, and I come across him here in San Francisco. Coincidence. Or maybe it was supposed to happen that way. The hand of the Lord guides us all, and we don't always understand the whys and wherefores."

"Mr. Weaver, what did that bombing massacre have to do with you?"

"One of the people he blew up was my youngest daughter. Twenty-two that year. Went to that flower shop to pick out an arrangement for her wedding. I saw her after it happened, I saw what his bomb did to her. . . ."

He broke off again; his strong voice trembled a little now. But his eyes were dry. He'd cried once, he'd cried many times, but that had been long ago. There were no tears left any more.

I got slowly to my feet. The heat and the sweetish tobacco scent were making me feel sick to my stomach. And the grayness, the aura of age and hopelessness and tragedy were like an oppressive weight.

I said, "I'll be going now."

"Going?" he said. "Telephone's right over there."

"I won't be calling the police, Mr. Weaver. From here or from anywhere else."

"What's that? But . . . you know I killed him . . ."

"I don't know anything," I said. "I don't even remember coming here today."

I left him quickly, before he could say anything else, and went downstairs and out to O'Farrell Street. Wind-hurled rain buffeted me, icy and stinging, but the feel and smell of it was a relief. I pulled up the collar on my overcoat and hurried next door.

Upstairs in the office I took Irv Feinberg's two hundred dollars out of the lock-box in the desk and slipped the envelope into my coat pocket. He wouldn't like getting it back; he wouldn't like my calling it quits on the investigation, just as the police had done. But that didn't matter. Let the dead lie still, and the dying find what little peace they had left. The judgment was out of human hands anyway.

I tried not to think about Nick Damiano any more, but it was too soon and I couldn't blot him out yet. Harmless old Nick, the happy whack. Jesus Christ. Seven people—he had slaughtered seven people that day in 1957. And for what? For a lost woman; for a lost love. No wonder he'd gone batty and developed an obsession for skeletons. He had lived with them, seven of them, all those years, heard them clattering and clacking all those thousands of nights. And now, pretty soon, he would be one himself.

Skeleton rattle your mouldy leg.

All men's lovers come to this.

*

SANCTUARY
A "Nameless Detective" Story

We were still twenty miles from Paradise when the skies opened up on us.

It was 7:30 on a Sunday evening in late October and Kerry and I had spent the afternoon driving around in the Sierra Nevada up near Lake Almanor. The sun had been shining when we'd started out from Paradise just before noon, but the sky had begun to cloud up in mid-afternoon and the first rain had begun falling at half-past four. We'd have started back before that, and been in Paradise long since—literally and maybe figuratively, too—except for the tire that had got punctured by some litterbug's broken beer bottle and the damned spare that had turned up just as flat. We'd had to wait for a good Samaritan to come along and take us into Almanor, and then to ride back out with a Triple-A truck and a new tire. The whole episode had cost us well over two hours and neither of us was in a very good mood. So then the rain had to change from a drizzle to a deluge so heavy the windshield wipers couldn't get rid of the water fast enough. Straining to see, I had to slow to less than twenty-five or run the risk of losing the car on one of the sharp turns in the two-lane mountain road.

Kerry said, "Oh God, just what we need. Can you see? It's just a blur out there to me."

"Ditto."

"Maybe we'd better pull over until it lets up."

"No place to go."

"The first place we come to, then."

"Don't worry," I said, "we'll be all right."

"Some Sunday," she said irritably. "Some terrific weekend."

I didn't say anything. My temper was as short as hers and I did not want us to start bickering; the road and that silver curtain of rain took all my attention. But the truth was, it hadn't been such a bad weekend until this afternoon. I'd had half a day's worth of wrap-up business in Chico on Friday, on a civil case I was working for a San Francisco attorney, and I had taken Kerry along because my job fascinated her—she fancied herself as having latent detective abilities—and because the timing was right for a three-day mini-vacation after my business was finished. That night we'd driven up to Paradise, a resort and retirement community in the Sierra foothills a dozen miles northeast of Chico, and taken a room in a first-class motel. The weather was good, with no early snow on the ground; it was the off-season so there weren't many other tourists in the area; and we'd been having a pretty nice time eating out, exploring, and making love.

Now we were paying for it.

The rain seemed to be coming down harder, if that were possible. It was like trying to drive under and through a seemingly endless waterfall. Close on both sides of the road, pine forest loomed black and indistinct; there wasn't even a turnout where I could pull off. I let our speed slacken to under twenty, little more than a crawl. At least there wasn't any other traffic: we hadn't seen another car traveling in either direction in the past five minutes.

The night was pitch black except for the shimmer of our head-lights against the rain. Or it was until we came around another curve. Kerry said, "Up ahead, look! It's some kind of roadside business place."

Through the downpour I could make out the reds and blues of a neon sign, the squat shape of a single log-and-shake-roofed building set back at the edge of a narrow clearing. There were lights in one of the front windows, and more neon that materialized as beer advertisements. The big sign on the roof said liquidly: *Kern's Woodland Tavern and Cafe.*

I eased the car off the highway, onto a deserted gravel parking area that fronted the building. There was nothing behind the place except more trees and an empty access road that vanished in among them. Directly in front were a pair of gas pumps: I stopped the car between them and the entrance to the tavern half, the part that was lighted. The other half, the cafe, had a Closed sign in its darkened window.

"The bar's open, at least," Kerry said. "Why don't we go in? I can use something hot to drink."

"Might as well. It's better than sitting here."

We ran to the tavern entrance, a distance of maybe ten feet; but we were both half-drenched by the time we pushed inside. Some hard rain, the kind you only get in the mountains and that might last anywhere from three minutes to thirty.

The tavern was one of those rustic country types, full of rough-hewn furniture and deer heads; this one also had a big American flag stretched out across the wall that bisected the building, one made before Alaska and Hawaii were admitted to the Union because it only had forty-eight stars. A three-log fire blazed hotly in a native-stone fireplace. Near the window was a musicians' dais, empty now, and a scattering of maybe a dozen tables. Opposite was the bar, rough-hewn like the furnishings; on the wall behind it were a lot of little burnt-wood plaques that had dumb sayings on them like *If You Don't Ask Us for Credit, We Won't Double the Price of Your Drinks.*

There were only two people in the place, both of them men. One, a middle-aged guy wearing a plaid shirt and a tight-fitting woolen hunter's hat, was passed out at one of the tables, his head cradled in both arms. The other man was upright and conscious, standing at the near end of the bar, on the customer side of it. He was a few years older than the drunk, short and wiry and pasty-faced; dressed in shirt and chinos and a loose-fitting barman's apron.

He came forward a few paces, hands on his hips, as Kerry and I entered and I shut the door against the force of the storm.

"Something I can do for you folks?"

"Lord, yes," Kerry said. "We need a drink. Another few minutes and we'd have drowned out there."

"You visitors in these parts?"

"Yes. We're staying in Paradise."

"Bad night to be out driving," the barman said. "Fact is, I was just about to close up and head home. Not many customers on a night like this."

"Close up? You're not going to send us back out in *that?*"

"Well . . ."

"We won't stay long," I said. "Just until the rain lets up enough so I can see where I'm driving."

"We *could* wait in the car," Kerry said, "but the heater's not working." Which was the kind of sneaky lie they teach you in the advertising business; the heater was working fine. "It's nice and warm in here."

The barman shrugged and said without much enthusiasm, "Guess it'll be all right. Supper'll wait a few more minutes."

Kerry smiled at him and went over to the fire. He moved to the door and locked it, just in case some other damn fools showed up out of the storm. And I unbottoned my coat, opened it up like a flasher to the room's warmth.

At the fire Kerry took off the wet paisley scarf she was wearing and fluffed out her thick auburn hair. The firelight made it shine like burnished copper. "I'll have a toddy," she said to the barman.

"Lady?"

"A hot toddy. A strong one."

"Oh. Sure."

I said, "Just a beer for me. Miller Lite."

The wiry guy moved around behind the plank. Outside, the rain was still hammering down with a vengeance; it sounded like a load of pebbles being dumped relentlessly on the tavern's roof. You could hear the wind skirling around in the eaves and rattling the windows, as if it, too, were seeking sanctuary from the storm.

"What was *he* celebrating?" Kerry asked the barman.

"What's that, lady?"

"Your other customer." She nodded at the drunk sprawled over the table.

"Oh, that's Clint Jackson. Good customer. He . . . well, he takes a little too much now and then. Got a drinking problem."

"I'll say he does. What are you going to do with him?"

"Do with him?"

"You're not going to let him sleep there all night, are you?"

"No, no. I'll get him sobered up. Wouldn't let him drive home in the shape he's in now."

"I should hope not."

"He can be a little mean when he's been drinking heavy," the barman said. That was directed at me because I had wandered over toward the drunk's table. The rasp of the man's breathing was audible from nearby, even with the pound of the rain. "Better just let him be."

"I won't disturb him, don't worry."

I turned over to the bar and sat on one of the green-leatherette stools and watched the barman set up Kerry's hot toddy and my beer. He asked me as he worked, "Where you folks from?"

"San Francisco."

"Long time since I been there. Fifteen years."

"It's changed. You wouldn't recognize parts of it."

"I guess not."

"You own this tavern, Mr.——?"

"Kern's my name, Sam Kern. Sure, I own it."

"Nice place. Had it long?"

"Twenty years."

"You live nearby, do you?"

"Not far. House back in the woods a ways."

"Must be peaceful, out here in the middle of nowhere."

"Sure," he said. "The wife and I like it fine. Plenty of business in the summer, plenty of time to loaf in the winter."

"You don't stay open during the winter?"

"Nope. Close down the end of this month."

Kerry came over from the fireplace, sat down next to me, and took a sip of her hot toddy. And made a face and said, "Ugh. Rum."

"Something wrong, lady?"

"You made it with rum instead of bourbon. I *hate* rum."

"I did? Must've picked up the wrong bottle. Sorry, I'll mix you up another one."

He did that. When he brought the drink I laid a twenty-dollar bill on the bar. He looked at it and shook his head. "Afraid I can't change that, mister," he said. "Already closed up my register and put every dime in the safe. You wouldn't have anything smaller, would you?"

"No, I wouldn't."

"I've got some singles," Kerry said. "How much is it?"

"Three dollars."

She paid him out of her purse. He rang up the sale and put the singles in the empty cash drawer and shut it again. Pretty soon he moved down to the other end of the bar and began using a bar towel on some glasses.

A couple of minutes passed in silence, except for the noise of the rain on the roof. I glanced over at the drunk. He still had his head buried in his arms; he hadn't moved since we'd come in.

The steady drum of the rain began to diminish finally, and the wind quit howling and rattling the window panes. The wiry guy looked over at the front window, at the wet night beyond. "Letting up," he said. "You folks should be all right on the road now."

I finished the beer in my glass. "Drink up," I said to Kerry. "We'd better get moving."

"What if it's just a momentary lull?"

"I don't think it is. Come on, Mr. Kern wants to close up and go have his supper."

"All right."

She drank the last of her toddy, and when she was on her feet I took her arm and steered her to the door. The wiry guy came out from behind the plank and followed us, so he could lock the door again after we were gone. I let Kerry flip the lock over; as she did I half-turned back toward him.

He said, "Good night, folks, stop in again——" and that was when I hit him.

It was a sucker punch and he was wide open to it; the blow caught him just under the left eye, spun him and knocked him off his feet, and sent him skidding on his backside toward the bar. Kerry let out a startled yell that got lost in the clatter of the guy hitting the bar stools; one of them fell over on top of him. He lay crumpled and unmoving against the brass rail, with the stool's cushion hiding part of his face.

Kerry said, "For God's sake, what did you do *that* for?" in horrified tones. "Have you lost your mind?"

I didn't answer her. Instead I went to where the guy lay and knelt down and got the gun out from where it was tucked inside his pants, under the apron. It was a .357 Magnum—a hell of a piece of artillery. Behind me, Kerry gasped when she saw it. I put it into the pocket of my coat without looking at her and felt the artery in the guy's neck to make sure he was still alive: I'd hit him pretty hard, hard enough to numb the first three fingers on my right hand. But he was all right, if you didn't count the blood leaking out of his nose, the bruise that was already forming on his cheek, and the fact that he was out cold.

Straightening again, flexing my sore hand, I crossed to where the drunk was draped over the table. Only he *wasn't* a drunk; when I took the hunter's hat off I could see the lump on the back of his head, the coagulating blood that matted his hair. I felt his neck the way I had the other guy's: his pulse was shallow but regular. But he was in worse shape than the wiry guy—the way that head wound looked, he had at least a concussion. He needed a doctor's attention, and soon.

Kerry was standing a few feet away gawping at me. I said to her, "Get on the phone, call the Highway Patrol. Tell them we need an ambulance. Tell them to hurry."

"I don't understand, what's going *on*——?"

"This man is the real Sam Kern, or at least somebody who works here," I said. "The one I hit is an impostor—probably either an escaped convict or a recent parolee. Tell the Highway Patrol that, too."

"God," she said, but she didn't argue; she went straight to the phone behind the bar.

I took another look at the wiry guy. He hadn't moved an inch, and the way he was breathing satisfied me he was going to be out for some time. In the pocket of his chinos I found a wallet full of ID that identified it as Sam Kern's; but the photograph on the driver's license was that of the wounded man at the table.

I went out into the rain, got the set of emergency handcuffs I keep in the trunk of the car, took them back inside, and snapped one cuff around the wiry guy's wrist and the other around the brass rail. I was over looking at Sam Kern again when Kerry finished with her telephone call.

"They're sending people out right away," she said.

"Good. This is Kern, all right, and I think he'll be okay; but you can't tell with head injuries. We'd better just leave him where he is."

She wet a cloth and brought it over and laid it across Kern's neck without touching his wound. Her eyes were big and her cheeks had a milky cast; she still looked confused.

"How did you know?" she said.

"That the other guy was an impostor? Half a dozen reasons. You're always trying to play detective; how come *you* didn't spot them?"

"Don't kid around, you. What reasons?"

"All right. One, he told us he was just getting ready to close up and go home, yet there's a big log fire blazing away in the fireplace. No tavern owner would stoke up a fire like that just before closing for the night.

"Two, he told us this man here was a regular customer and that he wouldn't let him drive home until he sobered up. But where's his car? It's not out front; the parking area was deserted when we drove in. There's no room for a car around back and there wasn't one on that access road either.

"Three, the hat the real Kern was wearing. How many men sit in a bar and get drunk with their coat *off* but their hat still *on?* And not only on, but jammed down tight on his head. Had to be some reason for the hat—to hide something like that head wound.

"Four, you asked the other one for a toddy; he didn't know what you meant at first. Then he made it with rum instead of bourbon. Could have been a mistake, but that's not likely for a man who has been serving drinks at the same bar for twenty years; that man *knows* which bottle is which. No, it's the kind of mistake somebody makes if he not only doesn't know how well the bottles are arranged but isn't enough of a bartender in the first place to know how to make a hot toddy.

"Five, he said he couldn't change my twenty because he'd taken every dime out of the cash register and put it in the safe. And the drawer *is* empty; I saw it when you paid him. But what kind of businessman empties his cash drawer *before* he locks up for the night, when customers like us might still show up? And how many businessmen clean out their cash drawers *completely?* All the ones I know leave at least the change in there and most also leave a few singles, so they won't have to bother putting it all back the next day."

Kerry no longer looked confused; now she looked a little cowed. She said, "You said he's probably an escaped convict or a recent parolee. How could you possibly know that?"

"That's number six," I said. "The color of his skin, babe—it's white, pasty. No man who has lived in these mountains for twenty years, as hot as it gets up here in the summer, could have a complexion like that; the only people who do are shut-ins, hospital patients, and convicts."

"Oh," she said in a small voice.

"I figure it happened something like this: He arrived here earlier tonight—hitchhiking, probably; which would make him a parolee, or else he'd have picked up his own set of wheels. He found himself alone with Kern and it was a set-up he couldn't resist. Maybe he had that .357 Magnum with him; more likely it belongs to Kern. In any case he used something hard to knock Kern over the head—out on this side of the bar, maybe while Kern was stoking the fire. Then he rifled the till. But he's not too smart; he forgot to lock the front door first.

"Then we showed up. When he saw our headlights through the window he didn't know who we might be. He could have done any of three things. Run and lock the door and pretend the place was closed—but what if we were friends of Kern's? What if we looked through the window in any event and saw Kern lying on the floor? His second alternative was to let us come in and throw down on us, rob us too and steal our car, and that's probably what he *would* have done if we'd been locals who knew Kern. But he didn't want to do it that way; it would only buy him more trouble, leave one or more people who could identify him as an armed thief a lot more easily than a man with a busted head. And he's not a killer, thank Christ, so that alternative was out. His only other choice was to find out if we were strangers—he asked about that right away, remember—and if we were, to run a bluff and get rid of us quick.

"He picked Kern up off the floor, draped him over the table, and shoved that hat down over his head to hide the wound. His own hat, maybe; it had to have been handy. Kern was probably wearing the apron, so all he had to do was yank it off and tie it around himself to cover the gun inside his belt. All of that wouldn't have taken more than thirty seconds—less time than it took us to stop the car, get out, and come inside."

Kerry was silent for a space of time. Then she asked, "You didn't know he had that gun, did you? Before you hit him?"

"Sure I did. It made a bulge under his apron when he moved around. Didn't you notice it?"

"Well," she said, "I . . . um, I guess I did, when we first came in. But I thought . . . I mean, I didn't look again because . . ."

"Because why?"

"I thought . . . oh hell, I thought something had aroused him."

"*Aroused* him?"

"I thought he had a damn erection, all right?"

I looked at her. And then I burst out laughing. "Kerry Wade, star detective," I said between cackles, "the female Sherlock Holmes. She can't even tell the difference between a gun barrel and an erection!"

"Oh shut up," she said.

I was still chuckling when the Highway Patrol and a county ambulance got there a few minutes later.